Vanish Like Water

Sam A. Mustafa

Copyright © 2021 by Sam A. Mustafa

All rights reserved.

ISBN: 978-1-7357633-2-3.

Sam Mustafa Publishing LLC
Boonton, New Jersey, USA

sammustafa.com

For Ursula Soyez,
in friendship and gratitude.

CONTENTS

You who will emerge from the flood
In which we have gone under
Remember.
When you speak of our failings
Remember also the dark times
That you have escaped.

— Bertolt Brecht, *To Those Born Later*

d'accord

West Berlin, Autumn 1989

1.

One October morning, about two years after he had moved to West Berlin, Daniel LeClerc awoke to police sirens and uniformed men ordering everyone out of his building. Daniel assumed it was a raid of some sort, and he thought about making a run for it. He had every reason not to want the police in his apartment. But he kept his cool and was soon herded, along with all of his neighbors and the residents of every building on the block, behind a temporary barrier at the end of the street. Men wearing thickly-padded black armor waddled through the foyer of his building and disappeared. Somebody had discovered the tail fin of an unexploded bomb just beneath the concrete basement slab.

Daniel stood and watched his neighbors, impressed by their patience and calm. They grumbled or made dark jokes, a few small children whined that they were hungry or bored, but nobody appeared surprised. An old woman waited peacefully with her hands folded against her stomach, her soft smile hinting that she had done this more than once. By evening the bomb was partially excavated, its remaining explosives drained away, its rusted fins sawed off, and a fresh patch of concrete was poured over the wound it had caused.

That night Daniel dreamt of bombs under all the buildings in the city. The people came and went, some indifferent to the geology of menace beneath them, others resigned never to know when they might explode. He awoke, slightly surprised to be alive, and thought: *this is a strange place.*

2.

Three weeks later, on a chilly November evening after wrapping up a complex deal involving a bundle of fake passports and a nervous French diplomat with a wallet full of smuggled South African diamonds, Daniel was walking to *d'accord*, the restaurant owned by his friend Sabine, when he realized that something was wrong. The West Berlin traffic was much heavier than normal, but not in its usual evening commuter pattern. The sidewalks swelled with chatty, excited pedestrians. As Daniel walked past bars and cafés he saw clusters of people huddled around televisions. By the time he got to *d'accord* he was aware that huge crowds had converged upon the checkpoints on the eastern side of the Berlin Wall and were demanding to pass through. Daniel felt annoyed. He had plans to get drunk tonight but apparently somebody had scheduled a revolution.

Daniel was neither a Berliner nor a revolutionary. He came from Paris, where people spoke of revolution as casually and frequently as they spoke of grocery shopping. He had grown accustomed to the precise and orderly Germans, who liked to plan everything months in advance. This passionate and spontaneous display of emotion took him by surprise. Having never experienced a German revolution, Daniel wasn't sure whether or not sobriety was required.

Sabine's television, mounted in a corner over the bar, showed an ARD special news bulletin. The broadcast alternated between an avuncular anchorman in a brown suit speaking calmly in a studio and raw footage of excited people confronting the East German guards at the checkpoint. Daniel sat next to Rudi, a plump, round-faced schoolteacher who lived across the street. From time to time people rose from their tables in the restaurant and wandered over to stand at the bar beside them and squint at the remarkable scenes unfolding on the screen.

"You know what Lenin said about the Germans?" Daniel asked. Rudi raised an eyebrow and waited obligingly for the punch line. "If a mob of Germans wanted to storm a train station they'd all stand in line first to buy proper tickets."

Rudi snorted. "Yeah, but those *are* Lenin's Germans. And I don't see any tickets, do you?"

"What are they expecting?" Daniel said as they stared at thousands of people jamming the checkpoint. Green-coated border guards, looking twitchy and worried, stood behind a metal barrier not much bigger or sturdier than that for a toll gate. They confronted a rising sea of faces, illuminated with hope, alternately chanting, singing, and shouting. The voices from the crowd betrayed a bit of fear and a lot of determination.

"Schabowski said the Wall is open, as of now." That was Charlotte, the waitress, standing behind him.

"Doesn't look open to me," someone said.

"No, look," Rudi said, "they're coming through. They're letting them through."

Sabine, who had been moving between tables with a tray of drinks, passed in front of the television. Balancing the tray against her waist, she stared at the screen and said, "Unbelievable."

"No," Daniel said, "What I mean is: what do they expect from *here*? They're coming over, okay, so now what?"

They were all silent for a moment, considering this, then someone said, "McDonald's?" and they laughed and shook their heads.

"Can't you just enjoy it?" Sabine asked. "All those poor people finally getting the chance to travel, or even to move around. I've been traveling most of my life and always took it for granted. For them, crossing a few blocks is like Columbus discovering America."

"Free drinks if the Ossis come here?" Charlotte asked, arching one eyebrow.

Sabine set a beer mug down on the bar a little too hard. "Yes," she said firmly. "If any of them make it all the way out to here, free beer."

"Free beer for the Ossis!" Daniel said, raising his arms.

Sabine probably said that only because it seemed so implausible. But every few minutes brought some fresh surprise. They could hear fireworks in the distance and people cheering and singing in the streets. Shortly after midnight, they started hearing the sickly farting of Trabant and Wartburg engines as the Ossis drove down the broad boulevard of the Kantstrasse. A fire alarm went off at the end of the block and the exasperated firemen came and then left. Someone explained that the eastern cars had no catalytic converters and their exhaust fumes were setting off everybody's fire and carbon monoxide alarms.

D'accord was located in the middle of the block, on a side street leading away from the Savignyplatz. Sabine had opened it only a few months earlier, having bought and renovated an old Italian restaurant that had been there since the sixties. Daniel, who lived nearby, wandered in one evening and immediately realized that Sabine's native language, like his, was French. West Berlin had a plentiful supply of everything except Berliners; everybody was from somewhere else.

Daniel's friendship with Sabine almost foundered upon the discovery that he worked for her ex-boyfriend Miguel. She assumed that Daniel had been sent by him as some sort of spy and it took two weeks of protest to convince her otherwise. Over vodka and wine, they watched the hopeful spring and summer of 1989 unfold, as people filled the street cafés into the early morning hours, drinking, smoking, talking. There was a lot to discuss. Great tectonic shifts coming from the other side of the Wall shook the ground beneath everyone's feet and people spoke of "openness" and "transparency" and "re-structuring." Some dared to imagine the end of the Cold War or perhaps of communism itself. The walled island of West Berlin, which had always made its inhabitants feel anxious and uncertain, now felt like a front-row seat at an extraordinary show.

There were parts of West Berlin that never slept, where parties never ended and nothing was off-limits, but none of the people in *d'accord* that November had ever heard their tranquil bourgeois neighborhood in Charlottenburg this wild and alive after midnight on a Thursday. They alternated between staring at the television and staring out the windows, trying to catch glimpses of the world changing. Some went out to walk without direction or destination to swim in it or to feel the sense of being carried by the stream. Others came into *d'accord* with huge grins and restless limbs, looking as if their neighborhood football team had just won the World Cup. How does one celebrate an unexpected revolution? They drank beer and assumed they'd figure out the rest.

Nobody was in a mood to go home, not even the tired cook and waitress who had been there for hours. Nobody wanted to be alone in that moment. The streets of West Berlin swelled with blissful, weeping strangers who just wanted to say hello and wander stupidly from one block to the next, dumbfounded by the scenery unfolding before them and ecstatic to be alive. They collided, literally, with western TV reporters, as if unsure anymore where their imaginations ended and the real world began. Daniel watched a middle-aged woman bump into a camera crew and burst into laughter, tears streaming down her cheeks.

At about 1:30 AM there was a sound of car brakes shrieking in the street, followed one second later by the loud *smack* of metal and plastic meeting some heavy object. Then the chalky squeal of a tire spinning for a second before the car departed, shifting urgently through higher gears as it vanished down the street.

People in *d'accord* looked around as if they could find the car somewhere in the room.

"Damn," Daniel said. "That sounded like it was right outside."

"Go look," Sabine commanded. "See if anybody's hurt."

When Daniel reached the door he saw that something had collided with the *Litfassäule* on the corner. The pavement around the base of the concrete cylinder was decorated with shiny red plastic, as if from someone's front bumper, and two of the posters on the column were torn. There was a black tire smudge not one meter away. Daniel was about to turn and go back inside when he saw a man lying against the wall of the hair salon next door. His rumpled gray clothes were comprehensively stained and in that moment Daniel wasn't sure whether it was by dirt or blood.

Daniel crouched down beside the body. It was an elderly man, his hair white and thin, his hands grooved and leathery. Daniel saw that his face was dirty and unshaven, with little cuts and scrapes all over.

"Is he alive?" Rudi called, his head poking out *d'accord's* front door.

"Yeah, he's alive," Daniel said, putting two fingers to the rough old throat, pressing against its surfeit of leathery skin to find the pulse. "I can't tell if that car hit him, or if he was sitting here the whole time. I don't see any blood." He gently tapped the old face a couple of times and frowned when he got no reaction.

"Come on," Daniel said, "I'll check him out. Let's get him inside."

They were surprised by his weight. Daniel and Rudi carried him like a long piece of furniture, entering with him feet-first into the room. They unfolded him into a chair near the bar. Sabine stood with one hand at her waist, the other on her mouth.

"Did that car hit him?" she asked.

"I can't tell," Daniel said.

"I'll call an ambulance," she whispered but didn't move. She seemed transfixed by the battered old face and it wasn't until Charlotte emerged from the kitchen, curious, that Sabine suddenly remembered what she said she would do. She shook her head quickly and reached for the phone.

Daniel felt around the circumference of the old man's head, which had slumped forward onto his chest. "Nothing bad back here. His skull seems okay." Daniel noticed a large scar in the shape of a fishhook on the man's left cheek. "That must've hurt," he said.

"Damn it," Sabine hissed as she slammed the receiver against its frame. "Fucking recordings."

"Hey mister," Daniel said as he opened the old man's shirt and felt along his ribcage. "You break anything? Scream or something if this hurts."

"What did he say?" Rudi asked.

"What?" said Daniel. "I didn't hear anything."

"No, he said something."

Sabine cursed again, slammed again, dialed again.

"Hey mister, speak up, huh?" Daniel felt the shoulders and throat.

...die blaue Straßenbahn...

"What was that?" Rudi asked. "I only got a couple of words of that. Tell us your name, can you tell us your name?" The old man's eyes remained closed.

"I don't think he's broken anything," Daniel said. "I can't find any wallet or ID or anything, though. Nothing, no papers at all."

Sabine's face was behind her hands. Daniel looked at her, puzzled.

"Sabine," Daniel said quietly. She didn't move. "I think he'll probably be okay."

They stood in silence. When at last she pulled her hands away, her eyes swam in water.

"I can't get through to an ambulance," she said, her voice cracking.

"Hey," Daniel lifted himself up onto the bar, swung his legs over and plopped down on the other side. He touched her arm. "It's not your fault. The whole city is insane tonight.

The world is coming to an end, remember? Or starting, or something."

She placed her hands to the sides of her face and took a deep breath. They were still regarding her silently when she said very firmly:

"I'm going to take care of him."

"That's fine," Daniel said, "We'll make sure he gets to a hospital."

"No," she said, staring at Daniel. "I'm going to take care of him."

They looked at each other, then to the gray figure in his dirty wrinkles, then back to each other.

"Okay," Daniel finally said.

"We'll take him upstairs to my flat," she said. "Are you sure he hasn't broken anything?"

Daniel shrugged, "I don't think so. Nothing obvious, anyway. But I mean, if it's a concussion or something, it could be bad and we wouldn't know. I can't tell if that car hit him or what."

"We can try for a doctor in the morning, but for now...."

Daniel nodded. He was too grateful to see Sabine restored to her usual state of bossiness to argue or protest.

"You men lift him," she said, opening the cash register and taking out a set of keys. "Follow me upstairs."

"This isn't how I thought I'd finally get invited up to your room," Daniel muttered as he and Rudi huffed and carried the body.

...muß die blaue Straßenbahn finden...

"What did he say?" Daniel grunted as he crested the final stair.

"I didn't hear it," Rudi said.

"Put him on my sofa," Sabine commanded, opening the door.

"He's a heavy old bastard," Daniel muttered.

"Doesn't smell so great, either," Rudi said.

"Yeah, but not booze, though. He's not a drunk."

Sabine emerged from her bathroom with several small wet towels. She knelt beside the sofa and placed one on the old man's forehead. His lips moved, mumbling, but his eyes remained closed. With another towel, she dabbed away dirt from his face. After a minute, she looked up at them standing behind her.

"I might be here a while. Go back down and tell the kitchen to close up, starting now."

Rudi didn't need to be told twice. He turned and fled at once. Daniel lingered, squatting down beside the sofa. He stared at the fishhook scar and was startled when the old man's eyes opened and he smiled serenely.

"There you are," Sabine said.

The old man placed his hand on Daniel's arm, which made him jerk backward and away, falling to the floor on his ass.

"Go on," Sabine said. "I can take care of him."

Daniel regained his balance and stood up. He looked at Sabine, then said in French,

"Are you going to keep him here overnight? Does your bedroom door have a lock?"

"Don't be ridiculous," she said.

"You have no idea who this guy is."

She appeared unmoved. "It's a new world. We're starting something new."

3.

Daniel came to *d'accord* the next afternoon and rang Sabine's upstairs bell. She buzzed him in. When he walked into her living room he saw the old man sitting up on the couch, calmly staring at him. Sabine had pulled a chair into the room, opposite the sofa, and Daniel grasped immediately that she had been up all night with him. He didn't need to see the dark crescents under her eyes to confirm it.

"You look better," Daniel said to the stranger.

"He doesn't say much," Sabine said, her arms folded across her waist.

"I assume you didn't get any sleep last night?" Daniel asked her.

"No. You?"

"I tried," he said. "There was a party in the street and it was too loud to sleep, so I went outside and joined them. I walked over to the Brandenburg Gate and I think everybody who has ever lived in West Berlin was there. They say Willy Brandt is going to speak tonight at the Ernst Reuter Platz."

Daniel realized with some discomfort that the old man was smiling and staring at him again.

"So, are we taking you to the hospital?" Daniel asked him. The old man shook his head slowly.

Sabine turned toward her kitchen and gestured with her chin for Daniel to follow her. They stood beside her oven, leaning conspiratorially toward each other and speaking in French.

"I tried that," she said. "No hospital. So I called Renate this morning."

"The, uh, the nurse?" Daniel said, squinting, trying to remember the face of one of the regulars at *d'accord*.

"She lives down the street," Sabine said. "She came by and checked him out."

"How did that go?"

"He was gentle as a lamb the whole time. You were right; nothing broken, no concussion. Renate thinks the car hit him; he has some bad bruises. It probably knocked the wind out of him. He just... doesn't talk. I can't figure him out. He doesn't ask for anything, no money or booze, not even food."

Sabine sighed and looked through the open doorway at the old man on the sofa in the next room. He stared directly at Daniel.

"He looks at me like he knows me," Daniel said. "It's a little creepy. Do we know if he's an Ossi or a Wessi? Did he come through the Wall last night?"

"No idea," Sabine said. "When he does speak, he sounds like he has an old Berliner accent."

"So what are you going to do?"

"I told him he can stay here for a couple of days."

"Why?" Daniel asked. "I mean, if he's all right?"

"I knew you'd ask that," she said. "I don't know. Part of me thinks that it's just my duty, you know, to be the Good Citizen. Part of me thinks it's what we should be doing right now, with the Wall being open and everybody helping out. Part of me thinks it's fate."

"Fate?"

"Don't say it like I'm stupid."

Daniel looked her in the eyes. "I've never thought you're stupid," he said. "You're the opposite of stupid."

"Maybe it's a test," she said. "Sometimes life throws a test at you: how will you react? Are you a good person? I wasn't there when my dad died, maybe I should have been, maybe I should have taken better care of him when I had the chance, but I had moved to Berlin and fallen out of touch with my family and was too young and immature to realize what was important when it was right there in front of me. Maybe I owe this to the universe."

"If you try to care for a stranger," Daniel said, "It's going to be hard and unpredictable and it won't be like caring for your father. There's no scorecard in heaven for stuff like this."

Daniel frowned. "Why is he staring at me?"

"Maybe it's a test for you, too?" Sabine said, smiling. That made Daniel grunt.

"I don't think so," he said. "My father was an asshole. I don't owe him shit. If anything, the universe owes *me* something for enduring him."

"Well," Daniel said, "Do what you need to do. But in case you were wondering, nobody has any doubts that you're a good person."

Sabine squeezed Daniel's elbow briefly then returned to her living room. She sat in the chair opposite the sofa. The old man smiled.

Daniel followed a moment later. "Do you need anything?" he asked as he stood near her door.

"No, we'll be fine. Are you coming by later tonight?"

"No," Daniel said, "I have to work. For Miguel."

That made her frown.

"All right, don't worry about us," she said. "I'll see you soon.

4.

Daniel's job kept him out of Berlin for nearly a week. When he returned he found the streets teeming with astonished Ossis who wanted to see, hear, touch, and feel virtually everything in the West, from bananas in grocery store produce sections to two-ply toilet paper. A middle-aged couple huddled outside *d'accord*, reading the menu on the wall and debating the meanings of several strange words like "tapenade" and "bisque." They gasped in shock at the prices.

When Daniel entered he didn't immediately see Sabine. He sat at the bar and waited. He was about to knock on the back door that led upstairs to her flat when he saw her emerging from the storage room. She was wearing her reading glasses but he could see that her eyes were red and sunken, not making contact with anyone. Her arms were folded around her waist and she looked as if she had been sick.

"This doesn't look good," Daniel said to her in French. He thought at first that she didn't hear him, that she might simply walk right past him, but she turned and said in German: "He's gone."

"He's gone," she repeated, growing angry. She turned partly away from him, her hands resting on her hips, then pivoted back, strumming the air before her chest. "I left him up there... I was working for, I don't know, not even three hours. And I went to check on him and he was gone."

She extended her arm to point at the front door of the bar.

"Tell me," she demanded, her hand shaking violently, index finger jabbing, "how he could have come down the stairs and gone out that door while I was down here working, and I never saw it? How? He didn't say anything, he never..."

Her hand rose to her mouth, snatched up a sob and flung it away quickly. When she saw Daniel's face, puzzled and uncomprehending, she became angry.

"You have to help me."

"Um," Daniel said. "Help you do what?"

"We have to find him," she implored.

"Why? Maybe he was feeling better and went on his way?"

"Daniel!" Several customers turned to look. Charlotte watched, alarmed, from the safety of the kitchen door.

Sabine stared at the door for a few seconds, then sat on a barstool. Her fingertips rose to her cheeks, then to her temples. She bit her lower lip.

"I can't let him die out there," she said, straightening and wiping her eyes. "I can't. We have to find him."

"He probably lives out there," Daniel said. "You did the right thing. You took care of him and now he's gone on his way. It doesn't mean he's not grateful. He's just... he's a street person."

Daniel found himself thinking about the fishhook scar on the old man's cheek and the way he looked at him, as if with pleasure or recognition.

"I'm sorry," Sabine said. She inhaled deeply, stood up, and exhaled. "I'm okay. I'm okay."

"Did you get his name?" Daniel asked.

"Johannes. That's all. He had the accent of an old Berliner."

"Maybe you'll see him again," Daniel said.

"I don't know."

The pair of Ossis who had been studying the menu for several minutes finally ventured cautiously through the door. Their faces and postures indicated fear or uncertainty as if they weren't sure they were allowed to be here.

"New customers," Daniel said. "Look at them. No matter what you serve them tonight, it will be remarkable. They'll talk about it for weeks. Isn't that a great feeling?"

"New everything," Sabine said. "And yes, it is."

She sighed. "Are you hungry?"

"I could eat," he said.

after he was nowhere

Berlin, Spring 1992

5.

Daniel loved to watch Julia eat. He loved to watch her hands, with their narrow fingers resting on the spine of a fork or knife. He loved to watch the lines of her mouth and neck as they shifted above graceful thin muscles. He loved the way she seemed to drift away while they ate, gazing around the room, unaware he was staring at her. For a long time, he never told her any of this, wanting her to sit across from him silent and unknowing like prey. Then one night they talked about the childhood game of assigning animals to people: if you were an animal, what would you be?

"I think you would be an owl," she said. "Definitely an owl; all by yourself in the dark on some tree branch, with big glowing eyes watching as the night things go by."

When he told her she reminded him of a praying mantis the observation struck her as anything but a compliment. No, he insisted. She was a perfect balance of movement and stillness. The silent poise, the measured sweep of her smooth arms, the fingers traveling in an arc to brush away cinnamon-colored strands of hair from her eyes. The way she tilted her head away so that her gaze rested upon nothing, so that she seemed perfectly *elsewhere,* hovering before him, entrancing him.

"Don't the females eat their mates?" she asked, arching one thick eyebrow, as she often did when amused by his enthusiasm.

"Right after sex."

"And this concept appeals to you?"

Daniel grinned sheepishly, and as he did so he saw Julia's expression change. She looked at him as if trying to understand something unfamiliar that had appeared in a place she thought she knew well. She had discovered that Daniel was in love with her. They both wondered how and when it had happened. Neither said a word. It occurred to him later that they had both chosen flying creatures, animals that might disappear at any moment.

Julia had made Daniel's dining table a few months ago. It was shaped like a splatter of liquid or the splash of a tear: an amoeba of thick, dark wood with odd protrusions and sudden curves. Across the surface were holes which ran clean through, some almost big enough for a plate, and it had taken Daniel a few weeks before he no longer absent-mindedly set his glass down on thin air, hearing it smash on the floor. Now he was accustomed to the oddities of the table's shape and was grateful that the holes afforded a view of Julia's legs and feet, because watching these was perhaps the only thing in the world he loved more than watching her eat.

She was eating the first time he ever saw her: plucking triangles of caraway gouda from a silver tray on a table in the front row of Club Maxim. Daniel had approached her without meaning to, certainly without preparation. He simply obeyed the pull of her praying mantis arms and their long hands and found himself before her. She looked up at him curiously, her head tilted almost perpendicular to her neck, studying him indifferently for a moment before smiling.

"Do I have any seeds in my teeth?" were the first words she said to him.

"No," he said.

"I have to go on in a minute," she said, reaching down to wipe her fingers on the tablecloth. She excused herself and slid past him, smiling quickly once again. It left him suffused with an inchoate sadness he had never experienced before. He felt planted there, waiting for her to return and explain what he was feeling.

She did not return. The table was taken instead by three men. Two were broad-set and elderly, with thick rippled faces and tentative sprays of gray-white hair. The third was Miguel DeSoto, Daniel's boss. Tall and strikingly handsome, of uncertain middle age, his perfectly-tailored suit moving effortlessly as he sat, DeSoto looked knowingly at Daniel before turning his dark gaze toward the expectant stage.

Julia emerged from the side of the stage through a door of hanging beads, walking *aux points,* so slowly that the motion of her legs was nearly as invisible as that of a minute-hand and the curvature of her muscles changed like creeping shadows advancing over land. As the music began Daniel had no idea how long he had spent watching her and had completely forgotten that there was anybody else in the room.

That was then. Daniel never asked her to dance for him privately. But sometimes, apparently randomly, when they were standing near each other, she lifted weightlessly upon the ball of one foot and turned in a liquid crescent, sweeping air downward with floating hands. In a second it would pass and she might smile or kiss him and move lightly away as Daniel stood speechless. He satisfied himself with these special windfalls like the convergence of a hole in the dinner table with his line of sight, which allowed him to see the narrow slope of her ankle. When they ate together he was silent, consuming the view.

6.

You're tall for a Frenchman. That's what older people usually told Daniel LeClerc, after praising his German grammar and pronunciation and remarking with surprise that he had only been in Berlin a few years. Tall, ash-blonde, blue-eyed: nobody would guess that Daniel wasn't from here.

Sometimes he answered, "I'm good with languages," and was relieved that the other person usually wasn't listening.

Younger people didn't notice or care. When he came to West Berlin in 1987 Daniel found a city in perpetual uproar. Nothing ever disappeared here. The beatniks and hippies were still going strong, the sweater-clad student cadres jostled against the soldiers on the sidewalks, the punks still haunted the subway stations, making the old ladies scowl at their spiked purple mohawks. Gay men came home from their offices in business suits and changed into shiny skin-tight leather. The yuppies on the Ku'damm rushed from meetings to boutiques and back again. For a place that was so weighed down by the past, walled-off and sealed up by conflict, Berlin was astonishingly young, noisy, and irreverent and nobody gave a damn where you were from because nearly everybody under thirty was from some place other than here. There were neighborhoods where people had sex in the street or walked around mostly naked except for tattoos and piercings, and where hard narcotics were available practically on tap. There were other areas where the chubby middle-aged owners of bookstores and vacuum-cleaner repair shops closed up at 5:00 and murmured down tree-lined residential streets past tasteful cafés, en route home to watch the evening news with a beer before dinner.

In those days streets ended suddenly and vertically. You could turn a corner and see a city block chopped clean across by the Wall. Absurd angles resulted. Front doors and windows that had once opened to a vast cityscape now faced this arbitrary end of the world. West Berlin was big but one never escaped the sense of being a prisoner. It was like being held captive by some half-mad circus. The lines between lunacy, fun, and danger were written in mortar, clear for all to see.

In the past five years, Daniel had established only a small circle of friends and relationships. He had dated a few women before Julia, had shared a few rounds with neighbors in *d'accord*, and was valued by his boss. But Daniel's kind of work did not lend itself to trust or transparency. It was better not to have friends than to have friends to whom one must always lie.

He had Eugene, his Russian partner and accomplice. And Sabine, the owner of his favorite bar and restaurant, where Daniel spent most evenings that he didn't spend with Julia. And he had Rashid.

Rashid was Daniel's healer / sage / therapist. You couldn't call Rashid a doctor. Not any more. In days gone by (Daniel never asked how many days gone by) Rashid had been a "real" doctor. In his native Syria, he had strolled hospital corridors in his white coat with the imperious frown of The Doctor beneath his thick black mustache. He had scribbled on charts and given solemn instructions. Like Daniel, he had come here a few years ago, seeing something like hope in the broken skyline and the churning streets.

The building that housed Rashid's office was small, converted from one of the rare homes that had survived the war. Despite the modest exterior, once Daniel entered Rashid's practice he always felt as if he had walked into a vast, white cavern. The rooms were immense, the ceilings high. Rashid's office was ludicrously too large for the plain brown desk which slouched in one corner a kilometer? — perhaps two? — from the nearest potted plant, a thirsty-looking cactus near the door. Daniel sensed that his friend loved the tan expanses of hardwood floor and the undecorated white walls. He imagined Rashid haunted by memories of sand between his toes or longing for endless shimmering horizons.

Rashid spoke German with a heavy Arabic accent and an orchestra of sighs that always sounded as if he was resigned to some tiresome but not quite terrible fate.

"Ah, this could be many things, my friend. Anything from just stomach acid to possibly cancer. It could even simply be stress. If you want the usual treatments you must go to a real medical doctor."

"The usual treatments."

"They could test you, to rule out cancer at least."

Daniel tried to avoid doctors and anyone else who might have the right to investigate his present or past too closely.

"I'm not going to go to a doctor," he said. "I have you."

"Ah, I can only address the pain."

"That's all I ever ask you for."

"And the pain is every day?" Rashid asked.

"Not every day," Daniel said. "Almost. Usually at night."

Rashid frowned as he turned and beckoned Daniel to follow him into one of the back rooms.

"It's been a lousy week," Daniel said. "I haven't been sleeping worth a damn. And when I do, I have bizarre dreams."

Daniel followed Rashid into one of the large, high-ceilinged white rooms, made to seem even larger by the complete absence of any furniture other than a narrow white table in the very center. Daniel pulled off his clothes, lumping them into one of the corners against the wall. There were no hooks or hangers. Rashid left and returned wearing an apron with several bulging pockets.

"What kind of dreams?" he asked as Daniel tugged at his socks.

"Water, mostly. Floods, drowning, waterfalls, rain, that sort of stuff."

"Ah, well, it has been a very rainy Spring. These things appear in our subconscious." Rashid offered this with a shrug as he removed three oblong pieces of wood from one of the apron pockets and cupped them in his palm. With his free hand, he removed a small flask of oil and doused the wooden eggs. He then closed his fingers around the pieces and seemed to crush them, but slowly manipulated them in his fist.

"No," said Daniel, climbing naked onto the table and lying on his stomach, "More than that. It's as if the water is coming for me personally, you know? Like, no matter where I turn or go, or whether I run or not, I can't avoid it. It's coming up from the ground, falling down from the sky, spilling out of the river, everywhere."

Rashid said only, "Mm."

"You know that thing," Daniel said, "where if you die in your sleep you're supposed to actually die. You know what I'm talking about?"

"Ah, I think that's just superstition."

"Well, it's never been *dis*-proven."

"Daniel," Rashid sighed. "Of course not. Dead people don't talk about their dreams."

"Well, for the record, earlier this week I died in my dream."

"Indeed?"

"See?" Daniel looked up at him. "If it's just superstition, how come you sound so surprised?"

"Well Daniel, if it were true I wouldn't be talking to you right now, would I? All right, so how did you die?"

"I drowned. I was caught in this river or... no, I was walking down this valley and there was a flood and I got caught up in it. I remember I kept thinking that I should be floating. You know, bodies float, right? But I kept sinking deeper and I couldn't hold my breath any longer."

"Ah, you had your head stuck into the pillow and you couldn't breathe, yes?" Rashid smiled.

"No, listen — I got to that point, right? That point where you're about to burst, and that's where you're supposed to wake up. Right the second before you die, you're supposed to wake up all sweaty and realize that you've been dreaming. But I got to that point and *I crossed it.* I lost my breath and I burst but I didn't wake up. And the water filled me up inside. I swear, I can still feel it right now. I could feel it all cold and heavy inside me. And I sank down deeper and everything got cold and dark and quiet. And you know what? This is the strangest thing of all. That whole time after I died I was still conscious, feeling it. And then I thought: 'This isn't so bad after all. I thought it would be worse.' I remember being dead and thinking that."

Rashid stood pensively for a moment.

"There's another possibility," he finally said.

"Yeah?"

"Ah, maybe you *are* dead and you're imagining you're here telling me this now."

"You're brilliant," Daniel muttered, sinking his head into his crossed forearms on the table.

Rashid placed the three wooden eggs on Daniel's upper spine, a few centimeters below his neck. Then he laid his hand on them and pressed lightly, slowly and steadily increasing the pressure.

"You don't believe any of this," Daniel said.

"I believe it all. But as I said, it could be stress. The cold weather will be over in a couple of weeks, a month at most. You should get away. Go someplace warm and quiet."

"I have work to do."

"Ah, *your* kind of work is always flexible."

"It's not that simple. I have obligations. I'd rather stay here and take my chances. Besides, what difference does it make where I am?"

"Are you still thinking of quitting and setting up shop somewhere?" Rashid asked.

"Yeah, I've been rolling some plans around in my head."

"Ah, I don't imagine you selling shoes or toasters or serving cappuccino."

"No," Daniel grunted with pain as Rashid pushed down on the eggs between his shoulders. "I've got some ideas that don't involve toasters. What do you think about private detectives?"

"Private detectives?" When Rashid was surprised his Arabic accent dramatically exaggerated all his consonants and made Daniel smile. "Like in the movies?"

"Legit and legal, but it makes sense. I know the city, I know how things get done here, I'm good at finding or hiding things, and I know how other people find and hide things. It's one of the only jobs you can do in this country without needing a special license. You just have to have a clean police file, which I do... in this country. Assuming I don't die from whatever this is, I was thinking of becoming a private dick."

"Ah, let's get to work, shall we?" Rashid said. "We can talk more later."

Daniel exhaled slowly. As he did the hand pushed downward, moving the eggs slightly upward, then down.

Time halts, comes to a standstill: stops as if catching on something, then disintegrates altogether in a silent shatter of dancing gray pixels like an ancient TV screen. He feels the hands, big warm brown hands, emerge and disappear, rolling on waves, hiding in folds, bobbing up, sinking down, out of sight, fading into other movements. There are broad yawning stretches of time, he has no idea how long, between motions. There are interruptions of pain that shout at first, like alarms through a fog, but which recede into their own echoes and finally dissolve as muscles surrender to the current of heat lapping around him. A warm drop of something, his own blood perhaps, on his bicep, drop-dropping away to land in some infinitely distant pool, a splash echo crashing when it strikes, but the sound dying on the long night journey back to him. Two outlines, soft and dark, take shape gradually as women, then girls perhaps, standing side by side staring at him without expression. Are they saying something? A single soft word, is it Flucht? *The German word for "escape" He realizes he was thinking in*

French. It is an echo now, pacing the room before investing itself in the walls softly, sinking in, absorbed, soaking, fading, drying slowly, vanishing.

And with it, laughter. Soft, feminine laughter in the growing kindness of light.

"Ah, there you are," Rashid said softly, waving two fingers before Daniel's eyes. "You weren't joking about bad sleep. It took you forever to fade out. But then you slept like the dead for hours.

"No dreams," Daniel said, smacking paper-dry lips.

"Good. Water?"

Daniel nodded emphatically.

Rashid stepped across the room to a sink which was set into the wall.

"How long was I out?" Daniel rose and drained the cup in one draft, holding it out for Rashid to take. Daniel collapsed back onto the table, still staring at the white sink and white shelf beside it, both attached to the white wall.

"Ah, it's about three-thirty now, so that's what, about five and a half hours?"

"Good God," said Daniel, closing his eyes again.

"How do you feel?"

"I don't know yet. How does it look?"

Rashid inhaled deeply before answering.

"Ah. There's a... *presence* inside you. Sometimes I think I see it, sometimes no. Sometimes it almost seems like a liquid, flowing through you, in your blood. It comes and goes like a tide. But I can't tell if I'm looking at high tide or low tide. I think that when it recedes it takes little bits of you with it. That's its method. Then it rests, lets you rest. And then it comes back for more."

"Am I dying?"

"Ah, everybody's dying. In your case, I can't guess."

"If I wanted evasion and riddles, I'd go to a real doctor. Am I in trouble?"

"It could take two days, two months, two years — I have no clue."

Daniel sat up and stared at him.

"That bad," he said at length.

"What do you mean, 'that bad...' I don't have any idea."

"The longest time you could envision was two years."

Rashid exhaled slowly. He shook his head, looked down at the floor.

"Ah..." was all he finally said, a long, descending sigh, a whole concerto of sigh. Then he looked back up at Daniel and spoke firmly: "Rest here for another ten minutes. When you're done I'll be in my office."

He turned and left through the sparkle of the beads.

Daniel contemplated his stomach, bare and bent, with a ripple of excess skin bulging along the latitude of his navel as he sat. The fold concealed most of the long scar that ran horizontally and tapered out near his left kidney. Daniel exhaled slowly and lay back down on the table, resting his hand on his flattened abdomen. He stared at the white ceiling until it moved tectonically, sections of whiteness detaching and rubbing against each other.

He remembered the laughter because he heard it again then.

Two voices, perhaps? Feminine, muffled, giggly like girls. He lifted himself on his elbows. The walls were barren and white. There was no window. His gaze drifted to the doorway, to the hanging beads. Daniel rose and dressed.

"Ah, there you are," Rashid said merrily as Daniel walked into his office. "Sleep well?"

"Yes, fine." Daniel stood beside the cactus, staring across the desert at his friend behind the brown desk.

"You were out for a long time," Rashid said, looking at his watch. "Five and a half hours. Did you just get up?"

Daniel stood silently for a moment before he realized what Rashid was asking him.

"I, uh — yes. Yes, I just got up. Were you in the room?"

"When?"

"Just, uh... just a few minutes ago. Did you give me water?"

"No," Rashid said cheerfully, "would you like some?"

"No — you gave me water. We talked. You said I had two years to live."

Rashid startled, then laughed.

"Ah, maybe you should go back and sit down." He rose from behind the desk. "You're still a little out of it. Let me feel your pulse."

"There were two girls," Daniel said, uncertain now, as Rashid held his wrist.

"Ah, you're still a little slow," Rashid said, "Go back and rest for a couple of minutes. I'll get you some water. Go on," he said as he shouldered past, leaving Daniel alone in the office.

He heard the falls of his friend's heavy black shoes against the hardwood, the striking growing distant as the Syrian moved away. He felt for his own pulse against his wrist, nothing. Against his neck, beneath the ear, nothing. Against his chest, the flat palm lying on his breast, left of center. For a moment he felt a strange calm and a sense of satisfaction. Very well, I'm dead. That wasn't so bad.

Then he felt angry, cheated, indignant. He stomped out through Rashid's front door onto the sidewalk. Outside, facing the skyline, staring up, he thought: a building is missing, did they think I wouldn't notice? A void gaped from the fraternity of structures like a black gap in a smile. He started walking but stopped at the end of the block.

There was the gap: an ugly heap of grey stones in the center of the next block. This was a five-story building, he recalled, maybe even higher. Now it was a saddle-shaped pile, slouching into the imploded cave of its own basement, which was filled with dark water. Afternoon sunshine blazed garishly from the shards of glass mixed throughout the potpourri of stone and wood. He felt the warmth on his face and knew he was alive.

7.

Daniel did not tell Julia about his health. But he told Eugene. Yevgenny. That was his real name, although Daniel only used it sometimes when they had been drinking. More accurately, when Daniel had been drinking, because Eugene was perhaps the one Russian on the planet who never touched a drop. He was small and thin with a face full of sharp angles covered in patches by a wispy and irregular beard, a narrow, pointed nose that seemed designed to intrude, and long red hair usually tied back in a ponytail. In the past year, they had become partners in business and peril. In a lifetime devoid of siblings Eugene was the closest thing Daniel had to a brother. They had had some improbable escapes and close-calls and agreed that in the interest of survival there would be no secrets between them. So Eugene knew.

They met a year ago, in 1991, in DeSoto's office, surrounded by the sort of paintings that people always describe as "priceless" despite the evidence that somebody had obviously found a price for them. Miguel DeSoto Ramos was an art dealer to the elite of West Berlin, or so his tax returns said. He did in fact deal in art and knew quite a bit about it but Daniel was never sure how much of DeSoto's time was actually devoted to this front. Daniel only ever dealt with the other Miguel DeSoto, apparently the real one, if one could use that word to describe such an enigmatic man. That DeSoto was the smuggler, drug supplier, money-launderer, weapons dealer, and probably a great many other things Daniel had yet to discover. Such mysteries notwithstanding, DeSoto had thus far been good to him and Daniel had no complaints.

Daniel began by moving goods for DeSoto: grey-market drugs, untaxed alcohol, sometimes elite cars, the occasional stolen piece of art. He never did any "cleaning," which was DeSoto's euphemism for murder. Soon Daniel graduated to smuggling weapons, a trade that expanded and prospered as the Wall came down and the East European militaries started cannibalizing their stockpiles. Desperately poor Polish or East German officers with access to warehouses needed somebody to "steal" guns, bombs, ammunition, whatever. That's where things stood in 1991 when Daniel was in DeSoto's office one morning, shaking hands with the new member of the team.

"Gentlemen, I trust you have not met before?" the Spaniard opened his arms, gesturing broadly to both of them. "Daniel, this is Eugene."

Daniel thought: DeSoto *hopes* we've not met before because if we had, then he needs to fire (or worse) his researchers. Before taking on any new employee DeSoto would surely have sent people scouring the earth for all traces of their lives, in case some rival or enemy had planted them in his organization deliberately. Miguel DeSoto doesn't make mistakes. Therefore he's still alive and wealthier than the Pope.

"Please sit, gentlemen," DeSoto continued with the broad gesture, encompassing the chairs in front of his desk. "The opportunities in our weapon trade have become so significant lately that I thought we could use a new team member, preferably someone who speaks Russian and who has some experience and proven discretion."

If that was a compliment intended to elicit a Thank You, Eugene did not rise to the occasion. DeSoto did not appear to mind.

Their first job was straightforward but involved a trip to Prague in an old Renault van that could barely hold its own going uphill at more than 60kph. For two hours they struggled through the *Erzgebirge*, the "ore mountains" that had once divided Germany from the Austro-Hungarian Empire. There was plenty of time to talk.

"You'd think he could afford better vehicles," Daniel said, shaking his head in dismay at the fumes and the chugging engine. The steering wheel vibrated so much that Daniel's wrists were becoming numb. "He probably thinks that it won't attract attention if it's run-down."

Eugene shrugged. "This isn't so bad. You should see what we had in Russia."

Daniel discovered that Eugene spoke fluent English and passable French, in addition to his growing facility in German. Into each of these languages, he injected an unmistakable Russian accent, swallowing parts of most consonants or diverting them through one nostril. They talked about their misadventures in France and America. Eugene had left Russia and gone to Paris, then tried his luck briefly in New York. Daniel had left Paris and gone to Washington. Their paths now intersected in Berlin. They found each other surprisingly similar: close in age (Eugene was a year older), equally borderless, and devoid of ideology.

They drove through Dresden. Daniel marveled at the lunar craters in the streets. The frame of the van heaved apocalyptically with each massive pothole. The façades of buildings were filthy grey-brown concrete, peeling away like old vegetable skins, crumpling and falling to the streets. There were blocks still in rubble left from the war, fenced-off, in the middle of the old city. These alternated with streets filled with Soviet-style slab housing, brutally flat and featureless.

"You see?" Eugene said as he pulled a cigarette from a pack in his shirt pocket, "This is what communism did. This used to be a beautiful city. Now it's shit."

"It's what the war did," Daniel said.

"The war was fifty years ago. They had lots of time to fix it up."

"Worse than in Russia?" Daniel asked.

Eugene lit the cigarette, took a long drag, and shook his head slowly as he exhaled.

"Russia is always worse," he said.

8.

I am twenty-nine years old. This is what Daniel kept repeating in each of the existential debates he'd conducted with himself over the past few weeks. It was unlikely that he was dying of cancer. But still. Young people aren't invincible and anything's possible and it *had* been getting worse, and.... Then he considered whether twenty-nine was in fact still "young" and reassured himself that any age that started with a "1" or "2" was young by definition, meaning: he had one year left. Next year he would be thirty and it was time to make some decisions.

He had been a smuggler for Miguel DeSoto for more than four years. He had done well for his boss and for himself. Daniel had money, stashed in various accounts under various names, spread across three countries. He had more money than he knew what to do with at the moment, and for the past few years, he'd assumed that he'd figure something out eventually. Before turning thirty.

When he told Eugene, his Russian friend's fatalism and pragmatism sounded like contempt.

"What is thirty?" Eugene groaned. "Thirty is nothing. Why thirty? Why not twenty-nine or thirty-one or thirty-three-and-a-third? Why pick a stupid number at all? You might live to be a hundred or you might get squashed by the bus tomorrow. Trust me on this," Eugene said. "When I turned thirty, nothing happened. The next morning I still had hair and teeth, I could still walk down the street, my dick still worked, everything. No message from God, no revelation, just another fucking day."

"It's symbolic," Daniel said. "People have ten fingers. They like to do things in tens. The number itself doesn't matter. The point is to have a goal. I picked thirty."

The goal Daniel had in mind was that by thirty he would retire from DeSoto's service and become legitimate. He would start a business of some sort, settle into a more stable line of work, come home in the evenings and watch dumb TV shows and ask his wife how her day had been and whether he needed to pick up their son from the football club tomorrow.

Something like that.

Eugene saw right through it. "This is about your new girlfriend, isn't it?"

That got Daniel's hackles up.

"What are you talking about? I don't need a reason to want something different."

"Yeah, but that's the reason, isn't it?" Eugene said. "That's why we agreed at the outset that it was best not to have any serious relationships. They're distractions and weaknesses that bad guys can exploit."

"Has it ever occurred to you—"

Eugene whistled and rolled his eyes.

"— that *we're* the bad guys?" Daniel asked.

"You know that's not true," Eugene said, his tone softening. "You've been in this game long enough to know that. We're pussycats compared to some of these maniacs. Some of those guys hurt and kill people for fun. They actually like it. We're just transporters. If they don't get nasty then I don't get nasty."

They were quiet for a moment then Eugene said,

"I can't believe you're dumping me for a redhead. You know they're all crazy."

That made Daniel laugh. "She's not a red-head. You're the red-head." He switched to English and said, "It's called Auburn."

"Aww-burn?" Eugene sneered. "What the fuck is that? Your English is better than mine."

"I'm not dumping you," Daniel said. "I'm thinking about dumping everything and starting something totally new."

"For some *Aww*-burn." Eugene giggled, then sighed.

There were times when Daniel wondered whether Eugene wasn't right. What is the point of all this planning for the future when he might be dying, when he might get shot by some bad guy, when Julia — with whom he'd had precisely zero discussions of this sort — might not have even the slightest desire to share her future with him. It was March and Daniel mused that if he really were sick he might not even live to see Christmas. And although he'd never given a damn about Christmas before, when he had these thoughts suddenly it mattered a great deal.

After the Wall came down Daniel was fascinated by the East. He went there almost every day for months to see for himself this forbidden, hidden place that had existed behind the great curtain. It was wretched, mostly, and its inhabitants seemed more eager to get the hell out than he was to get in. The buildings and streets were as sad as he'd ever seen anywhere and Daniel was no stranger to ghettos. Everything reeked of coal smoke, uncollected garbage, and backed-up sewer pipes. He walked up the hill into Prenzlauer Berg and got lost because of the endless repetition and the absence of landmarks or even colors.

Yet something kept bringing him back. Daniel felt that he had discovered a portal to an older Europe that had existed before his lifetime. He had lived only in modern, protean places like Paris, Washington, and West Berlin, and here he felt like a time traveler. Everything was so old that it was new to him. He had never seen a bakery (called simply "Bakery") that offered only four kinds of bread. Or a bar where "vodka" meant: the one brand, possibly the one bottle, they had. There was a simplicity and clarity that made him realize he didn't need to choose from seventeen varieties of toothpaste. As the East Berliners were streaming West to gawk at porn shops and stores where nobody ever ran out of soap, Daniel found it charming to be in neighborhoods where coffee was still considered a luxury.

East Berlin was a broken place but it was addictive and Daniel increasingly realized that he wanted to live there. Flats were so cheap that there was no point renting. He bought a place with cash and paid less than what he'd earned in the last two months. Getting people to fix the electricity and plumbing was a challenge at first but there were soon government programs for that and Daniel simply had to open the door and point, and the guys in blue overalls did the rest.

So he became an East Berliner. And as that grey world began to sprout some color here and there he watched the steel-grey winter recede slowly in March, seeping out of the landscape and the walls and trickling through the cobblestones to the water that always waited just below the sandy soil. Berlin stood upon sixty underground lakes and streams and every time the ground was punctured water flowed up to meet the intruder. Daniel saw rising water everywhere, eventually even in his dreams. The city started to grapple with the unimaginably vast job of repair and renovation, stitching the two severed halves of its body back together. The streets birthed cranes and drills as immense new pipes painted royal blue drew the water up and away.

Julia was now an East Berliner too. Her flat was not far away, perhaps ten minutes by bicycle. Daniel was not fond of it. Staying at Julia's place meant competing for space with her various projects and *objets d'art* in progress. In a city that was crumbling, she seemed oblivious to anything but her own private constructions. Her apartment swelled with oddly-shaped furnishings, with stark, brilliant paintings and sculpture, with collages of cloth and tempera adorning the walls. Sensing Daniel's aversion to decoration, she had given him only the most utilitarian of her creations: a table, chairs, a bed whose knotted wooden supports looked like roiling brown waves. Normally she came to stay the night at his place, where expanses of floor existed free of paint pots or carefully stained beer bottles. It was not their custom for her to call beforehand. Sometimes she came, sometimes she didn't.

"I brought bread," she said in the door. "Have you eaten?"

"No," he replied, glancing at her feet in sandals made of three pale brown straps, premature for the reluctant spring outside. "No, that's perfect."

She let her sack slide from her shoulder. When it plopped in the middle of his floor she opened the top and extracted a dense, sepia-colored loaf and placed it on the tearsplash table. He watched her walk to the kitchen, the long slit in her skirt opening as she hovered over the refrigerator shelves.

"Do you have any cheese?" she called without looking up. He had begun to peruse his wine rack (another Julia creation, it seemed to be made of creeping vines that had been turned to stone, paralyzed leaves and all.)

"I have some quark, that's it."

Access to fine wine was one of several fringe benefits of his profession and Daniel normally hoarded his fringe-benefits with squirrelish determination in secret spots all over the city. The best wines he came across went straight to his apartment and rarely lasted more than a week. Erasing the evidence, he told himself. Daniel selected an '82 Chateau Lafite-Rothschild.

The city was moonless and black when they finished eating. Window lamps from the opposite apartments offered a few pale yellow blooms in the atmosphere like dying stars hovering above the street. Daniel stood at the window for a few minutes, listening to Julia run water in the bathroom. He turned off the overhead light and looked down from time to time but no one ever walked the sad brown grass of the little courtyard below.

When he heard the water stop he turned to face the bathroom door. She emerged barefoot and without her blouse, the yellow light making her skin seem pale, the black frame of her bra cutting her torso into four slices. He watched her praying mantis arms as she tugged earrings from her ears and laid them on the table. She stood halfway across the room from him and then a narrow smile crooked one corner her lips and she leaned into the rising arc of an uplifted arm, sweeping the still air as she lifted and turned.

Daniel removed his shirt and walked a few steps forward, stopping where her dance concluded. When she came to rest in front of him he waited, breathing deeply in the air around her before he touched the narrow line of her shoulder, tracing with his fingertips down the soft rising curve of her small breast. She placed four fingertips on his chest.

Hours later, in the confusion of his blankets, she slept in a quiet rhythm of air rushing against his neck. Daniel lay awake, watching the minutes burst, one after the other, in the incandescent orange lights of his bedroom clock.

When he rose she didn't awaken. He slipped out, her arm trailing across his chest and falling to the sheets. He stood naked at the window, staring into the darkened courtyard below.

The two most important women in Daniel's life were both connected to him through Miguel DeSoto.

Sabine had been DeSoto's lover, for exactly how long Daniel had never been sure. DeSoto collected women as carefully as he collected anything. In his own way, he was a monogamous lover. But he admitted no one without their passing some test of ownership. That Sabine could have once been "his" and still herself was a testament to the strength of her will. That he had ultimately let her go without tumult indicated to Daniel that perhaps Miguel DeSoto Ramos allowed himself, however rarely, the indiscretion of love.

Julia never made those moves. She worked for DeSoto; he owned her in a different way. Their connection had been contractual, as most of DeSoto's connections were. Daniel took some cold comfort in that, whenever the thought forced its way past the barricades he had built around it.

The woman that Daniel LeClerc had fallen in love with came from Baden. She spoke with the elongated southern accent, particularly when she was contemplative. Her Yes stretched into a long *Yoah* whenever she wasn't entirely sure that Yes was what she meant to say.

Julia dropped out of college in her second year. When Daniel had asked her why, she recounted the precise moment she decided to leave. She was in an art history class, seated near the rear of the auditorium as the professor muttered and showed slides. Everything she loved about art was reduced to a flat image on a distant screen, untouchable, lifeless, two-dimensional. She decided that there was no more point in hoping that others could impart wisdom to her. Everything she wanted would have to come from her own hands and imagination. She became convinced that her life would be merely a series of sustaining activities to support these things, and she didn't much care what those sustaining activities entailed, as long as they left her with time to paint, sculpt, carve, or sketch.

She never imagined she would fail. Her faith in herself was so strong that she was unequipped to deal with that unacceptable vision when it finally would not be denied. When at last she woke in a strange, filthy apartment, naked and shaking in withdrawal, when she found herself in stupendous debt to half a dozen terrifying people, when the heat and water in her flat were turned off and she was unable even to remember clearly whether it was indeed her flat, or why she was in Berlin at all... then there was a tip, a path of last recourse offered, and DeSoto was there, Mephisto-like with his exorbitant salvation.

Two years, that was the standard contract. For two years you are his, you work wherever, whenever, and however he commands. He pays for everything. All the demons who are chasing you, all the vultures circling over you, he makes them go away. You don't want to know how. Then you're free, cleaned up, back on your own.

Yet somehow, and everyone knew it without saying it, you were always and forever his.

Daniel stared at the empty courtyard below his apartment and thought for the thousandth time about his exit. From this place, from DeSoto, perhaps from Berlin. Each time he thought about it, the sensation grew stronger that there had been a moment at some point in the past that he had not recognized at the time, at which there was no more getting out.

9.

"German kids yell and scream a lot," Eugene said. "When I was a kid, if we'd made this much noise, the teachers would have punished us."

They were standing on the sidewalk of the Bötzowstraße in Prenzlauer Berg, in the East, against the back wall of a large school. The inner court was a playground and the sound of children shrieking at play echoed throughout the neighborhood. Daniel's apartment was only a few blocks away but they were here because of what was directly across from the school: a Vietnamese grocery and convenience store. They took turns, one keeping his eyes on it while the other scanned up and down the street. At the southern end of the block was the entrance to the Volkspark Friedrichshain, from this distance simply a wall of green trees exploding into Spring.

"I don't like using this place," Eugene said.

"You've mentioned that," Daniel replied.

"It's too risky. If somebody tries something, if shooting starts, this neighborhood is full of kids."

"The kids are behind *this*," Daniel said, thumping the century-old brick walls with his palm. "But yes, I know how you feel about it. Talk to DeSoto if you want to make a change."

The first time Eugene brought this up, Daniel stared at him in astonishment. He knew enough already about Eugene's past, about the things he'd done, to marvel that his partner would be this worried about the unlikely possibility that a child might be an innocent bystander or catch an errant bullet.

"Not just the danger," Eugene had said, "Just, that isn't the kind of stuff that a little kid should see."

And this from a man who had murdered his own father.

That was the confession, about six months ago, that Daniel knew Eugene wouldn't have offered unless he truly trusted him. Among other people, it was the sort of thing one might hear only after a long night drinking (and indeed Daniel had been a bit drunk that night). But Eugene was sober, as always. He just said it.

"It was either him or me," he had said, outlining the history of his father Sergei the alcoholic, the man who beat all four of his boys, each until they were big enough to hit back, and yet each departed instead as soon as he could. Yevgenny Sergeyevich, the last and smallest child, got the worst of it. "Not to mention my mom," he added, squinting.

So he'd waited until the right night, when Sergei came home reeking, barely able to walk, and Eugene jumped him, gagged and bound him at gunpoint and led him with shoves and kicks, haltingly, crookedly, to the edge of the rail switching yard a kilometer from their apartment. That was where the police always found the usual suspects: the bums, gangsters, and ne'er-do-wells who were officially nonexistent in the Soviet Union. There, if there were any witnesses, nobody would believe them. There, seventeen-year-old Yevgenny shot his father in the back of the head with the man's own Makarov service pistol.

"The only thing my father left for me," he said with a snort.

This is why you don't drink, Daniel understood.

Of all the people Eugene could have confessed this to, he had chosen exactly the right listener. Daniel had considered doing the same thing to his own father on more occasions than he could count but had never found the courage. Maybe Eugene had sensed that, maybe Daniel had let something slip out once. Maybe Yevgenny Sergeyevich simply needed to be forgiven by somebody.

He'd applied for a deferment of his military draft. Caring for a widowed mother was an approved exemption. But Eugene had done it to avoid looking suspicious, knowing that with the Afghan War devouring a generation of young men, his request would be denied and he would leave at last.

After growing up like that, Daniel mused, fighting the Mujihadeen probably wasn't so bad. Yevgenny could have made a career in the army. But he left after his mandatory tour, left Russia altogether, went to Paris and began calling himself Eugene. He became a soldier for gangsters instead, then went to New York for a while, and then to Berlin. Born in a broken place, always looking for another broken place.

"There," Daniel said, nodding toward the store window. A teenaged Vietnamese boy flipped the cardboard "Open" sign on the door to "Closed." They scanned up and down the street one more time then crossed quickly and went straight inside, Daniel locking the door behind him.

The store was tiny and narrow, constricted by crates of fruit and vegetables and a single shelf of bottled drinks. By default these formed a corridor, barely a meter wide, approaching and then passing to the side of the register and into the back through a thin and dented aluminum door. And then, after all that, suddenly there was all the space in the world.

The back of the store was a large freight elevator, left over from the days when this whole block had been a single factory, before the war, before the communists decided that they needed apartments more urgently and subdivided such structures, adding walls throughout. The elevator was big enough to hide a couple of good-sized cars. It had two immense doors on opposite sides. Eugene and Daniel stood in one of these doors and across from them on the other side stood the Wisniewskis, father and son, waiting for them.

Although they'd done several deals, Daniel still didn't know their first names and called them "Senior" and "Junior" instead.

"Gentlemen," Eugene said. The Wisniewskis nodded. Senior had put on some weight, Daniel observed.

"Is that a new tattoo?" Eugene asked Junior. Senior's wince and head-shake indicated that Yes, Junior had been adding more ink recently. Daniel and Eugene crossed through the freight elevator and now all four men were standing in the other doorway. It opened to a secluded and very small loading bay, squeezed between brick buildings on all sides and with room enough only for one truck at a time. The lot then opened to the alley that ran behind all the buildings on the block. Daniel stood guard behind them, watching the alley. Senior pulled a tire iron from an immense pocket on his blue work overalls and pried a steel floor panel up a few centimeters. It took father and son, plus Eugene, to lift the panel up, opening the elevator's floor. That revealed the shaft below and its immense space, partially filled with stacked wooden crates.

Senior squatted with some difficulty and huffed as he climbed down the rungs on the side of the elevator shaft until he was standing among the stacks. From another huge pocket, he produced a flashlight and peered through the slats of several crates. Apparently satisfied, he shouted to Junior:

"Pull up the truck."

Junior turned and left down the alley. Daniel stayed and kept his eye on the southern exit that faced the park, and suddenly realized that somebody else was there.

At the end of the alley, perhaps fifty meters away, was a man in a long coat, standing perfectly still and apparently staring at him. Daniel began walking toward him carefully, his hand moving around his waist, under his jacket, to rest on his gun.

As he approached he heard the engine of Junior's truck cough into action behind him, puffing through the low gears as Junior tried to line it up in the tight opening between the buildings.

The figure didn't move as Daniel closed toward him. It was an old man in a filthy grey coat and oddly bright-green tennis shoes. His grey-white hair was thick and wild and Daniel suddenly recognized the face and its large fish hook scar.

"Johannes?" he whispered, incredulous.

Behind him, the truck grunted its rear axle over the curb as Junior tried to back in. Daniel glanced back to see Junior sticking his head out the window, waving and yelling, asking for help. One of the rearview mirrors scraped a brick wall. Junior shifted into first gear again, trying to pull out and straighten the truck.

Daniel turned and saw Johannes staring at him.

"My dear boy," the old man said.

From behind came the crack and scrape of the truck hitting a wall, followed by Junior screaming a curse in Polish. "Fuck," Daniel said, taking two steps back and debating what hand gestures Junior thought he needed in order to get through this. He turned again, was about to say, "Wait a minute—" but the old man was gone.

Daniel sprinted the remaining ten meters to the curb, away from the still-cursing Junior. He emerged on the boulevard across from the park, looked up and down the sidewalk, then across, in time to see a grey figure disappearing through the trees. Daniel sighed and turned back down the alley where Senior and Eugene were puzzling at Junior's inability to park the truck.

For once Eugene was oblivious. He giggled a little as the Wisniewskis yelled at each other in Polish. Senior managed to open the driver's door enough to squeeze his belly up and into the driver's seat.

"See, it's never good enough for dad, is it?" Eugene chuckled. "Anyway, I got the money. Did you pay the Vietnamese kid?"

Daniel shook his head. "I'll take care of him before we go."

The truck finally lurched into position in the loading bay and stopped with a heavy thump.

"Always so glamorous, these guys," Eugene said.

10.

Donatello was Eugene's favorite place to get breakfast. They made deviled eggs which, according to Eugene, were every bit as good as in New York. That was high praise indeed, and he often told the waitress about it, but she still stared at him when he placed a triple order:

"Three times?"

"Yeah, three orders. Just put them on one plate."

"I'll check to see if we have that many."

"Never mind, just give me all of them."

"All...?"

"Yeah yeah, however many you have, I'll take them."

Daniel ordered a coffee and toast. He knew that he had at most five minutes to finish his food before Eugene cleared his plate and came scouting on Daniel's side of the table to see if the Frenchman could spare any of his breakfast, so he kept it simple.

"Do you remember I told you once," Daniel said, "about the old guy who was hit by a car on the night of the *Wende*? And Sabine obsessing about him?"

"Mm," Eugene said. "She told me too."

"She did?"

"Ah, secrets!" Eugene said, smiling. Daniel frowned.

"I think I saw him yesterday."

"Really?" Eugene said. "Well, that will make her happy."

"I'm not going to tell her."

"Why not?"

"I'm pretty sure it's him, but I don't know where or how to find him again."

"Bullshit," Eugene said.

"What do you mean bullshit?"

"I mean, you're the guy who says he wants to be a private detective, and —"

"Don't talk about that around—"

"—Don't worry, your secret is safe with me. I'm just saying, you could find him if you wanted to. You just don't want to see her get all hopeful and excited again and then get let down again when it doesn't work out."

There was no need to tell him he was right.

The food and coffee arrived. The waitress took her time serving Daniel first, almost spitefully, as Eugene visibly watered, contemplating the mob of deviled eggs on her tray. At last, she set it down in front of him and his fingers danced over the plate, happy and unsure where to begin.

"Oh, I love it here," he said.

It was here in Donatello, nearly a year ago, that Eugene had suggested that they should consider doing some jobs on their own, without DeSoto. Daniel was skeptical. Eugene was dismayed by that; why *wouldn't* you want to do more jobs on your own? Choose the work, make the rules, keep all the money. Do you really want to be somebody's drone forever?

Daniel was worried about the possibility of crossing DeSoto without even knowing until it was too late. What if they messed up something he'd arranged or interfered with one of his deals? The Spaniard had his hands in all kinds of things they didn't know about, at least not yet. DeSoto probably wouldn't ask questions; he'd assume the worst and that would be that. Eugene thought that was absurd. There are four million people in Berlin and plenty of opportunities.

Eugene had had a plate of deviled eggs beneath him then, too, and he'd cracked his knuckles and licked his lips in anticipation. Then, lifting an egg, he'd told Daniel that he had an idea for a compromise:

"Let's do it in Paris."

"Paris?" Daniel said, swallowing a bite of toast.

"Yeah, there are ridiculously cheap flights now, you can get there in two hours, take a train or car back if we need to transport anything. We both know the city, we know people there."

"Do you have a specific job in mind?"

Eugene had vacuumed a deviled egg in one breath and winced, smiling in anticipation. "As it happens," he said, swallowing, "I do."

A week later they were in a tiny semi-secret bar beneath a basement near the *École Militaire*. It was a club of sorts, an invitation-only enclave of foreign smugglers and their local accomplices. They descended a corkscrew staircase that would have tested the slightest claustrophobe and emerged in a cave so small that there was room for perhaps only ten standing and ten sitting. Despite the elbow-rubbing proximity of all the patrons, everyone spoke in mutters of five or six languages and managed to have private conversations. Every few minutes the whole place vibrated severely as a metro train passed less than a meter below the floor.

There, Daniel met Eugene's contact, an East German: "Call me Ralf." It might have even been his real name; he was so awkward and feckless that Daniel was surprised he'd managed to stay alive this long in the Paris underworld. Call me Ralf was a doctor by training, a former medical officer in the Volksarmee, the nonexistent army for a nonexistent nation. And he had medical supplies to sell.

Daniel had the impression that Call me Ralf was a bit afraid of Eugene, or at least a bit too eager to impress. Nonetheless, they worked out a fairly substantial deal and a week later Eugene was inhaling deviled eggs happily in Donatello again with a self-satisfied 'Whatever were you so worried about?' tone and discussing how often they should be making trips to Paris.

Every few weeks, as it turned out. The money was good and Call me Ralf, against all expectations, kept coming through.

"You know," Ralf said once to Daniel, "You could be German. You look German, you speak it perfectly. Are you sure you're French?"

"I'm good with languages," Daniel said and changed the subject.

When Eugene suggested a drug shipment from Budapest to Berlin, Daniel initially vetoed it.

"Not Ralf," Eugene said. "These guys are Jamaican. They operate in Budapest. There's no way they're connected to DeSoto. We pick it up from one pair of Jamaicans in Hungary and bring it to another group of Jamaicans in Kreuzberg. Two days' work, look at this money."

What Daniel should have said was: Why do we need the money? We don't have anything to spend it on anyway. Instead he said, "Fine."

That was the night it all went wrong. Either the Berlin Jamaicans thought they were being betrayed by the Budapest Jamaicans, or the whole thing was a sting from the start, but Daniel found himself against a wall in Görlitzer Park with his hand across his stomach, where a hot red stream spilled out from his opened flesh. Three faces, so dark in the night that only their white eyes were clear to him, stared for a moment at the burgundy spreading across his shirt, oozing between his fingers. One of them produced a machete from his raincoat and held it at chest level for a few seconds as if he expected Daniel to revere the instrument of his destruction. He seemed about to speak when a bullet split open his throat with a crack that Daniel heard in every bit of his body. The others whirled frantically, their black cords of hair snapping around the sides of their heads. In the last two seconds of his life, one of the other Jamaicans saw what he was looking for: a small man with a red ponytail rising from behind the metal box of a telephone line connector. He saw this and he, too, seemed about to say something when his ribcage shattered with the crack of the gun. He gasped and heaved and tried to run but fell backward and convulsed on the grass. The third Jamaican stood speechless, unbelieving, as the small man approached in the expanse of a single breath, trained the Makarov on his forehead, and without even a change of expression, pulled the trigger.

"Where am I?" Daniel asks, his head rising briefly from the table.

"You're fine," says a strange voice, foreign, a composition of sighs.

Daniel turns his head and sees he is in a white room devoid of furnishings. A tall man with black hair and a thick mustache washes dark hands at a sink in the wall. Daniel turns his head the other way and sees Eugene sitting on a white stool, his sleeves rolled up, a bottle in his hand.

"Vodka," Daniel says. "You're drinking."

"Ah, you almost bled to death," the foreigner says. "Your friend brought you here. I stitched you up. Don't move your stomach. Lie still and rest. I didn't have any plasma to give you, so we had to do this the old-fashioned way."

"You're drinking," Daniel mumbles again at Eugene. His eyes are heavy, clouded with white shadows that appear to slough off all the walls. Before he closes them again he thinks he sees a patch of white on Eugene's exposed forearm.

11.

Sabine usually referred to Daniel and Eugene collectively as *"Les Boys."* They had never made any show of protest. Not that that would have mattered. Sabine owned the place and she could call you whatever she liked.

How did Sabine get *d'accord*? Miguel DeSoto had something to do with it. Not right away, not in the immediate wake of their breakup, but a couple of months later, after things had cooled enough and the resentment between them had receded to leave only the familiar terrain of good memories. Then she came to see him, and he surprised himself, finding that he was smiling as she entered the room. She didn't need much money, it was mainly the favor of a few pulled strings. He said he'd do these things for her then he kissed her on the cheek and she left. He picked up a telephone and a week later *d'accord* was hers.

The interior "needs work," the realtor admitted. It had been an Italian restaurant that opened in the early sixties, when the western half of the city had finally lifted itself from the ruins of the war. In those days, right after the Wall went up, it took some guts to come to West Berlin. The Soviets and Americans glared at each other from the turrets of tanks. Some fresh crisis every few weeks threatened everyone with Armageddon. The original owners must have thought: until World War Three breaks out, people still need pizza.

Sabine had no idea how the Italian restaurant had fared through the decades, only that by the time she bought the place it was depressed and wounded from years of neglect. The kitchen reeked of mold and garbage, the ceiling was peeling away and falling in chunks to the floor, the bathrooms were unspeakable. Leaky pipes had ruined much of the wood around the base of the antique bar. Buying the restaurant meant buying the cellar below and the second-floor rooms above. Sabine decided that it made no sense to keep a separate apartment somewhere else. If she was going to buy a place, then she was all-in. The second floor would be her flat.

Sabine grew up speaking French, her father's language. Her parents had wandered western Europe in the fifties and sixties, coming to rest when they found some remote spot where the air was fresh and the immigration officials visited infrequently. Then they would have a child, realize with alarm that they were becoming settled, and pack up the whole show: a family like an accumulating snowball rolling around the continent. A son was born in the Spanish Pyrenees. Another was born in the Dutch lowlands. A third came amidst the ancient vineyards of central Italy. Sabine arrived in a tiny hamlet in the Vaucluse, at the end of a winding mountain road east of Besançon.

By the time she was a teenager, she had wearied of the family's restless peregrinations. One night she was throwing darts with her brothers and several of their male friends. Near the target was a hanging paper map of Europe into which her brothers had placed colored pins for all the places they had lived. The boys were drinking and their aim was becoming haphazard. Darts were starting to miss the target altogether and hit the map instead. Her brothers later claimed it was pure coincidence but Sabine remembered being sober, stepping up to the line of tape on the floor, and hurling the dart deliberately at Germany. It struck Berlin, dead-center. Three years later, as they were helping her pack and load her things, her brothers presented her with the map as a going-away present.

She was thirty-five now, having traveled more by the age of eighteen than most people do in a lifetime. She had settled in West Berlin and never left.

Owning her own bar and restaurant had been her ambition for years but the first time Sabine used the front door key and walked in alone, on the morning after she signed all the closing and insurance papers, she felt as if someone was drizzling ice water down her spine. Somehow it looked and smelled a lot worse than when she had been there with the realtor, before she was so deeply in debt for it, back when she still had choices. After half an hour of stark terror, she saw the first of the contractors poking his head through the door tentatively, asking where he should drop off the plumbing fixtures she had ordered, and her world began to right itself again. She thought about the famous photographs of the tired, dusty women who cleared the rubble with their bare hands after the war, stacking shattered bricks and shards of lumber or hauling dirt away in wheelbarrows. You have to start somewhere.

Sabine spent five months repairing and renovating. She spent another month struggling through the maze of the city's permits and tax regulations, hiring a few people, and massaging the restaurant suppliers and liquor wholesalers. Summer stretched into autumn as the women on the terraces of the cafés pulled blankets around their shoulders. The temperatures fell and the evenings came sooner each day. When at last she was ready, she had missed the Summer café season. Undaunted, she opened in late September. She named the restaurant *d'accord* in honor of her French father. Behind the bar, she hung a map of Europe with a dart lodged in the city of Berlin, and a framed photograph of the rubble women.

Daniel respected her for all of that, especially the way she had started with nothing and maneuvered presciently so that each step was a step upwards. She never let anyone use her without using them also. When she was young and beautiful, dancing in DeSoto's clubs, she moved directly into his line of sight, knowing exactly who and what he was.

When Daniel walked through the door Eugene was sitting at the bar, talking to Sabine and stroking his scraggly red beard. His ponytail was tucked into his collar. They were leaning closely toward each other and their voices were very low, in the manner of lovers muttering secrets in a public place. Daniel had wondered about this from time to time, having found them in similar poses more than once. Sabine was a pretty woman: smart, mature, confident. Why wouldn't Eugene be attracted to her? But Eugene had apparently sworn off that pleasure years ago, as he had done with many, if not most, pleasures of consumption. All except the most fundamental, anyway: eating.

"Ah," Sabine said, smiling, leaning back when she saw Daniel. *"Les Boys sont arrivés."*

Daniel nodded at Eugene's glass of juice.

"You shouldn't give him too much of that stuff. He gets really wild."

Eugene smirked.

"Orange juice makes me horny," he said, sipping around the ice cubes.

"Hello, sweetheart," Sabine said. "Your usual vehicle tonight?"

"Of course," Daniel said, taking the stool beside Eugene.

"His usual vehicle to oblivion," Eugene said to Sabine's shoulder as she prepared Daniel's drink.

In *d'accord* Daniel drank only Russian gimlets: iced vodka and sweetened lime juice. They called them his "vehicles" after a long-forgotten joke having something to do with a man driving off a cliff in an ice storm. (Into "Oh-bleevion" Eugene said in English, his accent funnier than the joke itself when he told it the first time.) By now he had lost both the set-up and the punchline. Vehicles take you places, Daniel said, and a couple of good vehicles help you reach a certain velocity of mind and action that makes some formerly impossible things possible and other, formerly easy things, impossible. The trick was to find that place between the two phases: the moment in transit where you are in neither your old place nor your destination, but underway at an ideal speed, free and gliding upon the perfect If.

"Are you boys here to do your books?" Sabine said it with something that, while not quite a wink, revealed her knowledge of *Les Boys'* profession. "Because I can't condone any criminal activity in my establishment."

"We don't want any trouble with the authorities, *gnädige Frau*," Daniel said, producing a little black notebook from a pocket in his brown leather jacket. He set it down on the bar and Eugene picked it up, pretending never to have seen it before. He opened it and leafed through the pages, affecting bored semi-curiosity and making "la-la-la" noises.

They sat in a corner booth at Sabine's bar and "did the books" at the end of each month. They divided their profits by consensus in something approximating 50-50. That involved getting rid of goods by converting them into cash as quietly and efficiently as possible, although they each wanted to keep certain items for themselves. It was often a negotiated process because it involved things whose values were relative. Eugene didn't drink alcohol so he didn't care how much an exquisitely rare bottle of cognac was allegedly worth. Daniel didn't eat caviar, whereas Eugene would have bathed in it if he could. On one occasion they had to figure out how to "split" an 18th century cello. Most partnerships eventually foundered on these sorts of things but Les Boys had thus far made it work without a fuss.

The lion's share went to DeSoto, of course, delivered each month in a ritual of fealty that the boss reciprocated by treating them as mature partners in an enterprise. He knew how to be gracious. He also knew that it underscored how frightening he could be if that grace were ever withheld.

"How much of this wine did you set aside?" Eugene asked, adjusting a seldom-seen pair of wire-frame glasses on his narrow beak of a nose. He frowned at the notebook.

"What," Daniel asked, "The Sicilian?"

"If you say so," Eugene shrugged. "You know I don't do wine."

"Whatever it says there. Three cases, I think. Eight hundred D-mark, maybe eight-fifty. It's nothing. Julia likes it."

Eugene looked at him over the rims of the lenses. His moist brown eyes were motionless for a few seconds, scanning Daniel's guiltless face.

"What?" Daniel finally said. "How much of that caviar did you take?"

"Oh, a lot," Eugene nodded seriously, leaning back in the chair. "Quite a lot. Three, four thousand D-mark, I think. It was delicious. I still have some left."

"So?"

"It's for Julia?"

"It's for me. I drink it with my girlfriend."

"You know what I'm talking about," Eugene said, removing the glasses. "We don't even need to get into this."

"Fine. We won't get into it."

"We had our agreements, but if you want to change them now..."

At that, Daniel exhaled slowly, putting down his pencil. He reached for his drink, felt the clatter of the ice in the empty glass and turned to call over his shoulder toward the bar.

"Sabine, could I have another vehicle, please?"

They were silent for most of a minute then Daniel looked at Eugene and said evenly:

"Maybe I'm being naïve, but I can't even begin to see how this is any of your concern. What I do with my wine—"

"—Maybe you *are* being naïve."

They were both quiet until Sabine had come and gone.

"You're not listening to me," Eugene said, switching to American English, which he knew Sabine couldn't understand. "We have our cut, we take those percentages, fine. Same as it's always been. What you do with it beyond that — you're right, it's your business. We only agreed to place limits on anything that would jeopardize our safety."

Eugene sat and stared at him quietly. Finally Daniel said:

"My relationship with Julia does not jeopardize our safety."

"We said no serious relationships," Eugene whispered. "No commitment or entanglement that somebody could use to—"

"*Das ist absurd*," Daniel said, switching back to German.

"Are you forgetting what we do?" Eugene snapped at him, still in English. "Are you forgetting the places we go, the kinds of people we deal with? Do you think for a moment that somebody who wants to bring you down won't figure out you've got a girlfriend? And then he'll come for her. And what will you do then? Will you still be willing to work with me on some job or will you be there to protect her?"

"Have you lost faith in me?" Daniel said, straightening his back, his chin elevating over the tabletop. "Because if you have, just say so, and we can split this whole thing." Daniel grabbed the notebook and waved it in Eugene's face. "We can split it right now and go our separate ways."

They pulled apart, collapsing almost simultaneously into their seatbacks, sighing dramatically through their nostrils and looking away from each other.

"You're being stupid," Eugene finally said.

"*I'm* being stupid."

"I'm worried about anything that would affect your judgment," Eugene said. "Can't you understand that?"

"I am capable," Daniel said, "of keeping all aspects of our partnership intact and still having a girlfriend. Can you understand *that?*"

"You know how I feel."

"Fine, but that was your decision to live that way. I never asked you to justify it to me. I just trusted your judgment."

Eugene groaned softly. He tugged at the rubber band that constrained his ponytail and let a mass of red hair tumble around his face. He scratched at his scalp with all ten fingers.

"You have more important things to consider about our relationship," Daniel said. "This could be a moot point soon."

"Oh shut up with that," Eugene said.

"You have strange priorities. You're worried about Julia when all the while—"

"—It's not an issue."

"It's going to be an issue soon enough," Daniel said. "Have you talked to Rashid?"

"You're not going to die," Eugene whispered in English. "You're not some old dog with worms in his guts, so shut up with that. It's the connection at your dick that I'm worried about, not your guts."

"This is all about my guts," Daniel said quietly.

12.

DeSoto had it arranged so that he entered and left only through back doors. This was understood by all those who associated with him and respected in the manner of a quirk that matures into an obsession when a person becomes wealthy enough to turn personal oddities into imperatives. Even his favorite office, a small converted school building in Moabit near the old prison, had been re-designed so that both of its doors (and who knows how many other entrances only DeSoto used) felt like back doors. One of these two opened to an alley, and as Daniel approached it he saw that Eugene was already there, waiting for him and chatting with the two chain-smoking guards.

The alley was perfectly clogged by an immense black BMW 750il with black-tinted windows. The guards were dressed in matching navy gabardine suits, with matching uncomfortable lumps just to the left of the buttons on the front panels of their coats. They could barely fit between the car and the alley walls but they did not dare lean against the vehicle.

Eugene lowered his sunglasses long enough to greet Daniel with eyebrows raised in suspicion, peeking over the rims.

"What?" Daniel said, "I'm not late."

"Pushing it," Eugene scolded as one of the guards opened the door for them and nodded.

"You're getting old and square," Daniel said as they ascended the stairs.

"You're the one who's puffing," Eugene replied when they had reached the second-floor hallway and two more guards waved metal detectors around their torsos and groins.

"Go ahead," one of them said, retracting the U-shaped wand. "He's alone."

Still, they knocked.

"Come," said the voice behind the oak.

He smiled graciously and rose when they entered.

"Gentlemen," DeSoto said, "A pleasure, as always. Please be seated."

He was a statuesque man, a bit taller than Daniel, immensely taller than Eugene. His face wore the lines and edges of a man in his early forties, but it was otherwise unblemished. His hair was black, flecked with silver at the temples and here and there around the slightly thinning crown. It was perfectly coifed around ears and neck, neither short nor long. When he extended his right hand to Daniel and Eugene, an immense ring gleamed from his third finger: Cornell, 1972. When he seated himself again behind his single-piece oak desk, he smoothed the spidery silk of his burgundy tie.

"I won't waste this on *you,*" he said, nodding at Eugene, "but Daniel, I have come across a superb collection of Chambertin. The 1983, truly majestic. I thought you might like a case."

Daniel nodded emphatically.

"Try not to leave wet tongue-marks on my carpet," DeSoto said with a chuckle. "I'll have someone leave it with Sabine. If you're feeling chivalrous, you should do the right thing and share."

Daniel smiled. "Of course. That's very generous of you."

"Well then," he puffed, "Business."

DeSoto picked up the antique telephone on his desk. There was no apparatus to dial; he simply waited a moment until a female voice answered, and then he gave quick instructions in Spanish. A few seconds later, a woman in a charcoal grey skirt suit entered nearly silently through a door in the rear wall and handed DeSoto a leather-bound folder. He thanked her, and she vanished as quickly as she had come. DeSoto extended the folder to Eugene, who laid it in his lap.

"All the details are there. Technical things. I trust you are not averse to some homework. I also trust you can make yourselves available for a little excursion to the Oder on short notice?"

Daniel and Eugene nodded, expressionless.

"Some of my colleagues in Poland have made a very attractive offer on a shipment of munitions. They are Russian, but I've checked through some sources and the origins seem to be good. Eugene, if you will be so kind as to have a quick look at that, too... I've left the names and numbers for you. Make a few calls, pose as a Russian associate of mine — a competitor but not an adversary. I think all is in order but I would hate to waste your gifts."

DeSoto smiled. His black eyes shimmered and reflected the light above his desk.

"I'll take care of it tonight," Eugene said. "I'll call at a strange hour to make it seem as if I'm on Moscow time."

"Fine," DeSoto said, then appeared to remember something, glancing at his watch. "I'm still on London time," he said, smiling and adjusting it. The gleam of the gold drenched the glittering diamonds positioned at each hour on its face. As he fingered its dial the woman in the suit knocked twice and opened her door again.

"Forgive me, sir," she said in German, "you asked to have your breakfast brought in late?"

"Yes," DeSoto said with a nod, "We're almost done."

A man in a dark suit brought a small tray. It was white gold, supporting, among other things, an intricately-painted demitasse of coffee, several dark miniature slices of bread interleaved with pale disks of cucumber, and a matching white gold egg cup. DeSoto nodded and his waiter slid out silently, leaving the tray on a corner of his desk.

"I believe that folder should have all the details of the merchandise itself. The cases will be locked and we'll get combinations after a first partial payment, so they need to be hidden for a few days. Exercise proper circumspection. These are my colleagues, not my friends."

Daniel nodded once.

"I think this should be fairly straightforward," DeSoto said, moving his hand to the tray and lifting an ornate silver spoon with which he tapped the circumference of the egg, shattering its shell into tiny clinging fragments. "Do you have any questions?"

Daniel and Eugene shook their heads.

"Anything you've been wanting to discuss?"

Again they said nothing. DeSoto put down the spoon and lifted a china lid to reveal a diminutive bowl with four gleaming strawberries.

"Ah," he said, smiling, holding out the cup toward them. "A strawberry?"

les fraises

Paris, 1968

13.

There were strawberries in the springtime in the palm of his mother's hand. He remembered the word for them: *Erdbeeren*. In the second grade, the year after she died, he made that mistake over and over again, to the exasperation of Mme. Dupliex the teacher. *Die Erdbeeren. Non*, Daniel, the teacher scowled, her fleshy box of a face so unlike that of his mother. *Les fraises.*

The only memories he had of his parents together involved fights. They shouted at each other about things he didn't understand. He could tell that when his mother used the word "revolution" she meant it seriously and positively, and when his father used it, he drenched it in contempt. According to his mother, Daniel's father was "not a revolutionary," and this was apparently both a condemnation and a surprise to her, although obviously not to him.

Daniel's earliest memories were like metal shavings jangling around his head, occasionally getting stuck somewhere or rubbing against something else and causing a moment of discord and pain. Were the strawberries in her hand before or after the revolution? When did his father drive the Mercedes up onto the curb, flinging the door open, his trenchcoat like a sail as he pushed through the crowd and tried to grab Daniel's mother as she wrenched her arm free? Did he grab Daniel instead and throw him into the passenger seat? And then speed away? Daniel remembered his mother's face distorted, screaming, but was she screaming the slogans with the other revolutionaries in the crowd, or was she screaming for him, screaming at her husband, or both?

Did the world have color in those days? Later as a grown man, when Daniel occasionally saw photographs from that period, the black and white confirmed his memories. Only a few points of color remained. A fat red strawberry resting in her palm. The blue of her eyes as she laughed at him mangling the sweet fruit with his stubby fingers and baby teeth. The neighbor's delivery van, decorated with images of sky blue fish and yellow chickens. The rest of that world was grey. He remembered sitting on the sofa with her, watching television. He remembered hanging on her fingertips in a marketplace and panicking when he momentarily lost hold of her.

He had a few memories of her voice in normal speech. He remembered her accent, the heaviness of her consonants, the way she spoke haltingly when she was upset, which was apparently often. Then one day the whole city joined her in anger, out in the streets, shouting and marching and throwing things at the police. He remembered that feeling of losing his hold on her fingertips, over and over again, as she raised her fist and shouted with the crowd. He understood that there was something other than him that she cared passionately about, perhaps even more important to her than he was, and this terrified him.

One day she was there and the next she wasn't. That's all he could remember now. One of those times she let go of his fingers must have been the last time. When he was five the images froze. There were no new memories. The few remaining colors drained slowly away; her blue eyes became gray, her brown hair black. All but the strawberries and her smile, which were the same color now.

14.

In the summer of 1968, Alain LeClerc rushed back to Paris in time to find his wife dead: her name cataloged, her body zipped into a plastic bag and chilled in a freezer drawer amidst a stack of drawers that slid out atop, beneath, and beside each other like cigarettes in a pack.

"That's her," he said, trying to remove a cigarette from a pack.

"I'm sorry, Monsieur, I can't have the smoke in here. You understand."

LeClerc frowned at the corpse as if it was her fault. He exhaled explosively, slapped his hands against his hips, and asked:

"What now?"

"I need you to fill out the forms. What was her religious affiliation?"

LeClerc shrugged, still staring at the body, looking annoyed.

"I don't know," he said.

The coroner's expression changed from well-oiled condolence to unprepared suspicion.

"You have no idea?"

"I don't think she was a believer. She was a communist."

"Ah," the coroner said, nodding. "Well, do you know if she had a preference for a burial?"

"Just cremate it."

The coroner stared at LeClerc with his mouth halfway open. He waited, expecting something more, and finally got:

"What was it, again, that killed her?" LeClerc asked, "They told me some kind of virus?"

"It, ah, was a pathogenic stomach infection. We've been searching for any signs that there might be some kind of outbreak, but so far she seems to be the only—"

"—She ate bad food?"

The coroner took two small steps backward.

"Ah, that's a possibility, yes."

"Mm."

LeClerc shook his head, grimacing. He stuffed his hands into the pockets of his blazer, strode a few paces away from the compartment that held his wife's body, then turned and looked at his Rolex.

"Very well, let's do those papers then," he said to the coroner, who was still standing sheepishly behind the extended compartment.

"Did she, ah, have any other family that needs to be notified?"

"No," LeClerc said. "I'll take care of it."

Daniel was five years old when a new face entered his world: dark-haired, small, serious, with huge chocolate eyes.

"Daniel, this is Nour. She's your new nanny. She'll take care of you while I'm away."

When his father was safely out of the apartment, Daniel looked up at this small woman, so dark she seemed to be made of shadows.

"My mother died," he said.

"Yes, child, I know." Her voice was throaty and deep.

"I'm going to take a bath now," he said. "I don't need any help anymore."

15.

"His French is terrible," LeClerc said to Nour while he bent over and scribbled at a table with an ornate gold pen. "That was his mother's fault; she never spoke it very well. And now I hear him using Arabic words. Are you speaking Arabic to him?"

"It is possible," Nour said quietly, her eyes trained on the check LeClerc was still writing, "that he heard me speaking on the telephone with my family."

"I watched you give him a glass of milk and he said, 'shukrin.' Arabic. You must correct him — he has trouble enough. He has a learning problem of some kind. The last thing he needs is to get confused with Arabic in his head now."

Nour stood rigidly until the check was handed to her. The moment it was safely in her purse, she aimed her chin upward at LeClerc and said:

"The boy has no learning problem. He has family problem. He doesn't make friend in school. He fight with other boys. I tell him he should go out with me for a walk, but he'd rather watch the television alone. He's depressed, that's his problem. He's a bright boy, he does his lesson, but he's depressed because he has no family."

LeClerc glared at her, realized the pointlessness of fighting with her. Nour was competent enough that losing her would result in yet more hassle and wasted time finding a replacement. Alain LeClerc would endure a little lip from an employee to avoid wasting time.

"It wasn't my fault his mother died," he said, his voice uncharacteristically needling, "and I can't stay here. My job requires—"

"—Yes, I tell him all the time, 'Your father's an important man, a diplomat. He has to travel and meet with important people.' And do you know what he said to me? He said, 'I don't care if he come or not.' Imagine a nine-year-old child saying that about his own father. So Monsieur, the least you could do when you come is to act as if you'd like to see him."

LeClerc threw up his hands with an exasperated "Gah!" and walked out of the kitchen.

One evening, on the rare and unexpected occasion of his father being home, Daniel asked at the dinner table:

"Why don't we have any pictures of my mother?"

LeClerc paused in the midst of chewing a piece of red potato, stared at him for a moment, then resumed chewing.

"I don't have a camera," he finally said to his son.

"It's ridiculous not having any pictures," Daniel muttered.

"Not to have... it's ridiculous *not to have* any pictures. God, do they teach you anything at that school?"

"No, not a thing," Daniel said evenly, thin brown wisps of sideburn erect on his smooth jaws. "Nour, may I be excused?"

"No, Daniel, finish your dinner," she said quietly.

"You ask the *maid?*" LeClerc said. "When you want to be excused, you can ask me."

I don't give a fuck what you think, Daniel thought, and I won't do you the honor of asking you for anything.

"Where are his grades?" LeClerc asked after another red potato. "Where are your report cards?"

"I have a question for you," Daniel said.

LeClerc said nothing.

"What class am I in this year?"

"What do you mean?"

"I mean," Daniel said, putting down his knife, "what class am I in? The sixth, seventh, eighth, what? Do you know?"

"I know that your manners are atrocious," LeClerc said. "Keep your hands on the table."

Nour looked down at her plate.

"You don't have any idea," Daniel said, his voice soaking with contempt. "You don't even know where I am in school. What do you care about my grades?"

LeClerc contemplated his teenage son for a moment, expressionless. Then a quizzical flicker of a smile touched one corner of his mouth for a second before he resumed eating. Daniel froze in place, then felt himself deflating and sinking into the wood of the chair.

He had known he was right, that his father didn't care about him at all. He had known it before he had challenged him. But he had never expected the man to be willing to confirm it.

16.

Madame Arnoux, the English teacher in Daniel's school, had a reputation as a merciless task-mistress. She was as uncompromising and humorless as a drill sergeant and students avoided English class if they possibly could take some other language instead. Daniel actually wanted to learn English and had enrolled with some enthusiasm, which was now being beaten out of him by endless grammar exercises.

In the chair beside and slightly in front of him sat a diminutive Corsican boy named Gianni who fascinated Daniel by seizing every imaginable opportunity for rebellion, even when nothing was to be gained from it. Gianni deadpanned jokes and deliberately mis-pronounced words in potentially naughty ways, as if he misunderstood. He wrote on a "shit" of paper, and the lines were too "tit" together, and all felines were "pussies" and so on. It did not take much to bring out the anti-Corsican snobbery of the Parisian students and teachers, and Gianni had apparently decided to head off their scorn with his own.

One day, as Daniel walked across the schoolyard toward the building, he saw Gianni surrounded and pummeled by four much bigger boys who were laughing and shouting "Vive Napoléon!" at him between kicks and punches. Gianni went down swinging, lashing out at them when his short arms could connect, which only made them beat him longer and with more anger. By the time Daniel arrived, the boys had walked away, spitting on Gianni as they departed, and the little Corsican's face was already swelling and turning purple. His lower lip was split, his nose was bloody, his clothes were torn.

When Daniel stopped and stood over him, Gianni spat a slimy ball of blood from his mouth, rose on one battered arm, and said,

"So, you wanna fight, too?"

They were friends from that moment.

Gianni's father worked as a trade representative. A promotion from his native Ajaccio to a marbled Parisian office had compelled his wife and son to follow grudgingly. Despised as a *nouveau-riche* country boy and a pipsqueak with a ridiculous Italian accent, sixteen-year-old Gianni had long since tired of defending his good name. Originally proud to be battered in the defense of Corsica, by now he would have been considerably happier to sign an armistice of some kind. The other boys, however, did not appear to have any plans for a cease-fire. Gianni was still the conveniently different-looking and different-sounding intruder, the undersized magnet for every bully within reach.

He let Daniel use the hated nickname because he knew he meant it with affection. Soon it degenerated into "Nappo." Gianni would elevate his impressive chin and declare, "That's right — because I can fight like Napoléon!" Friendship pulled Daniel into the world at last, with its ugly imbalances and inequities: allied in Gianni's hopeless cause, sharing the battle with the little Corsican, bloody and hurling defiance.

When Daniel turned seventeen, his father dismissed Nour with a hasty final paycheck. She looked precisely the same as she had a decade earlier, even wearing the same troubled frown. She reached upward to kiss Daniel's cheek and padded silently out the front door, never to return.

LeClerc left his son alone in the apartment the next morning. At seventeen, he had his own bachelor pad.

Daniel and Gianni spent their evenings in the living room, drinking LeClerc's wine and fiddling with the new Minitel terminal. They would look up all persons with the last name Giscard and call, trying to get the president. They argued about the sexiest names for women and when they had finally agreed on one, they would look up the addresses of all the women with that name, swearing they'd search out and find the sexiest woman in Paris. Finally, bored and drunk, they would head out to a late movie or try futilely to squeeze past the doorman at a disco.

"Where does your father work?" Gianni asked one night as they were clicking at the Minitel, looking up all the people with the name LeClerc.

"He's a diplomat."

"Yeah, I know, but where?"

Daniel shrugged.

"Hell if I know. He's always gone."

"Hmm." Gianni scratched at the thick crop of black nose hairs bristling from his huge nostrils. "Hey, let's see if we can look up his office."

Daniel grinned.

"Yeah, we can call the fucker up and leave messages."

"LeClerc, this is Giscard," Gianni said in the president's aristocratic baritone, "You're fired, you pussy-faced slime."

Daniel exploded in laughter, then stopped, shrugging helplessly.

"But I don't think he works in Paris."

"He has to. The whole *Corps Étrangers* is here. My father's part of it, too. Even when he travels, there's still his office here, and you can call his secretary and leave messages."

They spent twenty minutes in fruitless attempts to find an office at the foreign service with Alain LeClerc's name.

"I'll get the numbers from my Pop," Gianni said, now committed to the project of rooting out Daniel's elusive father.

"Maybe it's secret or something," Daniel said. "You know he's never had a listed phone number. For years the phone was in Nour's name and now it's in mine."

"We'll find him," Gianni declared, his martial nose pointing proudly skyward.

"I don't know, Nappo," Daniel said. "He doesn't like to be found."

"What do you want to bet?"

"Bet what? That you'll find him?"

"Yeah," Gianni said, grinning malevolently.

"I don't know. I'll think about it. I don't know if I really want to find him."

Two nights later, Daniel came home after midnight to find the door to his apartment slightly ajar. Red-brownish splotches speckled the carpet near the bathroom door and the bathroom wastebasket bulged with stained tissues.

Alain LeClerc lay in his rarely-used bed, his breathing heavy and difficult. Daniel stood in the doorway silently, waiting just outside, watching him. Finally the man said,

"What?"

"What happened?" Daniel asked.

"Accident." He was clearly struggling to muster the energy to speak around the rhythm of his breathing.

"What kind of accident?"

"Later," LeClerc said through another tired exhale.

Later came later than Daniel expected. When he returned from school the next day, LeClerc was still in bed, apparently asleep. He woke enough to scratch out the word *"water"* from his desiccated throat. Daniel complied, bringing him a bottle of Vittel. LeClerc drained it and asked for more. Daniel had never heard the supplicant tone in his father's voice before. He silently attended to the requests for the rest of the evening, more out of fascination than out of reverence or compassion. He laid out bread and a pitcher of water for him as if feeding a prisoner. When Gianni called, Daniel told him to call back tomorrow. The next day he told him to call later in the week.

"But listen," Gianni said, "I found out something."

"Later," said Daniel.

The third and fourth days saw LeClerc elevate himself slowly, torturously, to go to the toilet. His entire midsection was wrapped like a mummy. It took him thirty minutes to defecate and complete the painful journey back to the bed. On the fourth night the telephone rang again. Daniel answered, annoyed.

"Nappo, I said I'll call you later — I can't do anything right now."

There was silence on the other end, then a deep voice with what sounded like a North African accent:

"Give me LeClerc."

Daniel carried the telephone into his father's bedroom doorway, forgetting that there was another on the stand beside the bed.

"It's for you," he said to the quietly pulsing form beneath the sheets.

"Close the door," LeClerc said as he grunted and reached for the receiver.

Daniel obeyed. He didn't dare listen on the receiver that rested in his hands. He leaned instead against the wall beside his father's door, hearing one-half of the conversation. It was strange: disjointed sentences and fragments, almost as if in a kind of code.

"Stage props set up?"

"Where's the drop?"

"Do whatever you think is right."

"No, I can't. Not for a week, at least, maybe more."

"He doesn't know. No, he's in Moscow."

"Take care of this and I'll make it right for you."

"No, this will be arranged *before* he gets back."

"Very well. Very well. *Je m'en fiche.*"

"No. I'll be back."

"Do whatever you think is right, but I'll be back."

"Good. Fine. I'll make it right for you."

"Good. All right. *Au revoir.*"

On the following Monday when Daniel finally returned to school, Gianni demanded:

"What the hell have you been doing? Where have you been for the last few days?"

"It's my father," Daniel whispered, as if protecting a secret in the din and mayhem of the school cafeteria. "He came home on Thursday all cut up or something. His whole belly is bandaged up and he can barely move out of bed. He's been there for five days."

"Shit, what happened?"

"Some kind of accident."

"You don't know?"

Daniel shrugged. "We don't talk."

"Yeah, obviously. Listen," Gianni's face brightened, "I've been trying to get you since last weekend. I talked to my Pop's secretary, all sweet-like, you know, like I needed to know for a project in school. And I got her to check the phone directory for the whole foreign service. The whole ministry, *mon vieux...* nothing."

"What? Nothing what?" Daniel squinted.

"No Alain LeClerc anywhere. Your old man doesn't work for the foreign service unless he's a top-secret spy killer or something."

Daniel had difficulty envisioning his middle-aged father as a Gallic James Bond.

"I don't know what he does," he finally said with a sigh. "He gets these phone calls at night. It's always guys with foreign accents: Spanish, English, I don't know. Always these short conversations, weird. Like he's in charge of people and they're checking up with him."

"Maybe he *is* a spy," Gianni said, eyebrows rising. "Maybe some Russian agent shot him and now he's hiding out. Man, this could really be cool!"

Twelve days after Daniel had come home to find his father in bed, he came home to an apartment full of people. He had grown so accustomed to the silence and solitude of the place that a half dozen large men standing and sitting around made it feel mobbed. One gigantic man with bristly short black hair and an ugly little mustache was sitting at the dinner table eating the strawberries Daniel had bought that morning. Daniel stopped in the doorway, astonished. Although all six of the strangers were staring at him, he saw only this black-headed monster at the table, calmly devouring his food. The man looked him up and down once, nodded, then returned his attention to the strawberries.

Somebody said, "Tell him the kid's here."

"We're ready," another said, "it doesn't matter."

"Who the hell are you?" Daniel said to the crowd, his schoolbooks still in his hand. "And get your hands off my strawberries."

Twelve eyebrows lifted around the room above six smirks. The seated man smiled at him, looked at a colleague, and said with a short burst of laughter,

"Er will seine Erdbeeren verteidigen!"

Then to Daniel, in French:

"Sorry, kid." He pushed the plate away from him on the table. "I'll save the rest for you."

Daniel had stopped listening after the first sentence.

"What did you say?" he whispered, but the six weren't paying attention to him anymore. Daniel stared, slack-jawed, at the big man seated at the table even as Alain LeClerc came slowly, stiffly, from the doorway of his bedroom.

"Ready," LeClerc muttered.

One of the others offered an arm under LeClerc's, but was refused.

"No, I'm okay," he said. "Let's go."

The men filed out, LeClerc barely acknowledging his son. On his way out the black-haired man smiled at the boy and said,

"Good strawberries."

"Say it the other way," Daniel whispered at his immense broad back as it filled the doorway for a moment, then vanished.

17.

"America?" Gianni said, surprised. He stroked the tentative black wisps on his upper lip, then nodded. "Sure, why not. The land of opportunity. Heh."

"It's far away, that's the main thing."

"California, yeah," Gianni said, grinning, his arms stretching out as if he was balancing on a surfboard. "Movie stars and everything. That'd be great."

"No, Washington."

"Washington? What the hell for?"

"Remember that program they talked about in school? You go to study in America for a year? It's in Washington."

Gianni frowned.

"But that was something like... I don't know, but it was really expensive, right? How are you going to get the money?"

"My father," Daniel said.

"Graduation present?"

Daniel snorted.

"Not exactly. More like a deal. I'll go to school in America for a year if he'll pay."

"What's the deal?" asked Gianni.

"That's it. If he'll give me the money, I'll go away. It's not that much money, actually, and when I'm there I can work. It's a good deal for him."

Gianni shook his head.

"You're going to leave me behind here and go off to America. You fucker. Well, you'll probably get shot."

"No, they only shoot Germans."

"So, what? You're not going to go to school at all?"

"I don't know. Maybe. We'll see. But I'm definitely getting the hell out of here."

"When are you going to ask him?" Gianni said.

"Soon."

"We've still got another year."

"Not in America," Daniel said. "They have one less year of school than we do. You can be finished when you're seventeen, eighteen. Hell, you can drive a car when you're sixteen. It'd be six months from now. If I get the money, I'll be eighteen by the time I go."

"He won't let you skip out early."

Daniel sucked the last smoke out of his cigarette and frowned at the butt as he crushed it in the tray.

"He has no fucking idea," he said, exhaling the smoke in a dense blue stream. "He doesn't even know how old I am. He couldn't care less where I go to school, or when."

"Course, your English is terrible."

"It's not so bad," Daniel said indignantly.

"Tell that to Madame Arnoux," Gianni said, laughing, then in their English teacher's stentorian drill-voice: "I *have* had... I *had* had... Had I had one, I *would* have had..."

Daniel shrugged. "It's a simple language. And in America it's basic, anyway. You can learn from the TV. That won't be a problem."

"So you're really going to do it, then."

"If I get the money, *mon vieux,* then I'm gone."

For two months Daniel's primary concern was that LeClerc would not return to visit home soon enough for Daniel to make the admission deadline for the American program. (Not that he was certain that he'd ever attend, but he wanted at least to ask for the money prior to the deadline.) At last Daniel came home one evening to find the familiar raincoat on the hook beside the door. LeClerc was sitting on the edge of his bed, leafing through newspapers.

"What do you want?" he asked when Daniel stood in his bedroom door.

"I need something from you."

"What?"

"Money."

"How much?"

"Twenty-five thousand francs."

LeClerc laughed explosively.

"Forget it," he finally said.

"Or five thousand dollars," Daniel said, "whichever is easier."

"Dollars? What, are you going to buy America?"

"I want to go to school there. There's a program—"

"—What the hell do you want to go to school in America for?" LeClerc said. "You're not even out of school here yet."

"I'm finished this term," Daniel lied.

He sensed his father's eyes trained upon his Adam's apple, scrying out the terrain of his throat, looking for something.

"Indeed," was all the man said.

"It's a good program," Daniel said, not too firmly. "My English teacher recommended it. And you can get excellent jobs with it, after only one year. You can get jobs in America, even, if you stay."

LeClerc remained silent, expressionless, staring at his throat.

"It's a good deal," Daniel finally said, hearing the tone of helplessness creep into his voice despite every possible effort, and with it, a thick blanket of shame. He sensed his father watching him languidly, giving Daniel all the time he needed in which to feel himself sink into impotence.

"I'll tell you a good deal," LeClerc finally said. "If you can get into a university, fine. If you can get into this American program, fine. University is three years, that's over a hundred thousand francs just to keep this apartment. Or this American program is what, twenty-five thousand? I'll give you your choice. I'll pay for this apartment for three more years while you study. Or I'll pay for this American program. But after that, I pay for nothing, understand? You want to decide now, fine. You want to think it over, fine."

"I've decided," Daniel said.

LeClerc rose and walked to a black briefcase that was lying on his credenza. He spun the tumblers and opened it with three snapping motions. To Daniel's stupefaction, he removed three tightly-bound stacks of bills and slapped them into his son's unsteady palms.

"That's thirty thousand francs," LeClerc said. And then, in American English Daniel had never before heard his father use, he added,

"Keep the change."

On the seven-hour flight from Paris to Washington Daniel felt the weight of that money in his hands. He felt it in his arms, all through his body down to his feet. It was the weight of his father's power. He was sure of only one thing that summer: that he never wanted to feel it again.

18.

He came at the height of the revolution of greed, to a nation ruled by a vague and hoary-headed septuagenarian who was revered for spending billions on nuclear weapons while cutting funding for poor children's school lunches. Daniel arrived in the capital, impressed by the heavy heat pushing down against the marble. Compared to Paris, Washington was a tense, purposeful place with a knot of austere columned monuments surrounded by a vast miasma of misery and murder. The Metro was cavernous and immaculate, so unlike its Parisian namesake. But more often than not it left you in a place devoid of any beauty: a sea of shimmering glass-fronted offices or an ungainly cluster of shouting storefronts. With the exception of the virtuous white edifices of the Republic, the buildings in America were strewn about carelessly, too ugly to concern themselves with order.

He had never dreamed of a society that could be so loud. Mobs of televisions screeched day and night over howling billboards and screaming electronic façades. A river of belching vehicles puttered through it all like sludgy blood struggling to reach the extremities of an obese body. The average Washingtonian seemed not significantly different from the average Parisian except that this fusillade of noise drowned everyone and made them all appear as if they were struggling to hear and be heard.

He checked into his dorm room, but the week before his classes were to begin, he had still not registered. He found instead a job at night, loading crates of food onto refrigerator trucks. Urgent notes appeared under the edge of his door, reminding him to set his academic affairs in order. He lingered there for another two weeks, his nocturnal habits and lack of a telephone sufficient to evade the mounting requests from the administration. Within another week these were accompanied by notices that he would be evicted if he didn't pay his back rent. On the day they finally used the office key to enter his room they found nothing there, not even trash.

He moved to a tiny efficiency apartment near Capitol Heights. His neighbors scrutinized him suspiciously, assuming that he was an incompetent and very junior narcotics officer whose boss had assigned him to their neighborhood as some sort of punishment.

Sometimes Daniel lingered after work in the first hour of sunlight, sitting in the alley with the other men, waiting for the truck drivers to arrive to haul away the night's labors. They smoked weed then went to get breakfast before heading home to sleep. They were a scruffy miniature UN, a dozen sweaty men from almost as many countries. They learned English from soap operas and commercials and music videos, and from each other's accented, awkward braggadocio. They talked about women and pop music and work visas. They told stories about running away and getting into trouble. Daniel bought drugs from a Haitian man named Étienne.

"Hey French, you pretty quiet, man," someone would say.

"I'm listening," Daniel always replied.

This is how it works: the police will stop you if your skin is dark. The cops themselves are black, Hispanic, it doesn't matter. Pale skin is a license to travel unmolested by the authorities. Pale skin is trust. You can become the ghost in the machine. You can carry things the other men can't.

Then Étienne says you're crazy to carry shit and not have a gun. So Daniel buys a gun and now he feels crazy to have one. But he walks right past cops, invisible, the barrel jammed against his groin, the dense fist-sized bag of cocaine against his breast.

America teaches you about power. Power is the heavy steel of the .38 swaying with his crotch, protecting the magic white powder and the rolls of money. The money buys a car and nice clothes. The car and nice clothes obtain the women. He has been nocturnal for two years when he enters an alley one second behind the swing of a crowbar.

It sweeps a finger-length before him, fanning air across his cheek as he ducks and stumbles backwards. The dark face behind it is furious. The metal rears back and upward, aiming for his skull. Daniel has heard gunshots before, but the blast of his own pistol is the loudest thing he has ever experienced and it splits everything open: the heat of the humid night, the air, the incessant noise of the city, the flesh of the man holding the crowbar. The man spins before Daniel once, twice, as if in an ancient dance, the force of the bullet having pirouetted him. Daniel pulls the trigger again, and this time it isn't so loud. This time it's followed by the clang of the iron falling to the street, covered by the collapsing body.

And he is cold on a hot night, his hand shaking around the dark metal of the weapon, trying to pry his fingers loose. He is shivering, wiping his fingerprints off, throwing it away, wanting never to touch it, never to hold it again. He is cold and hungry walking from the alley, leaving the gun at the bottom of a rain sewer. Hungrier than he has ever felt, open and cavernous inside with a hole as dark and roaring as the raging black face he murdered. He is cold despite the heat all around, drinking hot coffee in the all-night restaurant, ordering French toast, which comes to him in a glistening syrup, covered with bright red strawberries.

Daniel bluffed and lied his way through a renewal of his work visa, showing up in shabby clothes, swearing he'd been up late loading trucks, even though he hadn't done that work in three years. He had mastered the skills of subterfuge necessary to be a player: the small-time fake job to keep the tax people happy, the sleepy daytime poverty under the gaze of the authorities, the bluster of wealth at night.

During the half dozen years he spent in America he moved eleven times. He kept no telephone number other than that of his beeper, answered at convenience store pay phones like those of all the other players. Daniel cycled through women with each change of fashion trends. He acquired too many things, he became at last too obvious. He was in his BMW coupe, admiring his lycra-wrapped new girlfriend as they buzzed on Ecstasy, when the flashing blue and red lights signaled the beginning of the end of his stay in the promised land.

It had been nearly six years since Daniel had seen Paris, and he had grown accustomed to the American pace of change. The city of his childhood was shockingly unaltered. He got an apartment in the seventh *arrondissement* and spent a few days walking around, expecting to be surprised but disappointed that it felt so familiar. A few of the cafés were different, at least in name and/or decor, but most were exactly where he'd left them. He realized that he had returned to more or less where he had started. He felt much older than a quarter of a century, awakened like Rip van Winkle in reverse, in the beautiful old asylum of his boyhood.

Gianni, at least, had disappeared. That much was different. It was a relief not finding his name on the Minitel. Daniel didn't want to see him after all these years, afraid that it would be embarrassing. What if Gianni had become fat and boring, or worse, conventionally successful? But he felt compelled to search. Daniel lingered a month before he went to see the old apartment. He stood in the street and looked up at the third-floor window, wondering what was behind it, imagining every part of his childhood having vanished in the puff of air with his last closing of the door, just as every trace of his young adulthood had been left in the jet exhaust on the tarmac at Dulles.

Maybe you can't help disappearing, he thought.

That evening, spooning soup to his lips while reading a magazine, he saw an ad for a trucking company that needed drivers to run an express across West Germany, through the special corridors to West Berlin. Daniel didn't consider the truck-driving job but the thought of West Berlin lodged in his mind. Perhaps, after too much freedom, it was time to go someplace that was hidden away and walled-off like an invisible fortress. He decided to disappear.

to dance

Berlin, Spring 1992

19.

When Daniel came to West Berlin in 1987 he thought it was by far the grubbiest and poorest of the great cities in which he had lived. He had no idea that within two years millions of people would pass through the Wall from the East, gawking in astonishment and delight, having never imagined such wealth and ostentation. When the Wall came down, and Daniel saw the East for himself, he understood.

Three years after that event it still did not feel like one city. Huge swathes of what would be "downtown" in any normal place were open fields of sand with wooden plank pedestrian bridges passing through, in some cases secured with high fences on both sides because the minefields had not yet been cleared. The Berliners didn't break ground without considerable preparation; the city's geology was a complex stratum of ancient bombs, some living, some dead, all buried. Still, a few major new foundations had been sunk, causing water to boil up to the surface and run through the streets. One could navigate by orienting to the sea of construction cranes that represented where the Wall and death strip had once been and where the former East began. Or one could simply pick a direction and walk and eventually arrive at the old border, which was like crossing through a portal into the early 1960s: a black-and-white world before air-conditioned cars, deodorant, or bank cards. Everything was grey, uncertain, smelly, wounded.

From Daniel's point of view, the great advantage of Berlin's chaotic emptiness and vast abandoned spaces was the unlimited opportunity to hide. Daniel and Eugene each had a few stashes located in strategically-chosen points around the city so that no matter where they were, they were never more than half an hour from any of them. They were reasonably certain that DeSoto didn't know about most of them, in case that ever became important. In each, they kept a few basic survival items: guns and ammunition, forged documents and identity papers, some clean clothing, cash in a few different currencies. And sometimes, if a job for DeSoto involved a small quantity of something very expensive and/or dangerous, they'd leave it in a stash until they'd properly scouted the pickup.

A few months after he moved to the East Daniel had been standing on the platform of a station along the U1 subway line when he noticed an old door, flush with the wall and partially concealed behind a cigarette vending machine. He waited until he was alone on the platform and then tried to pry it open. He had to leave and find a crowbar, then return and try again. He discovered that it was the entrance to an unlit service tunnel that led to an abandoned branch line with its own small platform. It connected another similar service passageway that eventually led back to the main platform, but along the way were several alcoves with opportunities to conceal things. The service doors connected the tunnels-within-the-tunnels that were once used by East German security to monitor the subway lines. In some cases they enabled spies to exit a train, vanish to some meeting place, and appear moments later across the tracks on the opposite platform, ready to disappear onto the next train going back. There were security cameras in a few places but they were obviously long-dead. Daniel disconnected their wires then came back every week for a month to see whether somebody had reconnected them. When he was certain the place had been abandoned, he moved in, adding some locks to the alcove doors. The stash became a staging area for jobs that required something hidden for a couple of days, particularly something small enough to fit in the backpack or suitcase of anybody riding the subway.

"Have you given this one a name yet?" Eugene asked.

"You know I don't do that."

"That's unlucky," Eugene said. "Each stash needs a name. That way you can talk about them without anybody picking up on it. Like, instead of saying 'Meet you at my place behind the Turkish grill on the Schönhauser Allee,' you can just say, 'Meet you at Katrina.'"

"Katrina?"

"Yeah, I give them all girls' names. Lulu, Sabrina, whatever. Your girlfriend will overhear one day and get jealous. That's always good. Keeps them on their toes."

"My girlfriend is a dancer," Daniel said. "She's always on her toes."

They walked across the wasteland where the Potsdamer Platz had once been. With the wall gone, it was now a sandy marsh with bulldozers partially submerged in brown water. There was one corridor through the muck, running east-west on an elevated steel walkway, designed as a pedestrian access ramp to a little makeshift museum in the center of what had once been the plaza. In a design decision that now seemed like foresight, they had built the museum on huge metal stilts, so that it floated several meters above the sea of mud and sand. Daniel walked up the ramp and gazed inside as they passed. A gift shop offered postcards of Berlin tourist destinations, stuffed bears, and key fobs featuring the Brandenburg Gate or Trabis. Through the glass, they could see the huge scale model of what the new Berlin was going to become: a science fiction landscape of modern buildings in polished steel, white stone, and glass. Behind the model hung a two-meter-high photograph of what the Potsdamer Platz had once been in its heyday during the Weimar Republic: the Times Square of central Europe.

Standing two stories above the ground, one needed only to gaze east to see the filthy grey and crumbling reminders of how Berlin had spent the last four decades. Much of it was slated for demolition. But it would not go quietly. This whole expanse of earth was a festering wound of unexploded bombs and mines, God knows how deep. Daniel stared out over the plaza of mud and the long-abandoned city center. Then they descended the stairs and continued east.

"Let's call this one 'Nina'," Eugene said as they slid behind the cigarette machine and unlocked the exterior door. Closing it behind them, Daniel pulled out a flashlight and they began their descent into the service tunnel.

"All right," Daniel said when he'd unlocked the door to the alcove. "Let's get these guys out of here."

Inside this alcove, Daniel had arranged two flimsy metal shelves, each with four levels of shelving. Each of the two middle shelves was occupied by a large suitcase. Eugene pulled one out and put it on the ground.

In most transactions of this sort, with a locked case, they would have been given the combinations up-front, so they could inspect the goods immediately. In this case, with a new client and DeSoto's security precautions, they had picked up the cases still locked and Eugene received the combinations only after the first partial payment had been made. Now it was time to check the merchandise.

They knew already what it was: detonators. A dozen combat engineering detonators of recent Soviet vintage. Small bombs designed to trigger much bigger bombs. Each was an aluminum box, painted black, about the size and shape of a large book. It had a panel that popped out of one side, into which the explosive core and its wiring could be inserted. In theory, with the cores not yet inserted and hanging loose like this, they weren't dangerous. But according to Eugene, there was no "in theory" in the Red Army.

"We could blow up the subway with these," Eugene muttered as he lifted one carefully from the cardboard frame inside the case.

"This city has seen a lot worse," Daniel said.

"Shine the light here?" Eugene held up the box then cursed and put it down carefully. He removed his reading glasses from his jacket pocket and mounted them on his nose, then lifted the box again. "All right..." he said. "Where is your serial number, little bomb friend?"

"Did you ever use these in Afghanistan?" Daniel asked quietly.

"Me? No. I was plain old infantry. The guys who did this were crazy."

"There—" Daniel pointed. On one of the corners, the black paint had been scraped away.

"Mm." Eugene held it up to his nose and squinted. "Yeah, it's gone."

They put it back and checked the next one. There were six in each suitcase and they had to make sure that no traces of the serial numbers remained.

"Gone," Eugene said as he replaced the second and lifted the third. Daniel held the flashlight.

Eugene frowned at this one. "This is weird. Show me the second one again?" Daniel held it up with his free hand and shined the light on it.

"Am I being paranoid," Eugene said, "Or is it strange that the numbers are removed in exactly the same way every time?"

"What do you mean?"

"I mean, look how clean this is. Not scratched out with a screwdriver. One swipe, no cracked paint, a perfect rectangle."

They checked the fourth, fifth, and sixth ones. They were all the same. They checked the ones in the other suitcase.

"A machine did this," Daniel said. He stared at Eugene. "We're dealing with somebody who has a lot more of these than just a dozen. He has so many that he's created an assembly line for them. When you got the combinations did DeSoto tell you any more about the client?"

"I didn't get the combinations from DeSoto. I got the same briefing you got. It's a new client."

"We're going upscale," Daniel said. "This is the pro league."

20.

There was an announcement posted in the foyer of Daniel's apartment building, in the glass case beside the row of mailboxes. The *Hausmeister* announced that the building had been purchased and that the new owner was going to install an elevator. There was no explanation of where or when and Daniel didn't like the idea of workmen opening his walls. He snorted and started up the steps.

When he opened his door he saw Julia sitting in the middle of the floor in front of a skeleton of thin metal tubes, tugging at a wet cloth she was stretching to cover the imagined geometric face of an unfinished polygon. The cloth was one of Daniel's kitchen rags. Around her, spreading outward across the grain of the floorboards, were a dozen other objects of metal, glass, and stone, and the deflated shopping bag in which they had no doubt been collected. Daniel's mop bucket was filled with a pale, linen-colored slop the consistency of gruel. Into this, Julia dipped a hand and tried to coax the paste into acting as some kind of adhesive between the metal and the fabric.

"*Grüss dich,*" she said without looking up.

She wore a skintight black top, open around her neck but long-sleeved to her wrists. Her gingerbread hair had partially escaped the constriction of a red scrunchie and fell across one shoulder. At her waist clung a hot-pink skirt which was now hopelessly mired in mop-bucket sludge and the floor dirt it had befriended. Her legs were encased in the same sheer black as her arms. Daniel stared at her perfect bare feet against the ugliness of the floor and he wanted to tell her that he was certain she was the most beautiful human being he would ever know in his life.

"Hi," he said. "were you dancing tonight?"

"Yeah," she replied, snarling at a glob of gruel that had fallen away from the end of one of the pipes. "I was getting ready to go home, and I saw these pipes, you know, in the back room. And I suddenly had this inspiration. So I grabbed a bunch of stuff and came back here because it was closer."

She looked up at him for the first time since he'd arrived, and said,

"Hope you don't mind."

"Glad you're here," he said.

He puttered in the kitchen, threw away most of his mail without opening it, then went into the bedroom and took off all his clothes except his shorts. He pulled a bottle of Sancerre from the refrigerator and brought a glass to her, then pulled the cushion from his living room chair and laid it against the wall. He sat down on the floor to watch her. He was tired and she was absorbed in her slow act of creation. For a moment he thought about getting up and bringing a sheet from the bed but he decided to stay put. Within a minute he'd rearranged the pillow under his head.

She has finished the dance and the applause seems timid, as if the audience is afraid to disturb her. Daniel stands to the right of the stage, still staring at her. She curls her chin under her face, sweeping in a bow, and then she slices through the air and is gone.

Now he is directionless, wandering the room, colliding with angry waitresses who don't ask if they can bring him anything. He is still in this state of imbalance and sensory dysfunction even after finding a stalwart piece of wall to support him. He looks to the back, to the table with the three men. There she is.

The lofty, dark one, flawlessly handsome, takes her fingertips to his mouth and says something directly to her.

"You were astonishing tonight, always outdoing yourself. Magnificent."

With those fingers, he steers her to the side, toward the two older men, their faces and hands thick, their snowy hair thin. Now they take their turns with the fingers, smiling obsequiously: desperate hunger poorly concealed in their grinning jowls, their gushing words.

The dark one, the Spaniard, eyes moving pendulum-like from her to them, completing the transaction for tonight.

"Were you having a nightmare?" Julia asked as a lock of her hair fell down to his cheek.

"No," he lied.

"You were moaning like you were struggling or..." She smiled crookedly. "Were you dreaming of another woman?"

Daniel smiled, her image coming into focus now, bare skin hovering above him, her breasts downward, curving toward him, the perfect strokes of her shoulders and arms. They were in bed. He had no memory of getting there.

"Would you be jealous if I was?"

"Mm." She raised a thick eyebrow. "Maybe just a little."

"Good," he said. "But no, it was you."

When she shifted her weight, leaning backward, upward, away from him, he saw the brush in her hand. He was transfixed by the cinnamon cascade on her naked shoulders, so it was another minute before he realized she was painting him.

"What are you doing down there?"

She giggled. "I was wondering when you'd notice."

In uncensored half-sleep the truth spilled out clumsily across his tongue: "I was too busy looking at you. You were so beautiful."

"Sshh," she said, shaking her head. "You're a work in progress. Lie still."

She adjusted her legs over him and the brush disappeared in the shadow between her legs. Then he felt it against his testicles, warm and soft and tickling wet, stroking upward. She traced with the brush around the base of his penis and smiled as it swelled. When he opened his eyes and looked down the length of his torso, there was surprise in his voice.

"There's no paint."

"I'm painting you with something else," she whispered, her hand disappearing as she shifted her weight over him again. The brush was heavy and wet, warm against the base of his stomach.

His eyes were closed again when he felt himself vanish inside her. He kept his lids shut to complete the sensation of being closed into the depth and darkness where every movement brought him nearer some beginning or some end.

He was awake when the first light turned the sky indigo. His sheets smelled of her, a warm and reassuring funk. She was on her side, facing away, and he was on his back. He saw that the sculpture was only partly complete in the center of his floor but that it was clearly a head, a human skull, skin stretched tight over cold metal pipes. Hollow inside except for this skeleton of steel. He thought it might be the face of an old man or perhaps a death mask.

21.

From his apartment in Prenzlauer Berg Daniel rode a streetcar to the crazed Babel of the Alexanderplatz. In the past year, this grey and purposeful socialist commons had sprouted a McDonald's and a TGI Friday's. Huge, brightly-colored posters hung from the windows of the old buildings and promised imminent new capitalist invasions. People stood and admired the larger-than-life photos that heralded the arrival of a Beate Uhse sex shop. Frau Uhse's pneumatically-inflated breasts threatened to burst from a red lace outfit out across the plaza and into the traffic.

With hands stuffed firmly in pockets and steering an evasive course around the beggars and pickpockets, Daniel ascended to the S-Bahn platform and headed West. Between Friedrichstraße and Bellevue the buildings and cars abruptly transformed, becoming colorful and modern. He sometimes played a game with himself, closing his eyes and opening them after he knew they'd passed over the old border so that he went to sleep in one city and awoke in the other.

Just three years earlier this journey would have involved a stopped train, passport control, and a sweep by the East German border police to search for illegals. The mere fact that he could now ride from the Alexanderplatz into West Berlin still amazed him enough that he didn't object to the constant breakdowns and delays, the incessant glitches as the two transit systems tried to link a network that had been bombed to oblivion and then severed for four decades.

At the Savignyplatz he got off the train and descended to the sunny street with its buzz of restaurants and clubs. He walked the three blocks to *d'accord*. When he entered he didn't see Sabine. Eugene sat at the bar with a glass of juice and a newspaper, nodding as Daniel approached and sat beside him.

"Where's Sabine?" Daniel asked.

"Upstairs," Eugene said. "She's got Lotte waiting tables tonight and this new Russian guy in the kitchen."

Daniel's eyebrows went up and he leaned forward to try to catch a glimpse through the door behind the bar.

"I can't believe she hired this guy," Eugene said, pointing to a balding, thirty-something man who was arranging toast and slices of cheese on an appetizer plate. "I don't approve of hiring Russians."

Daniel glanced at Eugene's folded *Morgenpost*. The headline was partially obscured but he could see the words "—ploded bomb."

"Did they find another one?" he asked, nodding at the paper.

"Yeah," Eugene said. "A big British one, under the fucking foundation of a whole apartment building. Think about that for a minute. Some morons saw a big round hole all the way through a building and into the foundation and figured, Eh, just pour some concrete over it and it'll be fine. Amazing it didn't blow up the whole block."

"They did what they had to do back then," Daniel said. "Everybody was desperate for a place to live. A million bombs fell on this city, a lot of them were duds."

"Well, it's going to get ugly when they really start rebuilding around here. Some of those old ones are going to go off."

"I could use a drink," Daniel said, looking around for the waitress, finding only her vanishing back.

"You've been drinking a lot more lately."

"Well, comrade investigator," Daniel said, "It *is* a bar that we're sitting in. And I promise I won't let it affect my production of tractors this month."

"Don't get all pissed off," Eugene said. "I just worry about your health."

Daniel sighed. He tried again without success to flag the waitress.

"You think that Polish deal was too easy?" he asked.

"Too easy?"

"Yeah. Didn't you think it was a little odd to be so clean for a first-timer?"

Eugene shrugged.

"I guess they can't all be fucked up and complicated."

"I've been thinking about it," Daniel said. "They didn't feel us up for guns when we went into that warehouse. And the stuff itself — didn't it seem too good?"

"Too good to be Russian?" Eugene grinned.

"Just too good. Brand-new."

Eugene waved his hand as if shooing away a fly. "It's probably some Russian colonel, flat busted broke, selling off all the equipment in his regiment so he can get enough money to desert and make a break for it somewhere. Those two Polish guys who never said a word — they're probably already happy because they've dicked him for a fortune on the last couple of deals, and they don't care if we take a turn now. That's why the quality's good and the price was right. A buyer's market, comrade. You could start a decent little war these days for less money than Miguel DeSoto spends on gasoline."

"I don't know," Daniel picked at the wood of the bar with his fingertip. "It always gives me the creeps when it seems too simple."

"Not me," Eugene said. "I could take a couple more like—"

"Who's that guy?" Daniel asked.

They turned to look at a very tall, broad-shouldered man in a heavy black coat who had entered unnoticed and now stood almost perfectly at the center of the floor, facing them, his back erect, his head motionless.

"Are you looking for Sabine?" Eugene asked him.

"Mister DeSoto sent me," the man said, his head perfectly still.

"Ah," Eugene said, "What do you need?"

"Mister DeSoto conveys his greetings and requests your presence at his Moabit office at ten o'clock tomorrow morning."

"Fine," Daniel said. "Tell him we'll be there."

At last the man moved, inclining his forehead slightly before he turned and walked out through the door with something that in a smaller body might have been grace.

"That's odd," Daniel said. "Miguel is too important now to make a phone call?"

Eugene nodded in the direction of Sabine's back door, through which she was entering the bar. She blew kisses to *Les Boys* as she approached.

"Who was that?" she asked.

"One of Miguel's guys," Daniel said. "The world's largest messenger."

Sabine frowned and shook her head. "He does that," she said. "He could make a phone call, but he likes to check up on me, to send some goon to look around and give him a report. Nothing wrong, I hope?"

Eugene shrugged. "We'll see tomorrow."

Sabine began making their drinks and Eugene raised a hand as if to halt her.

"Nothing more for me," he said. "I'm leaving."

And when she looked at him with concern and a little pout, he added:

"I need my beauty sleep." He turned to Daniel. "See you at ten."

Sabine made a vehicle for Daniel and leaned against the bar. "What a day," she said. "I have to find another liquor distributor before the weekend. I'm sick of dealing with these assholes. How have you been?"

"I could use a bit more sleep," Daniel said.

"Something about you has been different lately," she said. "You haven't looked well."

"Everybody says that," Daniel said, "but nobody can put a finger on it."

"I've been wanting to tell you something," Sabine said.

"Mm?"

"I think I saw Johannes the other day."

Daniel was grateful for the low light and the distractions all around. There's a reason that poker is played in a darkened room, he thought.

"Our mystery man," he said. "You saw him?"

"I think so. I thought I caught a glimpse of him over near where you live, in the Bötzowkiez. I was over there the other night with Ulrich and Martina; there's a new restaurant in the Hufelandstraße."

"Did you talk to him?"

"No. He slipped away into the park," she said. "I can't explain; there was something, I don't know, familiar about him, something important."

Sabine sighed and stood up. She fiddled with some dirty glasses, moving them to the washbasin but not rinsing them.

"Do you think there's any way to find him?" she finally asked. "Just to... well, I want to know that he's okay. "

Daniel stared into his glass. "I suppose," he said. "Just tell me this: why is it so important to you?"

"Okay," she said, "but first, Miguel sent something for you." She searched briefly behind the bar and produced a bottle, followed by a corkscrew and two glasses.

"Ah," Daniel said, nodding.

"There's a case in the cellar waiting for you," she said, "But I brought this one up for the next time I saw you. Do you want it now?"

"Yeah, might as well. Celebrate the start of my new career as a Missing Persons finder, right?"

She looked up at him suspiciously as she drew the cork from the bottle of Chambertin. When it popped she admired the diamonds glimmering in its deep red-black nadir. She poured two glasses.

When Daniel reached for his glass, she frowned.

"You're not going to wait for it to open up?"

"I don't know if I can afford to wait too long anymore."

She scowled and shook her head.

"Are we ready?" she asked.

They smiled at each other but it was crooked, a weak little duet. They clinked the glasses and without pausing to inhale first, touched the wine to their lips. When they had swallowed their first sips and replaced their glasses they nodded simultaneously, eyebrows raised. "That's pretty amazing," she said.

He was staring at the bottle when she said,

"You're too young to be this old."

He squinted. "Well thanks, dear, I suppose."

"I miss the Daniel I used to know. What's the matter? Are you fighting with Julia?"

"Oh, no. No, not at all."

"What then?"

He frowned, drank another mouthful.

"I wonder how you men can be so lonely," she said. "Sometimes I think it's your own fault. Sometimes I see all these sad little boys wandering the earth, searching for the fathers they lost somewhere in themselves."

She poured them both more wine. They were quiet for a few minutes.

"What did your father die of?" he asked.

"Hm? Oh. Cancer. I found out too late. It was stupid, you know. I had sort of run away. I didn't mean to, that's just the way it worked out after I came here. I fell out of touch with them then I got involved with Miguel and I had that whole world. And it wasn't a perfect situation by any stretch but it was my world, you know? It was something I'd made, at least in part, and I felt like I should be true to it. I wanted to make my own place. I used to never be able to understand how my parents could move around so much, you know. How they could pick up and leave all their friends and everything. That was my dad. He couldn't be still. I think he must've thought that if he kept moving he could avoid being caught by all those things that catch us as we get older. But..."

She took another long sip.

"...he was kidding himself. It was following him the whole time, all of it. It was my oldest brother who finally found me and told me, almost a year later. To this day I don't know if I'd rather have been there in time or not."

"Did you love him?

She raised her glass and studied the burgundy meniscus with a sad little smile.

"Yeah, I think so. I mean, he was basically a kind person."

"That's not the same thing. I guess I don't get it," he said. "I never really knew either of my parents, and I never had any brothers or sisters. I've never understood this crazy romanticism people place on genetics as if you're automatically supposed to love somebody just because they share your DNA. You'd forgive them all sorts of things you'd never forgive a normal friend for. You cut your family slack just because they're family. And you've usually got friends or relationships with people who are better people, better companions, people you love and understand better... but you're expected to hold family above that, or you're some kind of traitor."

"Yeah, but it's your parents," she said. "There are special rules for them that don't apply to other people. They brought you into the world, they fed you long before you knew how to feed yourself. They put clothes on you and kept you warm and all that stuff. So it's a special kind of love, like an extra-bonus love that you're obligated to have or else you're a bad person. A cold person, maybe, or at least an ingrate. I mean you could really, truly love them in addition to that, the way you would love someone else. But at a bare minimum, you've got to give them that."

Daniel drank a long swallow of wine. The velvety warmth descended through him.

"If it's an obligation then it's not love."

"It's an obligation you live with on a level that's different from other obligations. It's built-in."

"It's not built-in to me."

"You never know," she said.

Daniel studied his wine.

"So will you help me?" she asked.

"Yes, of course."

"I need to find him," she said. "I don't have any future to save and I don't know what this fucking city is going to look like in a month from now, much less a year, but for Johannes... I don't know, I just know that there was a past here and it's slipping away and nobody cares."

"It's okay," he said. "I understand."

"Promise me we'll find him," she said.

"I promise."

The cork lay on the table between them, the wine diamonds winking at him in the light.

22.

Daniel and Eugene sat on the couch in DeSoto's waiting room as a woman stood before them, bending slightly at the waist to offer a silver tray with miniature cups and a thumb-sized pitcher of cream. Eugene picked a tiny swan made of sugar from one of the cups, held it carefully by its long neck, and dropped it into his tea. She remained motionless as he took a spoon and stirred the liquid and returned it to the tray.

"Thank you, Miss Garcia," he said.

"Mr. LeClerc," she asked, tilting her head. "Are you sure I can't interest you in tea or coffee?"

"No, thank you," Daniel said.

"Has he redecorated in here?" Eugene asked as she straightened at last and was about to walk away. "That painting there," Eugene said, nodding across the room. "That's a Goya, isn't it? I don't remember it from last time."

"It's a Gros," Daniel said.

"The painting?" she asked, turning toward Daniel. "It's French, yes."

Eugene frowned at his teacup as she exited, leaving them alone in the antechamber.

"Did Sabine ask you about the old man?" he finally asked, sipping at the edge of the porcelain.

"Yeah," Daniel said, his eyebrows arching. "How did you know about that?"

"She told me." And when he saw that Daniel was irritated, he added, "Don't look at me, I don't know anything about it, other than that she brings it up every few weeks."

Eugene sipped his tea again and asked: "So how are you going to do it?"

"Fuck if I know," Daniel said. "We both saw him in my neighborhood, so I'll start there. I'll ask some of the local bums and wiseguys, maybe the cops, the postman, that sort of thing."

"The cops?"

"Yeah, all right, maybe not the cops," Daniel said.

"What do you think she'll do if you find him?" Eugene asked.

"The more important question is: what do I do if the old guy doesn't want to be found? What if he tells me to fuck off?"

"Kidnap him," Eugene giggled.

Daniel shook his head. The door to the antechamber opened and Miss Garcia leaned through it.

"Gentlemen," she said, "Mister DeSoto can see you now."

They rose, Eugene setting down his teacup on an end-table. As they walked through the door, Daniel noticed that it was precisely ten o'clock.

"*Mes amis*," he said. He appeared to have been standing in the middle of the room when they entered, and he smiled as they walked through the door. He wore a double-breasted olive suit with gold buttons and cuffs, so silent on him as he moved and so flawlessly tailored that it seemed to be merely sketched in around the outline of his frame. He shook first Eugene's hand, then Daniel's, waving them toward the chairs as he turned and sat behind his desk.

"I was admiring your new painting," Eugene said. DeSoto looked at him quizzically. "The Gros," Eugene added, nodding toward Daniel.

"Ah," DeSoto said, smoothing his tie. "Not new. I acquired it a few years ago, actually, in Paris. I've always found him to be a bit obvious, Gros, but that's the period, I suppose."

DeSoto's gaze came to rest upon Daniel. He frowned.

"Are you unwell, my friend?" he asked.

Daniel shifted in his chair.

"No," he answered, unconvincingly and after hesitation.

"Perhaps you've lost some weight or some color, then," DeSoto said, still scrutinizing Daniel's face. "You seem a bit off."

"I was up past my bedtime last night," Daniel said, chuckling. "Sabine talked me into drinking a couple of bottles of that Chambertin you gave me."

"Well," he said, "she has a certain... persuasiveness with her causes, yes. So then," he said, finally lifting the weight of his stare from Daniel's face. "Business."

DeSoto leaned forward, steepling his hands at the edge of his desk.

"First, of course, I want to thank you for your usual precision with the Polish shipment last week. And second, I should add that it's very good of you to come on short notice. I have been availed of an opportunity recently that requires some alacrity in execution, and I have no intention of missing it.

"Last year, acting upon bad advice," he continued, "I made some arrangements with a pair of Belgians which turned very sour for me."

Daniel cringed at the thought of the consequences of giving DeSoto bad advice.

"I failed to exercise the proper degree of caution and paid accordingly. Not only were the goods I had purchased fraudulent, but the man who represented me at the transaction was cleaned. He was a long-standing associate, in whom I had full confidence, and his loss is still heavy on my conscience.

"It was apparent that the Belgians had made very thorough preparations. I was unable to track them, the goods, or the money. You can imagine my disappointment. I later found out that there was an intermediary involved the entire time, of whose existence I hadn't known." DeSoto looked at Eugene. "A Russian, actually, although he operates out of Paris. One Mister Scherbatov."

Eugene's eyebrows rose.

"Yes," Eugene said, nodding at DeSoto. "I know him. Or, I should say I know *of* him. He was big in Paris a few years ago."

"Indeed," DeSoto said. "I regret that I was not as well informed, then. But it seems that I am to receive satisfaction after all. A few months ago I began a very loose framework of offerings, made through second and third parties, to attract precisely the kind of men with whom I would not normally do business. The majority of these I quietly discarded, of course. But this week I learned from my intermediaries that my two old Belgian friends have re-emerged at last from their little hole in the wall, and appear to be nibbling at my cheese.

"I will place my confidence in you for the most delicate part of what is to follow. Posing as two associates of a Monsieur Bonfils, you will meet with one or both of these Belgians tomorrow evening."

DeSoto reached into a desk drawer and extracted a large portfolio made of thick black leather with a brass clasp. He leaned forward and handed the portfolio to Eugene.

"You are to make arrangements for a final meeting and transaction of a weapons sale for Bonfils," DeSoto continued. "We will, in fact, be using precisely the same weapons you acquired for me last week. We will be using them, however, for slightly less commercial purposes than our Belgian friends suspect. You are to arrange the time and place of the pickup and to inform me directly. When you arrive at the pickup, I will have additional men concealed and prepared to..."

DeSoto smiled wistfully.

"...*complete* our transaction."

"I realize," he added, leaning back in his chair, "that there is no opportunity for you to make your normal commissions on this enterprise. Nonetheless, I need to take advantage of your multilingual negotiating skills, to say nothing of your experience and good judgment. There is no one else I would trust with this. I will make the appropriate adjustments in your favor, of course."

Eugene tipped his head.

"Daniel?" DeSoto said.

"Yes?"

"You are comfortable with this?"

"Yes. Certainly."

"If you feel physically compromised in any way at the moment..."

"No," Daniel said, a bit too loudly. "This Monsieur Bonfils," he said, asking a deliberately stupid question to change the subject. "He's purely your creation?"

"Of course," DeSoto said, "All the information you need will be in the file, as always. Well then," DeSoto said, standing. "I will look forward to hearing from you after you have arranged the pickup. Use one of the scrambler numbers, of course. I will be in Amsterdam tonight and most of tomorrow."

Daniel and Eugene rose. They shook hands again, DeSoto's grasp feeling heavy to Daniel as if trying to feel for something concealed beneath the flesh.

23.

Eugene, predictably, was hungry, so they went into an Italian café for an early lunch. Eugene opened the portfolio discretely and leafed through it with the one finger not sticky from his sandwich.

"You want to look at these papers?"

"I'll look at them tonight," Daniel said.

"It's too complicated. I don't like all this tricky shit," Eugene said around a mouthful of bread and salami. "He should just send in a couple of guys to clean them, and that's that."

"That's not DeSoto's style, not when his pride has been bruised. These guys fucked him over once, and he wants to make them know it's him getting even."

"Okay, but why all this crazy gymnastics shit?" Eugene said. "He's gonna have a guy *inside* one of the crates, popping up like a fucking jack in the box."

"Or a stripper," Daniel said. And when he could see Eugene didn't understand, he added, "at a bachelor party. Didn't you ever see that when you were in the States?"

"A bachelor party? You mean when somebody gets married?"

"Yeah. You know, the night before the guy gets married, his buddies throw a wild party for him and they have this stripper hiding in a huge wedding cake and at the right moment she pops out."

"Huh," Eugene said, flicking a piece of bread into his mouth. "No, I missed that. I never got married over there."

"Never mind," said Daniel, shaking his head. "It's an old American tradition."

"Well, elaborate revenge must be an old Spanish tradition," Eugene said, sighing. "I don't like it."

"It'll be fine."

"And that's creepy, about Scherbatov popping up all of a sudden."

Daniel's face was blank.

"You never heard of him? Never, when you were in Paris? Weapons and shit. *Russian* weapons, like I was saying the other night. That's how old Nikolai Scherbatov made his fortune. He ran the whole show from Paris so it was less obvious. He was selling off Russian weapons even before Glasnost."

"How did he manage that?" Daniel asked.

"Friends on the inside," Eugene said, chomping his sandwich. "You know those guys in prison who always seem to have everything they need? The drugs, the booze, the special food... they can even have little visits with women. Really well-connected bad-ass prisoners, the guards are scared of them. Think of the Soviet Union as a big prison, and not a very well run one at the end, either. Scherbatov had friends in the party, supposedly all the way up. He could come and go whenever he wanted. I forget what his official reason was, something to do with the Olympics. Anyway, he could move anything into or out of the Soviet Union. Supposedly through Yugoslavia or Finland but who knows. When Gorby came to power he tried to crack down on those guys and that's one of the reasons he failed. Sometimes the prisoners control the guards.

"When I was in Afghanistan," Eugene said, "We would hear stories about units that suddenly 'lost' their equipment and nobody could explain it, but the commanding officer was supposedly getting a nice new dacha built near Moscow. That was Scherbatov pulling those deals, or at least guys like him.

"He was big for a while. I think he took some hard hits from some younger guys, toned it down a little. They say he owns a lot of clubs and casinos now. He used to be mostly weapons. I didn't tell DeSoto but I actually worked for Scherbatov a couple of times in Paris. I'm sure he didn't notice me. I was just a punk running some errands for him."

They stared at the street outside the café window. Eugene wiped his mouth.

"He could tell you're sick," he said.

"It won't make any difference," Daniel said. "We don't do any of the rough stuff. He has his pros for that. We just have to make the contact, arrange the deal, and then get these two guys in a vulnerable position."

When Daniel looked across the table, he saw that Eugene was gnawing on the knuckle of his index finger.

"What?"

Eugene shook his head, finally blurted out:

"Fuck."

"What?"

"Sorry," Eugene said, "I shouldn't have... I mean, it's not your fault."

At that moment Daniel's pity for him was bottomless. He wished he could tell Eugene that it didn't matter, that he didn't have to say anything at all, that he didn't have to take care of him.

After they had become quiet for a while, watching the street once more, Daniel said in French,

"It won't be the first time you've had to deal with my sorry ass at death's door."

"That's true," Eugene said quietly.

"We've been in tough spots before," Daniel said.

Eugene nodded, stroking his beard, staring at a traffic light as it changed to green.

24.

In 1990 Daniel met the night manager at a posh hotel who told him about an elite club in Moabit where gangsters went to make deals and to watch gorgeous women dancing on stage.

"They're not strippers," the man said, "more like erotic ballerinas; anyway, you just have to see it, it's exquisite. Smoke a little something beforehand, if you know what I mean, and you won't be sorry."

Daniel dressed up and headed to the club, which to his surprise, let him in without a fuss. The first two dancers were good enough but Daniel had decided that the hotel manager was either exaggerating or hadn't seen the Parisian clubs like this and didn't know better. He was thinking about leaving when the third dancer appeared.

She was small and graceful and Daniel watched the curtain of her thick auburn hair slide across her naked back. It was the girl from Club Maxim, whom he'd seen with DeSoto a few weeks earlier and hadn't shaken from his head ever since. He noticed after a minute that his mouth was open and immediately felt embarrassed until he saw that nobody was watching anything other than her. When she finished, the room shuddered as if everyone had been waiting to breathe.

Daniel asked waitresses and bartenders and eventually learned that her name was Julia, but little else other than the obvious fact that she was "with Mr. DeSoto." He usually managed at each performance to find out where and when the next one was, and he would watch her show and then watch to see whether DeSoto set her up that night with some well-heeled middle-aged man. Daniel weighed the balance between serving his boss faithfully and making a move on the new girl. He lost track of the number of nights he spent watching her, paralyzed by indecision.

She burst into laughter when Daniel's suggestion for a first date was a picnic. Then she saw something in his eyes, paused, and relented. They walked into Friedrichshain, past running kids, young men kicking footballs, and students reading books. They chose a spot on the hillside amidst the birch trees and spread their blanket.

"You're awfully quiet," she said. "Can't you talk and eat at the same time?"

"Mm, I was just enjoying it."

"So you're a gangster, too. What are you, American? Are you a cowboy?"

"No, French."

"Really? You don't sound French."

"But I did live in America for a while."

"Ah," Julia said, her eyes casting about for the glass of wine she had set down on the blanket. She raised it above her face, as if in a toast. *"Le cowboy français.* See, I had my obligatory French and English in school."

"Trés bien," Daniel said. "Did you get good grades? All-Ones?"

"No, 2.6. That was a point of pride for me."

"Two point six?" Daniel asked, grinning, "Exactly that? That was a point of pride?"

"Two point six was the perfect statistical average grade, nationwide," She said. "Getting that, *precisely*, was a point of pride. To be able to calculate it, like a science. Mediocrity is so complex, people don't appreciate it."

Daniel laughed. "People don't appreciate mediocrity enough?" He chuckled, readjusted himself on the blanket. "I don't know. Sometimes I think it's all that people appreciate."

"You don't understand," she said. "You've never tried, have you? To be perfectly, absolutely mediocre? Human nature goes against what we say is 'average.' When you try to do something, you're either trying to do a good job, or you don't give a damn, and you're barely trying at all. Almost everything we do falls into one of those two categories. And people give you grades, right, based on how well you attained *their* goals. And somewhere along the way, I ran out of the ability to give a damn about any of it anymore, so I decided to screw with their system. I denied them the satisfaction of failing me despite my best efforts to succeed, and I denied them the satisfaction of taking pity on my weak efforts by passing me along despite a lack of ability."

Daniel shook his head.

"Amazing. But what about art class? You must have given a damn there, must've tried to—"

"—in art classes it was the easiest of all," she said.

Daniel nodded sadly.

"Well," he said, "I missed my chance to go to university. I had the money, actually, and got accepted. That's how I got to America, but..."

"But you turned to a life of darkness and evil," she said, eyebrows bobbing.

"It's easier to do that in America than in other places. No, really, I mean I've been involved in businesses that aren't entirely legal or would be legal under different circumstances, but I'm not some gangster. I don't hurt people or do that machine-gun and squealing tires stuff you see in the movies."

"What do you do?" she said, "I mean, if you can tell me."

"I buy and sell things that people can't get otherwise. I always check out the goods and the people first. It's not as dark and evil as you think. Most of the people I deal with are straight-up guys. It's a business."

"Fine, but you could work in business with other straight-up guys doing legal things," she said. "What is it? Do you crave excitement? Do you owe Miguel something? Or do you hate filling out tax forms?"

"I don't know. I've just... never fit in, you know, with the real world. It's never made a lot of sense to me. It's like some big shiny building, and everybody looks like they're happy inside, or at least busy, and it's all pretty and impressive, and you walk around and around, looking for the door to get in but you never find it. I could never find that door, so after a while, I walked away. I do my own thing. Like you, in your own way. With your sculpting and painting and stuff."

"And stuff, yes, let's not forget the stuff. Well," she said, sighing, lifting her wine again. "Here's to doing your own thing."

"Yes," he said, and they touched the cusps of glass together.

"These strawberries are really good," she said, popping one into her mouth. "Here, I'll save the last one for you."

"Yeah, they're my favorites."

"*Les fraises,* right?"

Daniel laughed.

"Yes," he said.

"What, why are you laughing? Did I say it wrong?"

"No, you said it fine. It's just an old memory."

"Tell."

"No, nothing. It's stupid," he said. "When I was a kid I was a really slow learner for a while. I probably had more trouble learning French than you did. That was one of the words I always screwed up: *les fraises.* It's probably how I came to love them."

He lifted the last strawberry and stared at it.

"I mean, it took me so long to remember... ah, I don't know." He popped it in his mouth, exhaled through his nose.

"Miguel says you're one of his best guys," she said.

His face screwed inward in the closing of his swallow.

"He's discussed me... with you?"

"Miguel doesn't miss much."

"You're with him all the time. Are you his girl?"

"If you thought I was, would you have asked me out for a picnic?"

"Yes."

Julia shook her head and smiled, looking away at the buildings that rose over the park.

"Oh my, oh my... No, I'm not his 'girl.' But I owe him. He saved my life. It's an ugly story and I don't want to say anything more about it, all right?"

"All right."

"But why were you there so many nights?"

"I was following you," he said.

"Obviously. Why?"

"It's hard to explain."

"Apparently so."

He sighed, ran his hand through his hair.

"I saw you dancing," he said at last.

"And?"

"And the rest is where it gets hard to explain."

"Daniel, I don't take kindly to being followed."

"No," he said, his face rising in alarm. "No, not like that. I mean... I couldn't stop watching... I had to know... oh fuck, why is this so hard to say? All right, all right, I'm sorry. Let me try to explain...."

"Shh, it's okay," she said. "Don't say any more."

She frowned, chewed for a concentrated moment on her thumb.

"Daniel, we should be honest about this right now, you know. Right at the outset, because I don't want either of us to waste any time on false assumptions. I like you, I'm attracted to you, we can see each other from time to time, but I can't ever have a relationship with you."

"That makes no sense at all," he said.

"I have a hundred reasons. Your work, my work, the fact that you work for Miguel."

"Look," he said, rubbing his forehead. "Could we just set some of these things aside for now?"

"Yes. All right."

"And we could see each other from time to time."

"Okay," she said. A moment later he was surprised that she smiled sheepishly and bit her lip.

"What?" he asked.

"Your face," she said. "You have this little boy face. All your emotions play out on it. I'd love to sculpt it but I wouldn't know where to start. It's all so very warm and young but then you get to the eyes."

"The eyes?"

"Those are very old," she said. "They go back a long way."

They were walking out of the park when she said:

"It's better not to know too much about a person. I don't like knowing what someone wants or expects. Things just happen, they just come."

25.

There are millions of faces in the city, he thinks. You live there, what, a few years? You learn a few dozen of them, maybe more. It's like trying to remember the stars. Could you really tell any one of them from another? They could die, one a night for every night of your life, and you'd never know. And those two stars that seem close together in this moment are in reality so far distant on a third plane that light will never pass between them in a thousand lifetimes. They only seem close because you, too, are so hopelessly far away.

Daniel turned a corner and saw his partner waiting in the pre-arranged spot. Eugene stood, shoulders sloping, face downward but eyes upturned in the mendicant pose of the junkies. He was dressed slovenly, his hair loose and hanging around him like a stream of flotsam. He held a beer in his hand. Daniel smiled at that last part of the disguise. Eugene waited against the wall of a sweet-smelling Turkish *Imbiß* on the other side of the street from the door that Daniel entered.

It was a porno store with three bulging shelves of glossy specialty magazines against one wall and a dusty display of sex toys against the other, beside the cash register. Aside from the young man behind the counter listening to the radio news, there were two other customers. Both regarded Daniel for an instant without turning their heads.

Daniel found the booklet. It was called *Classic Combos,* written in English. The cover was brilliant orange, with a gasping bleach-blonde wedged between two distracted-looking men. He held it, cover outward, against his thigh as he walked the perimeter of the shop floor, gazing at the other booklets. A few seconds later one of the two men looked directly at him, nodded once, and walked through the door. Daniel put *Classic Combos* back on the shelf and followed.

"I am think there is the two mens." The German words fell out of this man's throat in misshapen chunks.

"We can speak French," Daniel replied. "What should I call you?" The man frowned.

"Sergio."

"Fine."

"I thought there was supposed to be two of you," Sergio said in French.

"My partner couldn't make it," Daniel said, not turning to look at Eugene creeping along the edges of the buildings in their wake. "He'll be there for the pickup. And you? I thought there would be two of you."

"My partner couldn't make it either."

"Fine," said Daniel.

"Let's go to this park up ahead," said Sergio, and they stopped to wait for a crossing light.

Sergio was older than Daniel had expected. Mid to late fifties, perhaps. His face was deeply lined and rough, topped with white-gray bristles. He was no taller than Eugene but seemed intensely compact beneath his leather jacket: broad-shouldered and full-chested. The white line of an old scar ran from the left corner of his mouth up his cheekbone, ending beneath an ear that jangled with two large silver loops.

When they crossed the street they passed not more than three meters from Eugene. Daniel couldn't tell if Sergio gave him more than a second's glance or not, or if, for Sergio, a second's glance was sufficient.

The park was a small triangle of trees, bordered by the streets and shading an immaculate green space. Daniel and Sergio were the only two men there. Two women walked babies in strollers and two others sunbathed topless at the far point of the triangle.

"I can have everything ready by Friday night," Daniel said as they walked the perimeter of the park.

Sergio frowned.

"No sooner?"

"I have to move things and I can only do that during the daytime. I'll have it in a basement warehouse. I have to use the loading equipment. The guard knows me, but I have to go slowly. It'll take more than one day. I've got it in several different places right now."

"Why can't you bring it at night?"

"They get night deliveries sometimes," Daniel said, "so there's a guard. But only Monday through Thursday. On the weekend nights, there's no guard. Just a security system and I have access to that."

Sergio was still frowning but he offered no objections.

Daniel continued. "It's a basement, locked. Secure until late Sunday night. The guard comes back at 6 AM on Monday. Transportation away from there is your concern."

"Fine," said Sergio. "Do you have the address?"

"Mühlenstrasse 93, in Pankow," Daniel said. Sergio squinted at the sudden foreign words, then pulled a little pad from his jacket pocket. He clicked a pen against the pad.

"Spell that," he said. Daniel did.

"Fine." Sergio replaced the pen and pad. "What time Friday night?"

"Midnight."

"Earlier is better."

Daniel shrugged.

"So, what? Ten?"

"Ten is fine. We're going to check it out, of course."

"Fine."

"The place, too. Before the pickup."

Daniel shrugged again.

"Whatever you want. It's secure. I'll have it unlocked for you by ten on Friday. When we get the money I'll give you the security codes so you can reset it and leave clean."

"Very well," said Sergio. "It'll be two men?"

"Me and my partner," Daniel said. "And you?"

"Just two."

"Fine."

"Do you have an abort signal?" Sergio asked.

"No. Nothing will go wrong."

Sergio stopped. For the first time, he looked Daniel in the eye.

"I never use aborts," Daniel said, indifferent to the cold stare.

"That means I have to carry."

"I assumed you would," Daniel replied, his eyes motionless.

"If that's the way you want it, fine."

"It's going to be a room full of assault rifles and grenades," Daniel said. "Do you think I give a damn if you carry or not?"

"Let's just do the deal," Sergio said, snorting, turning to walk again.

26.

"I should have taught you Russian," Eugene said quietly in English, stroking his beard. "That way we'd have a code language."

"It's too hard," Daniel said. "My brain is full already."

"Easier than German," Eugene said, shaking his head.

They stood in the shadow of a delivery truck, between its aluminum panels and a nearby wall with a service door. The street was to their backs, and they took turns peeking out from behind the truck every minute or so to see if the Belgians had arrived yet. It was 9:48 when Daniel said,

"There. See that Mercedes? That's him."

Eugene turned, peeked, nodded.

"Yup. You know, this has been bugging me, but I know that guy from somewhere. That Sergio guy you were talking to. Did he look familiar to you?"

Daniel shook his head.

"No, I don't think so."

"It's not a big deal. I think I might have worked with him once or twice back in Paris. Sooner or later all gangsters look the same."

He reached into his coat and unlocked the safety on his gun.

"Okay," Eugene whispered. "Welcome to our big show... you go ahead."

Daniel thumped his partner once on the back and disappeared through a door in the wall. He closed it silently behind him and scrambled down the stairs to warn DeSoto's men in the basement to take cover. Eugene stayed behind, watching the Mercedes and the two men in it. The car sat across the street, half a block away, for almost ten minutes. Then the two figures emerged, one carrying a thin attaché case. Eugene slipped around the back of the truck and waited. When they crossed the street he walked into the light of the parking lot. The Belgians froze, hands on their chests.

"Gentlemen," Eugene said in French. "Not to worry. Everything is prepared."

They lowered their arms slowly, walked toward him.

"Where's the other one?" Sergio asked.

"My partner is downstairs. We've opened some of the crates so you can inspect them."

"We'll inspect all of them," the second man said. He was the one with the attaché case, and Eugene had never seen him before. Earlier that week, when he had trailed Daniel's meeting with Sergio, Eugene had kept an eye out for anyone else who might be doing the same thing. The fact that he hadn't seen anybody worried him. It raised the ugly possibility that these guys, old and gray though they might be, were better at this than he was. This second Belgian looked older still than Sergio, taller and thinner but by no means weak-looking. He had a strong, square face with waves of silver hair and a pair of icy blue eyes.

"Come with me," Eugene said, swallowing hard, as he always did when he had to turn his back to strangers. They followed through the fence, through the main door, into the building.

"There's too much light on this street," Sergio grumbled as they stepped inside.

"It doesn't matter," the other one said. "Let's see the goods."

"Come with me," Eugene said again, held the door to the stairwell open for them and let them walk first. Their footfalls on the metal steps reverberated through the warehouse.

The basement was fully as large as the warehouse itself, which covered half of a city block. The ceiling was five meters high, affording plenty of room for the two electric forklifts that sat on the concrete. There were two large freight elevators at one end, leading to the surface. The whole place could easily have accommodated five times the number of crates and containers it currently held.

When they reached the bottom of the steps Eugene nodded toward one end, where Daniel stood waiting. The distance was such, in the limited light, that he appeared small and dark beneath the towering ceiling.

"That's yours over there," Eugene said to the two men, and they followed him across the floor. Daniel had turned and walked to one side so that he didn't turn and look until half a minute later when they were right there beside the two dozen waist-high wooden boxes.

"We should have a crowbar over here," Eugene said, "if you want to pry the tops off and inspect. I think you'll find everything in order. To save some time we can count the money while you do that." He turned to Daniel, seemed about to ask him something, then stopped.

"Ah— D..."

Because the look on Daniel's face was so ghastly, Eugene almost slipped, almost used his partner's real name. "Ah,

Maurice..." he said, swallowing quietly. "Where's the crowbar?"

"Maurice...?"

Daniel stood utterly motionless except for the excited rush of his breathing. His hands hung loosely at his sides and his face had become so pale that even the yellow warehouse lights couldn't conceal the startling lack of color. Eugene's mind was racing, trying to invent an emergency scenario, convinced his partner was about to collapse heaving to the floor when Daniel's lips parted as if he was about to say something but simply could not.

Sergio saw three things, all within two seconds: first, Eugene's sudden discomposure; second, Daniel's wordless pallor; third, the astonished and enraged look on his partner's face.

"What?" Sergio demanded, looking around at the three of them.

"No," his partner said, so low and malevolently it was almost a stomach growl.

In the handful of seconds that followed, three of them snapped their heads around at each other, uncomprehending and increasingly alarmed. Only Daniel remained motionless, silent, staring across the three meters of concrete floor at Alain LeClerc.

"No," LeClerc said again, shaking his head, reaching inside his coat. "No, this is horseshit—"

"Don't do that," Eugene said, his voice rising as he saw the hand vanish, his own hand moving to his waist.

Sergio looked incredulously at both of them, then grabbed at his coat. He pulled his gun just as the room exploded with a blast from behind them.

"Fuck!" Sergio screamed as a bullet flew through his forearm. He and LeClerc scrambled in opposite directions. Eugene bolted over a crate, landed behind it, pulled his Makarov, then flattened himself against the side of the box as he heard two more shots and then a third returning in the opposite direction. When he looked up again, he realized that Daniel was still standing in the same place.

"Get the fuck down!" he howled at him in English, and the words must have penetrated at last because Daniel turned and dove for a pyramid stack of crates as a volley of automatic weapon fire ricocheted through the warehouse, sending head-sized splinters spinning to the ceiling.

Eugene couldn't see anyone else. He knew that the Belgians and DeSoto's two men could see each other because as far as he knew, that's who was doing all the shooting. He was on his stomach, his head and shoulders propped on his elbows, when he saw a set of legs dash across the warehouse floor, setting off another volley of fire. He couldn't tell where the legs went or whether they had caught any bullets.

He crawled forward on his stomach a meter or two. The cavernous room had fallen silent again. He detected some kind of slight motion in front of him, behind a triangular mass of crates. It's Daniel. He wriggled forward another few meters like a salamander, then rose into a crouch. When he bolted the last two meters between his crates and the triangle, he drew no fire. He was less than a body-length behind not Daniel, but Sergio, who was squatting, holding a gun in one hand and clasping a bloody sleeve with the other. He turned his head to see Eugene, and the second he spent in wide-eyed shock before he moved was the second the Russian needed to bring the Makarov to his head and pull the trigger. Sergio's face collapsed inward as if sucked backward through his splitting skull, spreading out across the blonde pine boards of the crates.

Daniel can hear bullets. They're crashing through this place, but it's this roar in his head, it sounds like ocean noise on top of everything: howling waves of water pushing him down. Jesus, I surrender, give me the bullets, make it stop.

Then a hand around his arm, his head turns too slowly to see if it's friend or foe lifting him up, pushing him forward. It's Eugene, thank God. Get me out of here, he wants to say. Get me out before I drown.

Then they're on the surface, not quite running because he can't quite run. Stumbling, dragging his legs, his head seeming to come out last of all, depressurizing.

"You're going to fucking tell me what that was about."

"It was him."

"What?" Eugene demanded. "Who? What the fuck are you talking about?"

Daniel tried to inhale and dissolved in coughing. The roar faded as they staggered away. It became an echo, no less terrifying in the distance, in the background.

27.

This is not a dream because I can smell him.

Daniel stepped down the stairs from the street into the subway. Light has left him, afraid to follow here. But the water finds this place easily, flowing up from the foundations and innumerable tears in the earth, overflowing the blue pipes and pumps, running through the streets and streaming down the stairs into the subway stations. He splashed with each step. The edge of the platform flowed like a dark brown waterfall.

Daniel walked into the mouth of the service tunnel, stepping over a chain with a warning sign. He sensed the presence of the walls and the ceiling closing him in, completing his self-interment. He was alone in the blackness with only the stench of decay to pull him deeper, forward, downward.

"It's so dark," he said, thinking perhaps he could detect the outline of the fingers of his hand. "Turn on the lantern," he begged.

Light blossomed with the feline hiss of a match: a flash in front of him, then gone. And then an ovaline point of yellow, swelling slowly from a glass chamber. The glow spread outward, upward, and he saw the old man's brown hand around the cord from which he held the lamp.

He sensed that he was drawing closer to him without walking. He felt the water streaming cold around his feet and ankles.

"As you go faster it gets darker," the old man said, and Daniel felt himself falling forward but not hitting anything. "Are you still with us, Daniel LeClerc?"

"Answer," he commanded. Daniel began to feel himself choking.

"Answer, LeClerc."

"LeClerc, answer the door."

"What?" He was on his stomach, his head leaning over the edge of the bed. A silvery thread of drool connected his mouth to the floorboards.

He heard the sound of two fists beating upon his door.

"LeClerc, goddamn it, open up."

He rolled, fell, out of the bed, staggered to the door, slumped against the frame, and said, "What?"

"Goddamn, we've been beating on this fucking door for five minutes."

"I was asleep."

"It's morning. Time to wake up. Get dressed and come with us."

"Say the word," Daniel said.

"Orange."

"All right, all right. Five minutes."

"Orange" was a code word used by all employees of Miguel DeSoto. It meant: "Whatever you're doing at this moment, stop; this new thing takes precedence."

Daniel knew perfectly well why this particular orange was at his door and where these men were taking him. He didn't know why he wasn't afraid. Miss Garcia offered him tea or coffee, as usual. He declined, as usual. He gazed around the empty waiting room and contemplated the surfaces of his fingertips until she returned and told him he could go in.

DeSoto was seated behind his desk and this time there was no ceremonial rising to shake hands.

"Sit," the Spaniard said, tipping his excellent nose toward a chair. Daniel sat.

"Eugene was here last night," DeSoto said flatly, his eyes trained upon the immaculate surface of his desk. "You, however, have not yet shown the courtesy of offering me an explanation for recent events."

Daniel sighed. He sensed that he was supposed to be afraid, and he was indeed slightly alarmed that he had thus far failed to work up even a decent sweat. DeSoto was at his scariest when he was being nice. He could be positively terrifying in the midst of a smile or a gracious gesture. For some reason, this poorly-concealed anger wasn't so bad. But Daniel held no illusions; he knew perfectly well what the man was capable of doing.

"I wish I could give you a good excuse," Daniel said. "I don't know what Eugene said, but if he took any of the blame for himself, that's a complete lie. It was entirely my fault."

DeSoto's eyes rose now to meet his. They narrowed slightly as if absorbing and weighing the absence of fear.

"When I arranged the pickup I spoke with only one of the so-called Belgians. The other didn't show. When we met them for the actual pickup,"

"It was your father."

"Yes."

DeSoto shook his head.

"I could have spared him if you'd been thorough enough to do proper research on the clients and quick-minded enough to make the right arrangements with me."

"That wasn't it. I mean, you're right of course about my failure to investigate thoroughly enough. I didn't... I mean, I wasn't trying to save him."

DeSoto blinked once, slowly, as if falling asleep.

"I consider myself a broad-minded man, Daniel. But if you're telling me that you are indifferent to the life and death of your own father, then aside from a brief delay to exchange greetings, I fail to see how this discovery caused you to blow the sting."

Beneath the decorum, Daniel knew, DeSoto's anger was very real. He had stooped to using verbs like "blow."

"My relationship with my father has been... troubled."

"My relationship with many people has been troubled," DeSoto said, "but I do not allow that to interfere with my plans. You, however, allowed a very carefully-laid sting to fly to pieces, at great expense to me, which resulted in the wounding of one of my men. If I were observing the actions of a neophyte in this business, I would conclude that you were someone I had no desire to employ. But to think that this performance was the work — if it even deserves to be called that — of my two most trusted and experienced agents? Can you appreciate my dismay?"

Daniel nodded once. DeSoto sighed.

"In any event, he got away."

Daniel stared at him.

"Your father," DeSoto explained, "is still at large, and apparently unhurt. You're entitled to your own verdict as to whether that's good news or bad. You can no doubt guess my sentiments on the matter. Eugene, as you might have surmised, claims that the fault was his."

Daniel rose in his chair.

"What? No — that's—"

DeSoto pushed his words back with an abruptly raised palm, like that of a traffic cop halting a stream of cars.

"It is irrelevant."

That was the moment that Daniel realized he was going to live. Now he found himself slightly chilled to think that he had been genuinely unsure until that point.

"You're suspended," DeSoto said, leaning back into his chair. "If and when I need your services again, I'll send for you. If I *do* send for you, it will be because I have decided that your skills are valuable and, above all, *dependable.* If I were ever to be proven wrong about that again, the consequences would be grave and tragic."

He nodded as if adding the final punctuation. Daniel rose to leave. He knew better than to thank him.

28.

Daniel awoke and immediately rose in bed, then doubled over like a jackknife and retched over the side. Nothing came out except a mouthful of searing gas. He gasped and heaved again, managing only some slimy mucous that pooled on his lower lip.

He opened the drawer of his bedside table and found the jar that Rashid had given him. He opened it and saw three pills remaining. He took two of them, realized that he couldn't swallow, and got up to go stick his face under the faucet in his bathroom. He gulped them down.

When his breathing returned to normal and he could feel the pain beginning to recede, he looked into the mirror and surprised himself by thinking: *I am unemployed now.*

Daniel's job for DeSoto had never involved anything like regular hours, nor even any official acknowledgment of employment. As far as the state was concerned, Daniel still drove a truck for Ramiro Logistics, one of the mostly-fictional front businesses that DeSoto maintained so that his employees wouldn't attract government attention. Daniel considered this as he washed his face. Presumably his Ramiro paychecks would continue for a while. But he was aware that he was no longer committed to DeSoto and that perhaps this was the break he'd been waiting for.

Miguel had the chance to kill me and passed on it, he mused. *Maybe this... thing will get me instead.*

Daniel watched a brown whirl of coffee wind and twist into his cup and pondered the awkwardness of trying to tell Miguel that he was quitting. He always assumed that he would leave on a high note. The Spaniard would be gracious and shake his hand, there would be thanks and best wishes all around, perhaps even a case of Bordeaux as a going-away present. Sabine would probably throw a private party for him at *d'accord*. But if he quit now, DeSoto might assume disloyalty or at the very least might make things difficult in his relationship with Julia.

He walked outside in the cool, moist air. At the end of his block, he heard jack-hammering as another work crew tackled another water or sewer line renovation. He sighed and turned the other way, heading for the Volkspark Friedrichshain. Within a minute he encountered an old man searching through a trash can and Daniel asked him if he knew anyone named "Johannes." The man with the fish hook scar.

The great advantage of working for Miguel DeSoto is that he gives you all the details and instructions. Tactical decisions are left to your judgment but everything else is usually scripted. This is the opposite of detective work, Daniel knew, in which one starts with very little information and has to assemble all the rest, constructing a framework of understanding and context as one goes. Having lived in Berlin long enough to appreciate how easy it was to hide things in the vast chaos of this city, Daniel was under no illusions regarding how hard it was going to be to find someone, particularly if that person didn't want to be found.

After zig-zagging through the park Daniel headed east along Lenin Boulevard. The latest round of re-naming announcements had included this street, which had a couple of weeks remaining before it would become the Landsberger Allee. There was a strange joylessness in all of this rechristening, so different from the euphoria when the Wall opened. People waited now with impatience for new electrical or water lines, or just to have reliable heat. The city's efforts to scrub away the communist past felt like a poor substitute for those quotidian priorities. Travel no longer seemed magical, and the practical Berliners cared a lot more about whether the buses would run again than they did about the names of the streets on which they ran.

The green spaces in front of the huge apartment blocks were full of uncollected garbage as if Lenin was making his disapproval of the name-change known via a trash collector's strike. According to two of the old men in the park, an unofficial soup kitchen and shelter had been set up in one of the big condemned buildings on the north side of the boulevard. Most of East Berlin was "unofficial" in one way or another these days, with people seizing the opportunity to occupy some abandoned space or renovate without permits. This tested the patience of the authorities, and of Germans in general, who revere planning and use the word "improvise" purely as a pejorative.

When Daniel found the shelter and asked around, he got an earful from the two grey-haired women who ran it. They thought he was a plainclothes cop and thus he stood-in for the government in their eyes. Where was the renovation plan for this block? Are they really going to bulldoze it? How can they keep closing all the factories and moving people out of old buildings without adequate alternatives for work and housing? And No, we don't have a man named Johannes with a fish hook scar on his cheek, now kindly fuck off.

Daniel turned onto a side street that led, more or less, back toward his neighborhood. It had the same earthy, cloying funk of decaying garbage and steamed potatoes as his own street. At the corner was a Turkish *Imbiß,* a recent arrival here from the West, and Daniel walked in to get a döner and some tea and to ask about homeless men who might have come begging in recent weeks. The woman behind the counter seemed baffled by his question and brought her teenaged son out of the kitchen to speak German with him.

"They go past all the time," the boy said. "Sometimes they come in and beg for beer but we don't give them any. I give them the leftover bread at night, but mostly they want beer."

Daniel realized to his irritation that these people also assumed he was *Kripo*: a plainclothes Berlin detective. He couldn't decide whether this impression was an asset or a liability. He sat beside the window and ate his döner and watched the street. Within five minutes he saw a middle-aged drunk slouching along the opposite curb, coming to rest on his haunches, and urinating without first pulling down his trousers.

Daniel found himself thinking about his time in Washington. Here is what America promised these people, he thought: a place where you can restart at Zero, where the past is everywhere but doesn't mean anything or at least doesn't matter. But they should've paid closer attention to America because that is exactly how it all goes wrong. You cut loose from the past and you cut loose from everything, including yourself. Excitement and freedom are poor substitutes for a plan and a map. He wondered how many Ossis already had buyers' remorse.

He was sipping his tea when a grey figure caught his eye. It was an elderly man with thick hair walking with a slow but deliberate pace, half a block down and moving away from him. He couldn't make out the face. He slammed a 10 D-Mark note on the table and rushed out the door.

Daniel approached quickly but then slowed and kept a distance of about ten meters. He realized that the man was talking to himself as he walked but he couldn't make out more than a few words. Daniel thought he heard him say something about "flat metal objects," and "report to the civil authorities," and he thought he heard the word "unexploded."

There's no need to scare this poor old fellow, Daniel thought. He'll stop eventually and then I'll go past him and have a look.

Thirty minutes later Daniel was beginning to wonder about that strategy. The old man didn't stop for anything. Not to buy groceries, not to wait for a train, not to plop down at a café table or walk into an *Imbiß* to beg for a beer, not to speak with or visit anyone. He plodded ahead, taking the side streets whenever he could, his dust-gray fading into and out of the crevices of the city. His gait never changed. Daniel watched the motion rather than the man as if the man himself were invisible or perhaps did not exist at all outside of some mysterious mission that never pauses and never concludes.

They walked north around the perimeter of Prenzlauer Berg, through streets where missing cobblestones opened shin-deep brown puddles. They passed buildings whose façades were entirely gone; the fronts were battered red bricks so rough and irregular that they looked as if they had been gnawed by some ravenous giant. They passed a few building sites where bulldozers sat axle-deep in swelling brown pools and the blue pipes rumbled futilely, trying to pump away the endlessly rising water. Daniel's shoes were soon soaked.

Daniel realized that it was evening and that he was heading west into the orange and raspberry blast of the sun at the end of a long street. He had become disoriented and made the mistake of stopping to look around, trying to find street signs. When he turned again toward the fiery glow at the end of the block, the old man was gone.

This time there's no finding him. Daniel cursed, zigzagging the entrances of side streets and alleys, crossing and re-crossing the road into the descending sun in the West, like a sailboat tacking into a hostile wind.

At last, deflated, his feet sore and wet, he turned toward the Dimitroffstraße and when he reached the boulevard, saw to his exasperation that the subway station was closed. An unfriendly yellow sign announced that it was being renamed the Eberswaldestraße. He walked toward the Rosa Luxemburg Platz, wondering if either it or its name were slated for demolition any time soon. (Communists can't be too careful these days.) Along the way, the Senefelder Platz station, at least, was in operation. He descended the stairs.

The corridor was covered in graffiti and the overhead lights were barely functioning. The platform was mostly in darkness and he could see no one else. One of his shoes, already sodden, smacked a puddle of standing water.

After about a minute his eyes adjusted and he realized that somebody was standing at the other end of the platform. It was the old man, grey and silent, staring him down. Daniel recognized him instantly.

He waited for Daniel to see him, then turned and walked toward the mouth of the tunnel, where a narrow ledge acted as a service platform.

Daniel realized that Johannes had been leading him the entire time. He stood in shock, his hands still in his pockets, his mouth slightly open, feeling his breath in the silence of the tunnel. Then he jogged forward, shouting, "Wait!"

Daniel squeezed sideways through a safety barrier and edged onto the service platform. It was barely as wide as his feet, utterly dark, and led away beside the tracks. There was a hint of yellow light in the distance; something glowed vapor-thin ahead of him, but he had no idea where, on which side, or how far it was.

He had taken perhaps two dozen steps when he remembered something about the subways in East Berlin. The communists built the fronts of their trains artificially wide, to fill the tunnels perfectly, leaving no crawl space on either side of the tracks. This was a way to "deter" people from attempting to escape to the West by creeping along these service ledges. Now that the subway was unified it increasingly used the western trains, but Berlin was broke and couldn't afford to upgrade everything. If a train appeared from this direction, he might be in its way.

"Johannes, is that you?" he called into the darkness. "I'm a friend. I was with you and Sabine the night you were hit by the car, remember? I'm trying to help."

Daniel waited, trying to remember how often the trains ran on this line in the afternoon, and he realized that he wasn't even sure what day of the week it was. Then he heard a voice that sounded more ancient, more laden with grief than he had ever heard in his life:

"I don't know where she is," it said. "I don't know how I got out. The lights went out and then there was water."

Daniel leaned forward, trying to see him. Then he felt a cool breeze on his cheek. Air began to flow in the tunnel.

"We need to get out of here!" Daniel said, stepping backward, trying to turn himself around without toppling over onto the track.

"No," Johannes said. "I'm sorry. I shouldn't have run. The water's coming back and this time I won't run."

The tunnel rumbled as if a storm were coming. Daniel shuffled back along the ledge as quickly as he could, aware of the light blooming behind him. He made it back to the platform breathless, with perhaps three seconds to spare.

The train coursed out of the orifice like a sudden uncoiling wave. It stopped with a metallic whisper. It was indeed an older eastern model, wide with a "catcher" on the front, but Daniel saw no evidence that it had caught anyone. A dozen people got off and strode toward the exits. No one got on. When the doors pressed shut and it pulled away, Daniel stared back down the tunnel.

"I'm here for Sabine," he shouted, even though he had no idea if Johannes was still there, was alive, had found some secret alcove. "She wants to help you."

When there was no answer, he shouted his address into the darkness and added, "I want to help you."

Then he decided not to ride the subway after all, and he walked out of the tunnel and onto the evening street. The presence in his abdomen had returned, like a predator waiting for him to slow or tire, and it accompanied him all the way home.

29.

It was originally built as a bank. It had a deep basement with thick concrete walls and a subterranean barred vault for the safeguarding of money. It was finished just in time for the war, so its heavy stone foundations protected people instead of gold. Soviet artillery, pulled up point-blank across the street, fired repeatedly at the handful of German militiamen who were making their last stand on the second and third floors. When the communists came they renamed the main boulevard where its shocked façade still stood: *Straße der Befreiung.* Liberation Street.

The communists had more success renaming things than they did at rebuilding them. Many of the streets and plazas were still brooks and ponds of rubble when they received their new socialist baptisms with names like Rosa Luxemburg Boulevard, Karl Marx Way, Paris Commune Street. Reconstruction usually had to wait, and banks were understandably low on the communists' list of restoration priorities. The building lay wounded and festering for two decades, its second and third floors gutted, its ground floor filled with debris. Only the basement was habitable since it had no shattered windows through which the winter sleet could stream. It became a hideaway for the dispossessed and desperate. They huddled in this dripping enclave beneath the street, pressed against each other and against the bars.

At some point in the 1960s, a government bureaucrat returning from a stroll in the nearby park must have noticed a current of ragged people coming and going from that miserable doorless façade. His observation flowed up the complex network of surreptitious information which served as the blood and circulatory system for the East German state until it trickled back down the capillaries into the office of the appropriate Ministry of State Security department head, who sent a lowly *Unterleutnant* to check out the goings-on in the old bank building on Liberation Street. He arrived after dark and took his curious place in a line of people waiting silently on the street outside. It was an odd assemblage of twenty or thirty — certainly enough to constitute a counter-revolutionary threat to the government — but he was struck most by the wide variation of ages. There were only one or two people who, like him, were in mid-life. The rest were either young, perhaps a few even in their teens, or very old and white-headed.

There was an interminable wait, during which the number of people standing on the side of the street grew by three or four. The Stasi lieutenant was in a quandary. If he asked someone what they were all waiting in line for, he would reveal that he himself didn't know. And since this was obviously some covert assembly gathered for some nefarious purpose, if he revealed himself as Not One Of Them, they would not only refuse to tell him the truth but would single him out for the infiltrator he was. So he kept his mouth shut, resisting even the temptation to ask, "When does it start?" (For fear of hearing in reply: "When does *what* start?")

At last, well after midnight, when he thought his legs had frozen to the pavement, someone appeared in the open doorway of the building and the somnambulant crowd shuffled and stirred as they went in one by one. He had a moment of panic when he realized that there might be a ticket or fee or some other kind of entrance requirement, but he was waved forward like everyone else by two teenage girls in black who stood in the doorway. He followed the slow line of people through the wreckage of the lobby, down the stairs into the basement.

It was deeply dark, illuminated only by the yellow mist of two oil lamps against opposite sides of the room. Most of the steel bars had been ripped out, leaving jagged round holes across the floor and walls. Only a single barrier remained, dividing the room at approximately the two-thirds point so that the small crowd of people sat on the floor in the larger section, ghostly in the thin yellow light as they continued to wait in silence.

The Stasi lieutenant could make out the silhouette of the man seated on his left, though he was too nervous to give him a good look. The man looked to be around thirty, which made him one of the generational oddballs in the crowd, neither old nor young. He waited, sitting crossed-legged like most of the others, with his hands in his lap. He stared at the other third of the basement which was separated from them by the black prison of the bars.

A small figure emerged behind the bars, holding a lantern. She was dressed in black and walked on the balls of her feet, pausing to look around her, then taking a few more tentative steps, like a dark predatory cat. When she reached the center of what the Stasi man now realized was a stage, she put the lantern down and began to dance.

For the next hour, he was never entirely sure what he was seeing. The small cat-girl whirled in what might have been a dance of freedom but her joy was tempered by the way she held one arm as if it was wounded, as if it dragged behind her, trailing blood or slowing her. When the figures of two large shadow-men appeared behind her, she looked at them, looked at her wounded arm, and seemed to want anything but to cry for help. She danced away from them until she was pressed against the bars that enclosed the stage, the telltale pain of her wound refusing to let her pass. There were other small animal figures at the periphery now. They, too, stood silent and unmoving like the shadows nearby. She stared at the others for a long time and then she fell slowly to the floor, her thin dark body shaking with silent sobs. The shadow men advanced and extinguished the lantern in the center of the stage. Not a single word had been spoken, not a note of music played.

The crowd exploded into applause so loud that it terrified him. The Stasi man looked to his left, where the man he had seen earlier was striking his palms together wildly, his mouth open, tears streaming down his face.

Almost immediately the people rose to leave and the Stasi man found himself walking with his feet not quite connected to the pavement, carried out by the stream of the others, and left to float awkwardly in the gloom of Liberation Street at three in the morning. He found his way to the car he had left a few blocks from the park, but there was no way he could drive; he could not make his feet descend upon the pedals. So he walked home instead, even though it was four kilometers, and he sat at his kitchen table staring at the window until the light finally came up and the streetcars whirred into electronic life.

When he got to the office he immediately found his superior and told him he was sick. The superior took one look at him and agreed.

"I'll type up this one report quickly," he said, "then I'd like to go home and get some rest."

This is what he wrote:

CASE 441/IV/61. OBSERVING OFFICER: HM31. REFERRED BY: GJ664 (SEE APPENDED FILE)

OBSERVED REPORTED ACTIVITY ON STRAßE DER BEFREIUNG 47. GROUP OF APPROXIMATELY 30, AGE, OCCUPATIONS VARY. STRONG STUDENT ELEMENT. ACTIVITY IS LOCALLY-ORGANIZED DANCE THEATER. NO BLACK MARKETEERING INVOLVED. NO OBVIOUS CRIMINAL ELEMENT. PERFORMANCE WAS A DANCE INTERPRETATION OF VARIOUS WORKS BY BRECHT AND OTHER SOCIALIST WRITERS. NO BOURGEOIS OR COUNTER-REVOLUTIONARY MATERIAL. RECOMMENDATION: OBSERVE AGAIN IN ONE MONTH, INSTRUCT ORGANIZERS TO OBTAIN PROPER STATE THEATER LICENSE.

Two days later he returned from his sick-leave. He made sure the report had passed all the offices it needed to pass, then he quietly misfiled it in a cavernous storeroom which housed the dental records of the entire ministry. It was still there in early 1990 when his neighbors found him swinging softly from a rope tied to one of the exposed pipes in his bathroom ceiling.

er hatte die Augen zu

(he had his eyes closed)

Berlin, March 1945

30.

Johannes was too young to remember when the war began, but he could recall when it got bad. At night the city became black and silent, power shut off in obedience to the angry posters on the walls: LIGHTS OUT! THE ENEMY IS WATCHING. On the posters, a leering demon straddled the back of a diving bomber, hurling fiery missiles at an innocent town. And thus they came night after night, as the vast city waited in darkness for the howl of the sirens which signaled their terrible approach.

Increasingly they came by day, too, and the sky hummed with the fleet of their engines as people clambered down into the subway tunnels, weary and tight-lipped. The anti-aircraft towers pounded above their heads, a sound which was comforting to some, but not to Johannes, who thought of it as a tocsin. He closed his eyes and counted, and then the city shuddered, the emergency lights in the subway flickered and flashed, and, though they were muted by the protective layer of earth above him, he heard the crashes of buildings falling into the street.

"If they come while you're at school, and you get lost afterward," his mother said, "remember that you have to find the blue streetcar."

She seemed to age quickly as the winter came on, the worst winter he could remember. She was a widow already, her husband fallen in Russian snow the previous year. Johannes remembered his father only in still-life: a tall man in a gray uniform tousling his hair, squatting down and instructing him very seriously on how to care for his mother. A few rare visits on leave. Then there was the day she finally saw his name on the lists they hung outside the post office, where all the women gathered in dread each week, their eyes scanning to their letter of the alphabet, screaming or turning away with a gasp, shaking hands clawing at their faces. She hated the others who said a dry-throated prayer of thanks that day, though she had been one of them for several years, too grateful that other women were weeping instead. She always knew her turn would come.

Johannes was eleven, and his mother tightened his coat more frantically every day as she sent him off. Her lips grew pale and thin each morning as she walked him to the corner, where the rubble had been cleared from the streetcar tracks. They stood and waited, breathing air full of dust and cordite, heavy and cold. When it appeared around the corner she always pointed and reminded him:

"There, that's the one that brings you home, all right? Just remember, if you can find the blue streetcar, you'll be okay."

Then she would kiss his head once more and scurry away before the tram stopped so that he couldn't see her coming apart.

Johannes was paralyzed by fear when the sirens began and the bombs fell. It required all of his mother's strength to pull him from the stairwell of their apartment building and drag him to the subway entrance. But once they descended, he calmed immediately and began to breathe normally. His mother released her grasp on his little fingers, which she had squeezed so tightly that they were white.

He was with her the night in March when they tumbled out of bed to the wail of the sirens and ran to the subway's mouth, shuffling down with the others. Everyone wore the dusty coats and shoes they kept beside their front doors for the night alarms. Beneath these, they were a multitude in pajamas: bed-rumpled hair and sleepy eyes, squeezing into the caverns alongside the tracks. The tunnel was warm, a miasma of perspiration and bad breath, and the red emergency light fell oddly upon wrinkles of cloth or angles of their faces and made them look as if they were swimming in fire.

The anti-aircraft towers began to thump nervously overhead. Johannes closed his eyes and counted their recoils. When he had counted to 187, he heard the first crashes. Someone always tried to estimate where the bombs were falling.

"In the north," a man said quietly. "The power station, probably."

They always said things like that, always trying to convince themselves that, no matter how close the massive, skull-rattling blows might be, it was not their neighborhood that was collapsing in spasms of fire and dust.

"The bridges," another said. Johannes kept his eyes shut, counting the explosions.

The lights went out. They were used to this. There were duplicate and triplicate back-up systems. They waited in the sweat and darkness, but the lights didn't come back on.

"Great," someone said. "Anyone have a lantern?"

"I do," said a woman. "But let's wait a bit first and save the oil."

For a minute they could hear only their breathing in the blackened tunnel. Then someone said,

"What's that?"

"What's what?" a man asked, irritated. But then he heard it, too.

Johannes felt a low rumbling, vibrating up from the floor and walls of the tunnel. He opened his eyes but could see nothing. In the distance, it sounded as if someone were rolling a barrel down the tracks. The hot, thick air of the tunnel began to cool and move. A few people muttered.

"Quiet!" a man shouted. "Listen..."

"Oh my God..." a woman said. "It's the Spree. They've hit the tunnel...."

"Turn on that lantern," someone shouted, but the woman was already fingering it, and a slight yellow glow pulsed from their midst.

"Hold it up," someone said.

"We have to get out of here," a woman said. "It's the Spree — they've hit the tunnel under the river."

"Shut up," someone said, "they're still up there. Wait for the All-Clear."

Johannes looked up at the lantern, whose thin light painted the ceiling and walls of the tunnel. He was too short to see over the people to all sides, but he realized that the rumbling had become very loud and the tunnel was shaking as cold, wet air blew through. He felt his mother tighten her grip on his hand.

"Get out of here!" a woman shrieked and tried to shove her way through the mob.

For the rest of his life he would not be sure how he remembered seeing it, but the bodies parted for a moment and Johannes looked up the tracks in the direction of the wind, and he saw a wall of black water bursting from the mouth of the tunnel and slamming into the crowd of people. For a second he heard and felt nothing but the roar.

In the moment that the black wall appeared to him, screaming toward him as if seeking him alone, Johannes felt his mother close her hand around his, and he heard her say his name.

Then he tore his hand away from hers, turning, and tried to run.

The black wall of water struck him in the head as if it were steel, and he was flung against another person, slammed away again and into the wall face-first, torn away again and spun while the water scoured his body, tearing his coat off, filling his nostrils and ears. He thought he struck the ceiling of the tunnel with his forearm, then was flung away. Johannes closed his eyes and held his breath. He had no idea how long it lasted. He felt himself upside-down and his lungs about to collapse. He thrashed, completely submerged, as his legs dragged across some jagged surface, and then he sensed that he was shot upward. He felt air against his skin but then was submerged again. And when he was close to blacking out and ready to gasp the water into his chest, he felt himself rolling on the ground. He opened his eyes.

Johannes was on the street. Water coursed from the mouth of the subway entrance. He breathed in, choked, felt the water all around him again, and stood up shakily in its current. He ran, stumbling through the street, splashing in black water ankle-deep. He gasped, choked out water as he stumbled, felt it inside his head: in his nose, his ears, even behind his eyes. He ran through the middle of the avenue as the spotlights scorched the sky in fiery white columns and the black city flashed with the bursts of the flak guns and shuddered with the annihilating crunches of the bombs. He ran until he couldn't draw enough air into his half-soaked lungs and then he fell to his knees on the cobblestones and vomited.

He looked up, heaving, and saw the open faces of the stricken buildings, façades torn away and lying in heaps on the pavement. When the lights of the explosions flashed, the ground glittered in a thousand shimmering pools of shattered glass. He was bent over and retching again when he felt a hand around his bicep.

"Are you hit?" The voice was deep and male. Johannes looked up to see a big man in a fireman's uniform, one arm lifting him to his feet, the other tucked into a sleeve from where a metal claw emerged instead of a hand.

"What are you doing up here?" the fireman demanded. "They haven't sounded the All-Clear yet."

"I'm sorry, sir," Johannes said. He was shaking.

"You're soaking wet," the fireman observed, looking curiously at the boy shivering in his sodden pajamas. He squinted at Johannes' face and touched his cheek. "That's a nasty wound you have there," the man said. "You're going to need stitches. Come on, come with me. We can't send you back to your mother looking like this."

"I'm sorry," Johannes said.

"Where do you live?"

They paused in the street. The fireman scowled down at the boy, who placed his hands against the sides of his face and concentrated. Johannes realized that his left hand came away from his cheek covered in blood.

"The blue streetcar," he said. "I have to find the blue streetcar."

The fireman sighed.

"Come on, let's go to the station. We'll get you home after that."

They passed a knot of firemen leaning helplessly against their engine, shaking their heads at the futility of a street running with water, and not a drop coming from their pumps. A block away, a big apartment building tumbled to the ground in an orange burst of flame and black smoke against the deep red of the sky. The firemen watched it fall and said nothing. Johannes and the man with the hook arm walked along the streetcar tracks in the center of the dying city.

31.

Shortly after Johannes' twelfth birthday, the world ended: pounded and pounded and pounded into dust and gravel until the streets were powdery canals through a land of crumbled stones.

The pounding had increased as the weather warmed, from frequent to incessant, finally becoming a shaking roar like a horde of ravenous animals approaching from all directions until their jaws were gnashing against every point of his head at once. And then, all in a single afternoon, it stopped. In the absence of that roar, he could now hear the screaming. Half the day and all of the night the women screamed, their torn voices ricocheting off jagged sections of walls, mixing, commingling with other screams, running together like brooks to a river until they formed a vast sea of pain and shame. It flowed over him in the hole where he hid, submerging him beneath the weight of agony that bled out from between women's legs and ran in butchers' currents, and he imagined that the pulverized canals where the streets had once been would become deep red veins.

He was alone in his secret underground space at the bottom of a shattered flight of wooden stairs. In his perpetual darkness, he knew of the passing of day and night only by the rhythm of noise that flowed above his head. When his food ran out and he could no longer bear his own stench, he finally rose, picking his way up the shards of wood from the sub-basement through the dust-choked cellar, up into the light. He fully expected that now he would be killed. He had grown tired of living anyway.

Johannes stood, swaying, unsteady, in the doorway of the wrecked apartment building. He rubbed the burning away from his eyes. The light came like a hot haze which seeped in through his entire head as if he was pocked and perforated like the dead buildings. The first images he could see were frail gray creatures: people climbing carefully over piles of jagged stones.

Johannes walked through streets that were no longer straight but turned and flowed now around mounds of debris like streams at the mercy of rocks and earth. There were no longer city blocks, but currents which intersected by accident, winding around the same hillock of shattered concrete to collide in dusty surprise. He did not know how long he had meandered when he saw a soldier standing at one of these confluences, resting his forearms on a stubby, black machine-gun.

He was a small man, seemingly too young to be a soldier, and his uniform was all wrong. Instead of gray, it was rust-brown, with a long brown coat and a rounded helmet. The young soldier turned and saw him. He shook his head and said something Johannes couldn't understand.

"To eat, to eat," the soldier said in clumsy German, opening his mouth like a baby bird and stabbing at it with cupped fingers. Then he gestured down the length of another street and finally waved at Johannes to move in that direction, scooping the air like a traffic cop summoning a stream of cars. Johannes plodded forward through the passage between the skeletons of buildings and the crust of rubble caked against them. At length, he approached a weary-looking crowd of people. They formed a line, waiting for a group of soldiers to hand them slabs of bread and tins of soup. Johannes was only partially aware that he was standing in the line until he felt the warm metal in his hands, and the smell of the potatoes rose to his face. He stared at the soup.

"Are you alone?" a voice crackled. Johannes looked up to see an old man, a piece of bread clutched awkwardly in a hand that was missing two fingers. With the other, whole hand the man held his tin of soup.

Johannes said nothing.

"Why don't you come eat with me," the old man said, silver bristles on his cheeks shifting over the thinly-covered bones. "Come on. I have a good place."

Johannes followed the ragged figure through the street, the two of them holding up their soup tins like offerings at a temple. The man stopped, turned to make sure that Johannes was still following, and then stepped slowly through the rubble.

"Come on," he said when they approached an opening in the ground. "Be careful on the stairs. It's dark."

The room was sunken and unlit but Johannes could see a bed smothered in dirty blankets, a cold and lifeless wood stove, and three crates with various things lying on and in them: old magazines, a paperback Bible, a worn clothback book, a teapot, a few ragged hand-towels, some cakes of soap, a few framed pictures. Beneath one of the towels, poorly concealed, the unmistakably cold blue-gray of a pistol.

"Not so bad a place, eh?" the old man said, clearing the surface of a crate and nodding at Johannes to sit.

They drank the soup from the tins and sopped up the potatoes and the remaining broth with the bread.

"My name is Albrecht," he finally said. "And you?"

"Johannes."

"Your family?"

"They're dead."

"You're all alone."

Johannes said nothing.

"Well," Albrecht sighed. "I'm all alone, too. Maybe we should stick together, you and I, eh? Help each other out, watch each other's back."

"What happened to your fingers?"

Albrecht looked at his hand, surprised.

"Oh," he said, smiling, the loose drapery of skin on his jowls stitching together. "In the war. Not this one. The first one. Before you were born. What about you?" he said, nodding at Johannes' face. "How'd you get that wound there?"

Johannes shrugged as if he didn't understand. He gazed around the dark little room. Albrecht asked,

"So do you think you'd like to do that? To stay here with me?"

Johannes was silent.

"You see," Albrecht said, leaning backward with a heavy grunt. "I need your help with something."

He reached behind the bed with difficulty and finally extracted a small metal cage.

"I need your help to take care of *him.*"

Inside the cage was a tiny brown rabbit, its deep black eyes imploring Johannes with fear and hunger.

The reserve of strength and control which the boy had kept with him, hoarded through the horror months of the winter and spring, finally cracked open and spilled out, leaking away and gone.

"Now," Albrecht said quietly, putting down the cage. "Now...." He held out his good hand, touched the thin shuddering arms and shoulders. "Now we must be strong," he said, his words dissolving in the rusty folds of his throat.

"We must be strong, you and I."

Johannes would not remove his hands from his face. He shook dirty sobs in channels of mud running between his fingers. He would not weep again for sixteen years.

32.

Years later, when he was dying and didn't care anymore, Albrecht cursed himself for not having left the city and gone west. We had the chance, he would say. We had the chance and I was too stupid, too old to dare, and you were too young to know better. It's my fault, he told Johannes, who gritted his teeth and wished the old man would be quiet.

That first year they foraged down one street, then another, wherever they could find food, soap, clothing. The rumors about the Americans turned out to be untrue; they weren't all jolly and laden with gifts, like camouflaged Father Christmases in half-tracks. Sometimes they gave you food, sometimes they waved you off with curses. The British were too far away, the French too unforgiving. The Russians at least had a line for you to stand in. A boy and an old man looking for food: go stand in line. They weren't young women, so the Russians didn't harass them. It was the same every day. Potato soup if you got there in time. By his tenth birthday, Johannes had eaten potato soup so many times that he smelled it in his sleep.

So they stayed in the Russian sector and they were given worthless ration cards, with coupons to redeem at the non-existent food stores and bombed-out bakeries. They scavenged, traded, bickered with the black marketeers. They were fully occupied with the work of living but they noticed the rising tension between the various garrison troops. They didn't usually go far enough into the West to see the barbed wire curling up around the edges of the ruined Potsdamerplatz, between the scarred columns of the Brandenburg Gate. They couldn't afford a radio and thus were deaf to the shrill accusations and threats which darted through the airwaves, twisting down the wrecked streets. Though they sensed the escalating twitchiness of the foreigners, they gave their attention to the politics of soup lines, to the diplomacy of cigarette traders. Johannes remembered a line of people standing not for food, he was told, but for an election. He waited long enough to make sure they weren't lying to keep him from discovering some concealed food cache, then he went looking for rabbit feed.

They kept their hovel as clean as they could, Albrecht teaching the boy soldier's tricks for staying warm and dry, teaching him the skills of squirreling away one's valuables in the smallest and most inconspicuous places.

"Is this you in the first war?" Johannes asked once, dusting a photograph.

"Hm? Ah, yes. That was a long time ago."

The reflective sheen of the glass in its frame caused Johannes to see his own face with its large, ugly fishhook scar and he quickly put it down and picked up another.

"Is this you, too?"

Johannes held this frame up to Albrecht's face. The picture showed another young man in a gray uniform. Albrecht's throat pulsed once beneath its bristles.

"No, that was my son," he said.

"He's dead now," Johannes said.

"Yes, he is."

"Were you married, then?"

"Oh, yes, yes."

"She's dead, too?"

"No. I don't think so. I don't know. She... left some time ago."

Johannes nodded and replaced the photograph on the crate.

Sometimes at night the old man took out a flaking volume of *Poetry of the German People* and read aloud until Johannes was drifting off. Then he tucked the book under Johannes' pillow as if it had some residual warmth or comfort that might travel with the boy out across the broken terrain of his dreams.

The city finally cleared away enough rubble to make the streetcars run. The subways were more difficult to fix because many had been flooded. People navigated their black channels in rowboats, like the gondoliers of Hades, grateful for the darkness so they wouldn't see the ruined bodies which sometimes thumped gently against their oars. When at last they drained it all out they found hundreds of the missing, shockingly preserved in the cold black liquid of their tomb.

Eventually the tunnels were repaired and the trains began to run again. Johannes still stayed away. Albrecht walked with him to the streetcar in the mornings to see him off for school.

One night Johannes showed Albrecht the flyer from the Free German Youth that he had been given by his teacher. "German Youth!" It shouted in huge, garish red letters, "You're not allowed to sit on the sidelines!"

"It's horseshit, you know," Albrecht said. "Slogans. Complete horseshit. Listen, don't let them ever hear you saying this, all right? Do as they say and nod and obey them, and memorize their stupid slogans. But remember:

you can't trust those people. They don't care about you. You're just cannon fodder for them. They'll count on you feeling alone and frightened and tired. They'll offer you their hope and faith and beliefs like a drug — they'll say if you swallow it, you'll feel better. You'll belong. You won't have to worry or doubt anymore."

He leaned very close to Johannes' face, his gray whiskers prickling as he drew in his lips tightly. Then he said,

"You must be strong and not let them see what you have inside. But one day, you must learn to love. You will have to find someone you trust with your thoughts and your pain."

They were quiet for a long time, then Johannes finally asked him,

"Read to me from the book of poems."

Albrecht opened to Heine:

> *The night is still, the streets are at rest,*
> *In this house my love once lived*
> *She left this town long ago,*
> *Yet here is the house, still in its place.*

On the day they buried the small brown rabbit, Johannes and Albrecht stood solemnly, staring at the cardboard box with the body.

"Would you like to say anything?" Albrecht asked.

"He was a good rabbit," the boy said.

"Yes. He was a survivor. He lived all through the war and died of old age. That's what counts. He held his own. He died when he was good and ready."

He looked down at the boy.

"You're not sad, are you?"

"No," Johannes said, shaking his head slowly.

"Good."

They were walking home from the riverbank after the burial and Albrecht said,

"One day you'll have to do that for me."

33.

Johannes was eighteen when the old man began to get sick. Albrecht coughed into his handkerchief, thinking Johannes didn't notice the blood in the soot-gray sputum. After a while Albrecht simply acted as if he could conceal the symptoms, knowing he couldn't. Johannes saw it happening and said nothing. Albrecht knew the boy knew and said nothing. Thus they passed most of a year.

They had an apartment by then, a tiny cube in a rectangular block of flats. They lived in a space not much bigger than the basement where they had shared their first meal. At night Johannes lay awake, listening to Albrecht hack and gasp.

One morning, when his voice gave out and he could only whisper, Albrecht stopped pretending.

"Sit down," he crackled, barely audible.

Johannes looked over his shoulder at the door, as if he had only a few seconds through which to escape to safety. At length, he pulled out a chair and joined him at their tiny kitchen table.

"I have cancer in my throat," the old man whispered. "I can't swallow anymore."

"You've seen a doctor?"

"No."

"There must be a doctor we can find."

"It's too late anyway."

"How can you know?"

"I know."

Johannes looked away, down to a corner of the floor.

"You're young and strong," Albrecht said. "You know how to survive. You're going to be fine on your own."

"Stop it."

"I won't be around much longer."

"Stop it."

"I'm just stating a fact."

"I have to go to school."

"Yes, go on."

Johannes didn't move.

"You're young; don't let yourself become all alone. Things are getting better, finally. In your lifetime, they're going to fix up all this mess. Go out and make some friends, be nice to people, try to—"

"Stop it!"

Johannes jerked backward, standing up as the chair slid across the floor.

"Well, go on, then. Go to school."

Johannes stood in the center of the floor, staring at him, breathing slowly through his nose.

"Would you like to say anything?" the old man finally asked.

When he returned from school that afternoon, Johannes walked into the kitchen and set his books down on the table. He noted with frustration that there was no bread in the cabinet. He slouched in the chair, staring at the old man on his bed in the adjoining room. For a long time he said nothing. Then Johannes sighed deeply and began to speak.

"It's all right. I have no right to judge you. You've had a hard life but you always pulled your share and then some. You took care of me when I was just a kid and didn't know any better. You didn't have to be mother and father to me but I guess you did a pretty good job bringing me up. I can't complain. And if it got really bad for you, I mean, if I was in your position..."

Johannes shrugged, bit his lip.

"...I don't know. But I have no right to judge."

He rose from the kitchen chair and walked slowly until he was standing beside the bed. Carefully, he loosened the dry fingers from around the blue-gray metal. When he lifted the gun, the old hand fell away.

He had lain on top of a blanket and shot himself in the chest, so there wouldn't be as much to clean up.

34.

He did, once, go back down there. After the old man died, after he was alone. It was the spring of fifty-three, when the tanks came and crushed the revolution. The young people shouted and marched in the streets, but not Johannes. He went down into the subway tunnel.

The entrance was black, unscrubbed of the ashen rain which had coated it during the bombing. In the cavern the natural light drained away almost instantly, leaving him descending, one shaking step at a time, into the decayed lamplight: yellow washing over black, running into the shimmer of puddles that shattered as his feet found the water.

This is where it happened. The river was gone, the flood dammed up, sucked away, held in check again for now. Dribbles down the cracked plaster and smacking footfalls in the little pools on the floor mocked it all, made senseless the effort to keep it at bay forever.

Johannes walked slowly to the mouth of the tunnel and stepped over a chain onto the ledge that ran along the tracks and disappeared into the darkness. He took a dozen careful steps forward until there was almost no light left from behind.

Mother, he whispered, then turned and fled, his feet stamping invisible water, terrified that she might call out to him, that she might say his name.

35.

By the time Johannes finished school the rubble was cleared away and East Berlin was a sprawling patchwork of empty sandlots separating blocks of wounded buildings. The communists had begun a few grandiose projects, rows of immense apartment buildings along a few big boulevards, but most of the city remained in its war-damaged condition. A battle-scarred wall might be covered with a huge red poster extolling the virtues of the working class, but the state gave priority to new construction, typically factory complexes and administrative buildings. People crammed into the old 19th century brick apartment buildings if they had no party connections that afforded them better, more modern housing.

Johannes wasn't surprised when his school administrators informed him that he had been slated for electrical engineering. All of the trades that could be directed toward building and construction received priority. Johannes was never tracked for academics. He hadn't joined the FDJ, the communist youth league, and his grades in political education were mediocre at best. The director of the graduation panel reminded him of this, not particularly gently:

"Your notes indicate aptitudes in mathematics and sciences, but your lack of political awareness rules out consideration for higher education. Nonetheless, an excellent starting position is available, for which you should be very grateful."

He learned that he was the new assistant to the electrical engineer in charge of a renewal district. He thanked the director and turned to leave. The remainder of his life, apparently, began on Monday.

His apprenticeship ended after a year and Johannes got promoted to a certified electrician. He was transferred to another district in the Summer of 1961 and promoted again. The perpetual tension in Berlin had risen to another new peak. Rumors swirled about some sort of new security measures, perhaps even a war. Sensing a closing window, people fled into West Berlin in ever-increasing numbers. The regime was humiliated and angry and also not inclined to press its valuable remaining skilled workers on their level of political commitment. Johannes' promotion occasioned another meeting with another panel, informing him — more gently this time — of the inadequacy of his socialist engagement:

"Comrade, we applaud the high level of performance of your work brigade over the past two years. Sometimes workers think that the party doesn't notice this sort of thing, but we do."

Johannes stood impassively, contemplating the red-and-gold emblem on each of their lapels.

"Have you considered joining the party?" one of them asked.

"I focus on my work," Johannes said.

"Nonetheless, because of your excellent record, a new position is available, for which you should be very grateful."

"Thank you," he answered them.

By the age of twenty-eight, Johannes was director of a work brigade tasked with urban renewal. He arrived on the first day to meet his new team and was introduced to "Lutz," the party liaison. Johannes grasped two things immediately. The first was that Lutz had been assigned because the bosses didn't think Johannes was capable of providing adequate political motivation to his brigade. The second was that Lutz's real name obviously wasn't Lutz.

His promotion earned Johannes a new apartment. The bureaucracy failed to notify him. He learned about it by listening to the grumbling of his subordinates, nearly all of whom were older than he was, and didn't appreciate this taciturn youngster giving them orders. They worried that Johannes might be one of those ambitious go-getters who tries to further his career by pushing his subordinates to greater efforts. The men had long since become accustomed to the sludgy pace of work and the consensus that rather little got done with a great deal of supposed effort. Someone said that Johannes must be fast-tracked, and that couldn't be good. Getting a new, modern apartment without party membership was "a miracle." Another man snorted that the state had officially abolished miracles a few years ago, so Johannes must have friends in high places.

They could not have been more wrong. Johannes had no friends in high places; he had no friends anywhere. He did, however, have an apartment in a high place. It was one of the new series of pre-fabricated flats in units that were built for party members and high-skilled professionals. Johannes could only assume that he got it because so many people in the latter category had fled to the West. Thus he had three rooms to himself on the sixth floor just below the roof. The apartment was on the edge of the neighborhood that his brigade was restoring, so Johannes' morning walk to work required about two minutes. When his work was done he came home and sat in his chair at the kitchen table and stared at the smudged expanse of the table's surface until it blurred and moved and shifted beneath his gaze.

Two weeks after he moved into his new apartment, they started building the Wall. Johannes awoke one morning and knew immediately that something had changed. Traffic patterns were different, people everywhere were nervous and whispering. Lutz was uncharacteristically silent for a couple of days. Then, armed with the Official Version, Lutz informed everyone about the necessity of the new Anti-Fascist Protective Barrier.

Ever since his childhood ordeal in the bombed cellar Johannes had been slightly claustrophobic and didn't like close or airless spaces. He had a single window on each side of his apartment, east and west, and he often left both open to create a breeze. It gave him a sense of motion in what was otherwise so stationary an existence. Sometimes, at night, he stood at the rear window, six stories above the street. The East was dark and silent, with specks of light here and there, and the whisper of an occasional car. At the edge of his renewal district, he could see one of the war-damaged buildings they had yet to demolish. It was a big old demi-block of apartments, a sturdy brick fortress that had taken a direct hit and been gutted. The bomb had fallen through the roof, shattering beams and plaster and, in the crushing descent of floors, bones and flesh as well. But the old brick walls were stubborn and refused to fall. They stared out through empty sockets of windows at the changing street, gathering grime and water with the years, always too heavy and difficult to bring down this year. Perhaps next year.

In the distance from the other direction, standing at his western window, Johannes could see the crazed yellow blur of West Berlin; a Babel of light and traffic. The murmur of its life hummed softly up into the purple sky, lisping echoes reaching his ears on windless nights. He could see spotlights marking the path of the Wall and its ongoing construction sites. The lights created a brilliant yellow borderline between the two halves of the city. Johannes smoked cigarettes and let the butts fall to the pavement, his eyes following the descent of the glow down through the cool air.

One night he stood at his rear window and saw a shade of motion on the street below.

Two figures walked along the sidewalk, tucked in close to the walls, across the street from Johannes' apartment. They moved slowly, heads sweeping the street around them, like the half-interested gazing of people strolling in a park. Their hair was black, long, and straight, falling halfway down their backs. They were women, small, perhaps teenage girls.

Johannes watched them stop, then he saw one reach into her coat and pull out a hand-sized object. It was a spray-can, Johannes realized, and she was spraying something on the wall.

It took only a few seconds, and then she replaced the can in her coat. She reached outward, fingers splayed, until the other one took her hand. They continued their leisurely pace down the street. Johannes craned to watch, sticking his neck out the window, but lost sight of them a couple of seconds later as they turned a corner. He squinted, trying to read what she had written. From six stories up it was barely legible, but he made it out. It said:

Escape

Lutz was, of course, the first to notice it. "What's this?" he said urgently, his brow crumpled. He looked at Johannes with an expression of betrayal, as if the new boss had done something that would get them all in trouble. He glanced up at Johannes' apartment window, then realized that he shouldn't know that and looked quickly down to the street.

Johannes crouched a few meters away, peering into an opening at a gutted basement through which his men were running new pipes and wiring. He frowned when he heard Lutz's voice, nervous and accusing.

"It's graffiti," Johannes said.

"I can see that it's graffiti. What is it doing here? In our district?"

Johannes shook his head.

"I'll have it removed," he said.

"We *have* to have it removed," Lutz said, his tone incredulous as if he couldn't believe that the new boss was this dense. "This is our section. We're responsible for this. If you can't keep hooligans out of our renewal districts, then they'll find someone who can."

"Will they?" Johannes said, turning to look at the political liaison. Lutz's Adam's apple notched once and he swallowed. He knew he had gone too far.

"Perhaps the party would be so kind as to get us that exterior paint that we ordered two months ago from the chemical Kombinat, then?" Johannes said. "Perhaps you could make yourself useful by seeing to that?"

Lutz backed down, literally, stepping off the curb and turning to go.

Rather than initiating the elaborate process of paperwork that could theoretically result in a work crew being made available to him by the end of the month — perhaps even with the right tools — Johannes took some sandpaper and a wire brush and decided to do it himself, after dinner.

He dawdled over his food. He fidgeted with the radio, listening to news broadcasts in which he had no interest. He loitered at the window as darkness fell, staring at the wall and its garish one-word command in black spray-paint. When he had stood so long that his legs were asleep, he trudged down the staircase in the darkness, walking out onto the street, and stared at the graffiti a few centimeters from his face.

It was late. There was a good chance that Lutz had reported him and Lutz's supervisor had detailed someone to watch this block, and Johannes' movements were now being recorded for some Stasi case-file on hooliganism. No doubt he was the chief suspect, purely by having had the bad fortune to be the one identifiable person present when blame needed to be cast. He sighed and raised the sandpaper to the concrete. The word vanished beneath the strokes of his hand.

He was about to use the wire brush to smooth out the discolored patch of wall when something caught his attention just beyond the periphery of his sight. He turned his head and was so startled that he jumped and dropped the brush.

The girls were staring at him, in a leisurely pose that suggested they had been staring for some time, from the opposite side of the sidewalk a block away. In the darkness, all Johannes saw was their outline, coats, and posture, but he was sure it was the two he had seen before.

They stared at him for a few seconds then turned and walked down the block, finally disappearing into a ruined building. Johannes watched them go then walked quickly across the street, jogged the six stories up to his apartment, and bolted his door behind him.

The next day, with his hard-hat and work clothes on, in the protective busy glare of daylight, he walked past the building into which the girls had vanished. It was an old bank, still wrecked from the war, near the bottom of his list for renovation. It had no front door and no windows, and from what Johannes could see from outside — for he dared go no closer than the sidewalk, and then only for a few seconds — there was nothing and no one inside.

36.

Because he stood at the window in the darkness now for several hours each night, it was inevitable that he would see them again.

They walked to the spot where he had erased the word, turned, and stared right up at him in his window. Johannes shuddered. They exchanged this stare for most of a minute then the girls turned away and kept walking.

Johannes strained his neck to look down the block and saw that there was a line of people forming in front of the old bank building: old and young, mostly in rough clothing, looking very much like the ragged survivors in the bread and soup lines Johannes remembered from his childhood after the war.

As he pulled on his coat, as he closed the door behind him and walked slowly down the stairs, Johannes knew that he was crossing over into a new landscape, perhaps irrevocably, across the night lands of his heavy dreamless sleep and into the hole that he had opened when he removed the word from the wall.

About twenty people were standing silently in a line leading away from the front of the old bank building. Johannes approached them from behind. He couldn't see the girls anywhere but he had resigned himself to wait in the line with the others, knowing that the girls' purpose and these peoples' were the same. Perhaps it was his own purpose now, too.

He lost track of time standing in the line. A few others came and stood behind him. Johannes was aware that he was a bit incongruous in this company; virtually everyone was either under 20 or over 60 years old. When he thought to look at his watch, he realized that he wasn't sure when he had left to come here. He had no idea how long he had been standing in the line when the people abruptly shuffled and moved forward toward the doorway of the old bank building on Liberation Street.

And there they were. The girls stood at the door, one on each side as if guarding the portal. Their faces were round and smooth, eyes narrow and dark. Johannes stumbled slightly when he saw them, but they only nodded once at him, as they did to everyone else, one perhaps turning up a corner of her mouth slightly in a knowing half-smile.

The basement was cold and damp and barely lit. It smelled of mildew, stale tobacco, and sweat. Johannes forced himself not to think about the way it reminded him of air raid shelters. He sat on the floor, as they all did, while some of the youngest helped some of the oldest to find places in the dark. Virtually no one spoke. Most people simply stared ahead at the smaller section of the room behind the steel bars.

At last it began. Two young men emerged on the "stage" behind the bars, each carrying a lantern. They set them down at opposite ends of the stage and turned slowly to face each other. As they stood perfectly straight, staring at each other while thin streaks of light illuminated their backs, she entered. She was small, with long brown hair pulled into a ponytail. She placed one foot precisely in front of the other until she had walked to the bars, facing the audience.

When her blue eyes fell upon him, he shuddered and grasped himself by the arms. It had been years, perhaps since his childhood, since he could remember a gaze that was this warm.

The dancers moved without music, without any sound at all except the muted slaps and scrapes of their bare feet against the stone. The two men strutted like matadors around the perimeter of the cage, glaring at each other through the figure of the woman-child between them. The men lunged and jabbed at one another, sometimes frightening her and making her cringe. Sometimes she hid her face in her hands, and Johannes gasped, desperate in the sudden cold without her eyes. He found himself cursing silently at the men as they turned and maneuvered. He realized that perhaps they were not fighting over her at all. Most of the time they didn't even notice her presence; they fought to fill the space between them, they fought to feed the hunger of fighting, itself. Only when they drew inward, threatening closer, did they sometimes notice her in their midst, trapped between the spans of their surging muscles.

All through the basement, the people sat like Johannes, their eyes locked on the stage behind the bars, their mouths slightly open. He couldn't see the others because it never occurred to him to look around the room, so consumed was he with the dancing girl and her imprisonment between the two men. He didn't feel the room swell with the breath of thirty shaking chests, didn't feel the crashes of their hearts against their ribs. They were all deeply alone even though they felt everything together: each blow of the men's arms, each gasp of the trapped girl. And when the warmth of her gaze penetrated the deep stillness of the basement, cutting its way through the coldness to him, it shook him. He trembled at the recognition of the sensation of hope.

At last, when the tension was so terrible that Johannes' tongue scraped dry against the back of his teeth, the two men lunged at each other, their broad arms connecting and sliding around each other's throats. And she, in the middle, suddenly burst forward as if she had been squeezed out from between them. For a second it seemed that she might finally escape, and her face bloomed candescent as she slipped from the midst of their death struggles. But her trajectory placed her against the bars. And there she hung, her thin arms between the black steel, her fingers sliding down, her face smeared with soot from the collision with her imprisonment. She opened her mouth in a final silent cry as her eyes closed for the last time and she lowered to the floor. Behind her the men, locked in their final agonies, took each other down, neither one ever relenting, even in death, the pressure against the enemy's throat. In their final seconds, they never turned to see her lifeless body a meter away. Their eyes froze over with infinite icy hate, until closed and dead.

All that remained were the lanterns, spilling yellow light across the floor without warmth or hope.

The people erupted in applause, Johannes the loudest. His mouth hung open as he struck his palms together furiously and cheered. The three dancers stood, linked arms, and bowed. Johannes felt the warmth pour across him one more time before she turned and fled.

The audience began to leave. Young ones helped the old ones to stand and stretch stiff legs. Johannes looked at his watch and was shocked to realize that the performance had lasted nearly an hour. He rose and moved through them, finding his way up to the street. As he stood in the door, breathing heavily, puffing smoke into the cool pre-dawn air, he became aware of a presence behind him. He turned to see one of the dark girls, who nodded once and smiled.

"Miriam," she said quietly.

"What?" Johannes asked, then suddenly understood.

"Her name is Miriam."

Johannes staggered the two blocks back to his apartment, fell into his bed without even removing his shoes. He carefully pulled the fragile book of poems from its safe place in the bottom drawer of his closet and placed it beneath his pillow. He lay wide awake until his alarm clock went off three and a half hours later.

37.

By the next night he was exhausted but still couldn't sleep. Johannes lay awake in his bed, red eyes scouring the ceiling. At last, he sighed and sat upright. There was no sense putting it off; he knew what he had to do.

He rose and dressed, then went down the stairs to the street, making no effort to be quiet. He used his key to open the fence and enter the worksite, then entered the warehouse shed and turned on the lights. Johannes dug around until he found what he was looking for, then he shut the place and went back to the wall on the street across from his apartment.

On the roughened patch where he had erased the word, he painted it now in blood-red letters:

Escape

No one noticed. He looked over his shoulder at the wall a dozen, two dozen times the next day. It was quite possibly the only graffiti in all of East Berlin, a city whose ugliness was so scrubbed and buttoned-down that even a smudge seemed like decoration.

Surely everyone sees it, he thinks. Surely they know it's me. My guilt must be smeared all over me like some stinking layer of filth. They're all keeping quiet, he decides. All keeping quiet because they know I'm a marked man. Any minute now Lutz is going to show up with two Stasi sergeants and I'm going to be called aside and asked if I could come down to some office somewhere to "explain a couple of minor things" to them.

But the day passed without incident, and he lay awake again that night, rising to stare out the window at the word on the wall. The handwriting, the word itself, they were his own.

At the end of the next block, he could barely see them. The line was starting to form.

Johannes dressed and vaulted down the stairs into the street. He jogged the block, slowing as he approached the line of people. He recognized a few faces, but aside from meeting his eyes for a handful of seconds, no one communicated with him, nor he with them. He passed the interminable wait on the sidewalk as the night deepened and the crowd slowly gathered. At last he went in, passing the girls in black at the door, down into the basement where he sat on the concrete, his mouth slightly open, his breathing slightly·accelerated.

She was not there. He realized, halfway through the performance, that she wouldn't be coming. It was a different dance altogether, with five performers he had never seen before, and he was so shattered by the discovery of her absence that he stopped paying attention. When he left an hour later, he wanted to ask where she was, but the girls weren't waiting at the door. Johannes trudged out into the darkened street as the other audience members slinked away in a dozen different directions. He found himself at the graffitied wall, staring up at the lonely window of his apartment. Then he began walking, jogging, running until he arrived breathless at the door of the warehouse. He struggled with the key and shouldered the door open noisily. He turned on all the lights. He rummaged, clanging tools around until he found a can of black spray primer. Johannes left, slamming the door behind him, and walked to the block which bordered his in the opposite direction of the old bank building. And there, on the wall of another building, he wrote the word again, in letters nearly as tall as his body.

He became an almost entirely nocturnal creature, walking the silent streets at night. He went to work late and often slovenly: half an hour late one day, an hour, two hours late the next day. His hair was wild and unwashed, his clothes rumpled. He slept at his desk and neglected to make inspections. Forms lay unfilled, unsigned, in his desk tray. And every afternoon he walked past one of the walls with the forbidden word he had painted across the stones and plaster. Each week he added it somewhere else until it was sprouting like crazy vines growing on all the vertical surfaces of the city.

Did no one see it? Or perhaps they saw it and said nothing? Or perhaps they didn't understand. Maybe if an idea is forbidden long enough it dies and rots away, until it is only a vague ugliness, like the unrecognizable corpse of a long-dead animal on the road. Or, he considered in the darkest part of the night when he despaired of retaining the last tendrils of his sanity, perhaps I am no longer living among these other people at all. Perhaps I live on the other side of a two-way mirror; I can see them, but I have become lost to them in the comforting image of their own reflections. And I have escaped through the pane only to a new prison. I am writing my own slogans now, on the invisible reverse of the walls where they can't see — where they look and see only their own words reflected back at them.

He stayed awake all night, almost every night, for fear of missing a single performance. He stood in the line with the others and waited for hours, only to sit in the basement and find that she was not there. One night he saw one of the dark girls. She was standing at the far end of what had once been the bank lobby, leaning against the wall in her black coat.

"Miriam," Johannes said, nothing more. She nodded slowly.

"Soon," she said. "She'll return soon."

He went out in the streets in the last hours of darkness after the performance, to find another barren section of wall on which to scream out his only word.

He told himself that she would return when she saw it. He had to keep writing the word until she found it, or until the word found her, as it had found him. Then she'll know, he said to himself. Then she'll come back.

When every wall he passed was covered with his lettering and still he had not heard a single word from his superiors, or even from his underlings, he knew he had failed. It was then that he happened to examine a calendar. Nine months. He had passed most of a year waiting for her return.

I am a fool, he decided as the sun set. I've escaped only the visible prisons, not the invisible ones. I'll never find my way out of those. I've gone where no one can hear me now. I'm nowhere. And from nowhere, there's nowhere to go. He opened the closet and then the lowest drawer, where he kept the book of poems and the old pistol. He breathed slowly, standing at the window, turning the blue-gray metal over in his hands and watching as the street sank into night. "Tonight," he said, "is the last time."

In the usual hour, well past midnight, they began to shuffle inside the wrecked doorway, through the debris-strewn lobby, down the stairs into the basement. It was very dark, even more than usual, with only two oil lamps in the audience area, and none on the stage. Johannes sat cross-legged, his hands in his lap. He stared at the bars and waited.

Because there was no introduction, no preliminary noise or motion, he didn't realize at first what he was seeing. The small figure emerged behind the bars, carrying a lantern, walking silently, carefully like a cat. When she reached the center of the stage, she looked up at him.

Johannes gasped as the warmth flooded across his face. She began to move.

She was dressed all in black, and the yellow light of the lanterns across the bars made her a shadow covered in stripes. She was an animal, pacing her cage, staring longingly at the space beyond the bars while behind her other silent animals emerged, all pressed against the confines of their own imprisonment, waiting to see what she would do.

And she escaped.

She flung herself at the barrier, and it must have been unprepared to meet such determination, such strength from so tiny a body. The barrier shattered and she was free. But it didn't break without a struggle, and in that struggle, in the moment before she broke through to the other side, it wounded her. Clasping her damaged arm as she spun away from the cage, she ignored the pain: turning, leaping, silently screaming out her name into the free air, as far away from the cage as she could get.

The pain followed her. It dragged and tugged at her, and as she moved, it became impossible to ignore. Her turns became less joyous, her leaps became smaller. She filled her small lungs with difficulty, breathing around the aches from her damaged arm.

At one end of the stage, two dark figures appeared. They were large, standing with folded arms, staring at her with a terrible patience, watching as her energy began to fade. One held in his hand a length of chain. She looked at them, then at her wounded arm, and she redoubled her efforts, dancing upward and away, grimacing through the pain, unwilling to cry for help.

At the other end were the animals, still standing in their cages, watching. As she faltered, as it became clear that she could not get away with her life and that she would not return to captivity to save herself, the other animals reached through their bars and joined their hands together. They lowered their heads.

At the end, as her strength was failing, she turned to see them, their fingers locked together, and she realized the dreadful mistake she had made. She watched them, and her little body collapsed in silent sobs. Slowly, she sank to the floor. When she moved no more, the two shadow-men advanced and extinguished the lantern in the center of the stage.

As the audience cheered, Johannes screamed out, striking his hands together wildly, his mouth open: tears, for the first time in sixteen years, streaming down his face.

Johannes stood before her, feeling naked and clasping his palms across his groin. He stooped a bit because he was so much taller than she was.

"Oh yes," Miriam said, smiling. "Of course I saw you."

"It was very beautiful," he finally managed to say.

"You're kind to say that," she replied.

"No, really. I — I don't even know what to say to tell you how much — to, ah, to say what it *felt* like to me."

"What's your name?"

He told her.

"I suppose I should tell you..." she said, tipping her head toward a distant body in a black coat, "They told me that you had been coming every week for months to see me dance."

Johannes swallowed.

"Oh my, you're blushing. I didn't mean to embarrass you. No, I think that's wonderful, that's so very sweet."

"Why don't you dance more often?"

"Oh, it's difficult for me. I only just finished school, you see."

She giggled at the sudden convergence of lines across his face.

"Yes, everybody reacts that way. Nobody believes it, but I'm only eighteen."

"Ah..."

"I hope you don't mean to say that I look *old.*"

"Oh, no—" Johannes frowned when he realized she was mocking him.

"No, there's another thing..." She leaned upward toward him and whispered. "...You see, I'm in the FDJ, too. And they're always watching, so it's hard to get a safe time to do this. If they found out..."

Johannes shook his head. "Why do you do it?" he asked.

"How can you ask me that? After seeing it tonight?"

"No—" He lowered his voice when she raised a finger to her lips. "No, I know why you dance. I can *feel* why you dance. I meant, why are you in the FDJ?"

She smirked.

"We can discuss this in someplace better, no?"

38.

"Don't you have to be at work?" Miriam asked, puzzling at her watch.

"Lunch break," Johannes said.

"It's been two hours."

"Nobody checks on me. Nobody does anything, actually. What about you? Haven't they given you a job yet?"

"I'm going to university in a couple of months," she said. "My father's in the party. He got it all worked out. I've got some time off until then."

Johannes nodded, contemplating the remains of their picnic lunch.

"This is such an ugly park," she said.

"It was once pretty. When I was a little boy. Back before all the bombing."

She laughed.

"I know, I know," he said through a long sigh. "I'm an old man."

"Oooh, twenty-nine isn't so old! You're only as old as you want to be."

"I forget sometimes that I'm only twenty-nine. I guess I've always felt old."

"Here," she said, removing a paper bag from her purse and opening it on the blanket where they sat. "I brought you something. I hope you like them; they're hard to get."

Johannes looked at them quizzically.

"Strawberries?" he finally asked.

She arranged them in her hand.

"Yes. You don't like them?"

"No, no — I want to try."

"You mean you've never had strawberries before?"

"No, actually I haven't."

"Oh my. Twenty-nine years without a single strawberry. You poor man. Well, you're in for a treat. Here."

She held them out in her hand and they glistened red: wild and tart like illicit kisses. She watched as he took one and placed it in his mouth. When his eyes widened in surprise and pleasure she laughed out loud.

"Yes?" she finally asked.

"It tastes," he said, "like poetry."

She stared at him for several seconds. Her face became serious.

"What?" she asked.

"It burns a little, but it's full of sweetness. And right as you learn the beauty of it, it's gone."

She continued to gaze at him with a look that was somewhere between worry and admiration.

"Yes," she said.

"Mm, I think I'd like another."

"Here." She took one from her palm and held it to his lips. He hesitated, wanting to savor everything, bathing in the warm stream of light from her eyes. When he swallowed it he realized she had been staring at him the entire time.

"There's a place," he said. "I want to take you. But you have to come at night. Late at night, after everyone is asleep."

"What is it?"

"Poetry," he said.

39.

"Where are we going?" she asked.

"Ssh. Be patient. Watch the stairs - some of them are loose."

They ascended the iron stairs between Johannes' attic and the service passage beneath the roof. The night was moist with dew, and the last flight was slippery. They had to watch their steps carefully and didn't see the view until they had arrived at the roof.

She gasped when she saw the shimmering yellow cascade of West Berlin.

"Look at all the *lights,*" she whispered. "They're so... alive."

The roof was flat and rectangular, with a single square column rising from the center for the chimney flues. She didn't notice for several minutes that Johannes was behind her, standing beside the wall of the shaft. When she turned to see him, she saw the word written on the wall, in red letters two meters tall.

"That was *you,*" she said. "The word — all over the city. *You're* the one who's been writing it."

"You noticed?" he asked, his face broadening with astonishment. "You've seen it."

"Yes," she shook her head, incredulous. "Of course I've seen it. Every day. Everywhere. I thought...."

"What?"

"I thought it was a madman."

He sighed.

"I thought perhaps it was, too."

"Why?" she asked. "What made you..."

"I don't know how to dance."

He could see she didn't understand but as he opened his mouth to explain, the words spilled out, colliding awkwardly.

"The cold, I mean, it's so cold always, everywhere. All I know is that when I saw your eyes, when you were dancing that first time, it was warm. And I was afraid I'd never see that, I mean feel that, again. I wanted, I was writing to you. I wrote it to you because you danced... poetry. About escape. And until I saw you, I didn't even know that I was trapped."

"Ssh..." she said. She had advanced across the space between them as he spoke, and now she reached up to place two small fingers over his lips. His mouth fell still like water becalmed by oil. And when she took her hand away, it was to lean up to kiss him.

They stood on the roof, the tips of their noses touching until she shivered in the cold. She was the one who suggested going back down to his flat. She was the one who approached him again, who touched him.

Her eyes rose to his when she felt the flesh of his chest, felt it trembling.

"You've never done this before," she said.

"I've never done anything."

"Ssh...." She placed her fingertips at his temples, kissed him again. Then she lifted her dress, tugging it from the neck, out and upward. Tiny hairs on her arms sparkled golden in the thin light passing through Johannes' room.

Their clothing slid off into mounds on the floor as they moved together. She told him to lie down, and he watched as her small body rose above him. He gasped when she lowered herself upon him.

Though he was rising into her, he felt as if he was being born. As if, moving up through this darkness and warmth, he was entering life for the first time.

"Wha?" he slurred, waking.

"I have to go," she said, leaning down to kiss his nose. She had dressed as he slept.

"Why?" He pinched at his eyes.

"It's almost morning. My parents." She produced a key from her purse, waved it before him like a talisman. "This is my passkey — if I get in before they wake up, all is well."

"I'll walk you home."

"No. You're sweet. But I'm going now. It's fine."

He rose on his elbows as she blew a kiss from the other end of the room. The last thing he saw was the morning-sky blue dress with its white flowers, fluttering once in the breeze of the closing door.

He collects on a favor from a man he knows in the Beautification Bureau.

"How many?"

"I'll need about a thousand," Johannes said.

"A thousand!"

"That's the month for them, right? August?"

"Come on, I can't give you a thousand. Your district is—"

"—isn't on the priority list, I know. But listen, as a favor, you know...."

"Oh, fuck, Johannes."

"I can requisition a truck and pick them up myself."

"All right, all right. Next Friday, after five, but not long after, understand?"

"I'll be there."

Passers-by saw a man bent over with a small shovel, crouched beside a wheelbarrow on the sidewalk. He worked without light in the shadows of the buildings, into the late evening hours. They didn't know how good his night vision had become, how rarely he slept anymore. He pulled up loose paving stones, neatened the holes, dug a little deeper. He planted the bulbs and covered them carefully. He moved on. A block, two, sometimes three in a night. Until the winter was past him and he was all the way there.

40.

With the game optimism of a child, Johannes attended the first party of his life at the age of twenty-nine. He puzzled briefly over whether to wear anything special, then looked in his closet and decided that he had nothing special. He cleaned his shoes, ironed his best trousers and shirt.

It was the Summer of 1962. The newspapers mocked the belated American entry into space and quoted Kennedy calling for more nuclear weapons. Johannes sensed that they were doing everything they could to avoid marking the coming anniversary of the Wall. People's reactions to it had ranged from bafflement to anger, and Johannes noticed that Lutz never mentioned the "Anti-Fascist Protective Barrier" in his weekly inspirational political meetings for the work brigade.

Johannes arrived at the party to find the young people buzzing, moving with a verve and confidence that seemed almost foreign. When they saw him, their faces drew downward in mistrust.

"Ah," one of them said around a narrow cigarette that threatened to dribble ashes across his black sweater, "*the masses* are here."

"Someone better tell Miriam before he gets any more confused."

Johannes surveyed the room, recognizing a few faces from the theater. He was the oldest in the room by several years, plaintively conspicuous in his inconspicuous clothes. When Miriam saw him she waved excitedly. Johannes tried to mimic the motion but felt idiotic.

She introduced him to the young man and woman standing beside her.

"What kind of *work* do you do?" the male asked.

"I supervise a renewal district."

"You're an apparatchik," the female said, blowing smoke upward across her arched eyebrows.

"Um, no, I'm not a party member."

The two snickered.

"No," Miriam said, taking Johannes' arm. "What Thilde means is that you work for the bureaucracy."

Johannes shrugged.

"Oh, of course."

"Of course," the male said, turning his head away, looking over the sea of black sweaters, trousers, and boots.

Later, Miriam took him aside.

"They're just a little snobby," she said, lowering her voice. "They reject the conformity of the party doctrine."

"But they're all Young Communists," Johannes said.

"Oh I know, but that's a front. In reality, we're all left-socialists, like Novotny."

"Maybe I should go."

"No, stay." She pouted, tugging at his hands. "Stay, please. Won't you? After Uta reads her poetry," she said, lowering her voice and leaning up toward him, "we can take a walk...."

He smiled.

She left him in a corner for another two hours. He watched the Young Communists all rejecting the conformity of the party doctrine, arguing for "Socialism with a Human face" while they disdained his face as apparently being somewhat too human for their taste. At last, she collected him and they escaped through the back door.

"It's so dark in here," she said, rummaging in her purse.

He stood before her, silent.

"Ah, here it is..." She grinned, pulling the bag out. "Your reward for being so patient tonight. These are so hard to get this early in the year. I stole them from my father."

She removed a tiny strawberry from the bag and placed it against his lips with a happy cackle. Then she lifted the straps of her dress and it slid to his floor.

An hour later, her breathing was steady beside him in his bed. His mouth tasted of sour berries and the salt of her musk. He ran his hands over his face, inhaling deeply, washing in her scent. He only said it because he thought she was asleep:

"I love you."

"Ssh," she said, placing a finger across his mouth. "I have to go soon."

41.

"I can't," Miriam said, "Not tomorrow night. I'm going to the Conference on Socialist Brotherhood."

"Can you come by afterward?" Johannes asked.

"Mm, maybe. If it's not too late. They usually have beer afterward, and people talk."

"I don't understand why you do all this when you don't even believe in any of that stuff."

"Oh, my dear, simple Johannes...."

She saw him draw upward and back, his face hardening.

"I'm sorry," she said. "That was harsh of me. I didn't mean you're simple."

When he was utterly silent, she said,

"Come on, forgive me. That's not what I meant to say." She sighed. "I meant that it's not such a simple thing for me. I have to go to these things; I'm in the FDJ. We're all going. There' will be foreign speakers, even from the West. My father's in the party," she said, tilting her head with the exasperated expression of someone explaining the obvious. "It's expected. My political education professor from the University will be there."

"That's fine."

"Oh, now you're all mad at me. Look, I'll come by afterward, I promise."

She kissed him quickly and glided through the door.

For a while he stood at the window, staring at the wall. His graffiti was beginning to fade after a winter's ice and the spring rains. He went up to the roof in the long summer evening. The sun was deep in the West and he stared at the fiery glow it ignited behind the buildings of West Berlin. This was the anniversary of the Wall, he recalled. This was the night they started and his life began to change at last.

He climbed down then went out onto the street. At the far end of his district, the ruined brick apartment building was finally fenced-off and rigged for demolition. He wasn't sure when they were pushing the button, but soon the last trace of the war and his youth would collapse gasping into its own dust. Yellow signs on the fences warned people to keep their distance.

Johannes walked past his words, his single word, written on all the walls. He walked the circumference of his neighborhood as if he was afraid to escape its confines. He wanted to write on the walls all night, to spray forbidden words up on all the stones and plaster until the city was nothing but his single sentence: his voice wrapped around every corner. But he came home instead to lie awake in his bed until at last he heard the scrape of her shoes in the hallway, and then the soft blows of her hand upon the door.

I don't know how I know, but I know. Tonight, when I was deep up inside of her, in the moment before it all rushed together and then burst from me, I knew. At the end of her tunnel, the depth of her warmth, the egg of my child waited. And we have done this now, made this thing. Somewhere inside me — in a place I never knew existed inside me — there was enough of that which is good in me to give a part of it to her. And it is within her now, though she doesn't realize it. I have given her the most secret part of me and she carries it, invisibly, written in forbidden letters on the dark interior of her walls.

"There was this man from France," she said, shaking her head. "At the conference. He said he was a French communist, and he gave this little speech — in perfect German — about the rising tide of socialism in the West. And you know what it was? He was just a black-marketeer. He comes over to the East, and he's probably bribed everybody on both sides of the border, and he talks this great talk about socialist brotherhood, but all he's doing is selling his contraband Western stuff.... He's so incredibly obnoxious with that flagrant, decadent bourgeois attitude."

Johannes nodded.

"Is that where you got that bracelet?"

She had been fingering the bracelet the entire time she spoke, and now she smiled.

"No — you know what it was?" She leaned forward across the table, her hands clasped in the center. "I went up to him and told him what I thought about what he was doing, and how obvious it was, and that he wasn't fooling me. And he *gave* me the bracelet. Oh! You should've seen the smug look on his face. I hate him."

Johannes nodded.

"I have a surprise for you," he said. "I've been working on it for a long time. It's almost ready. In fact, by this weekend, it should be perfectly ready."

"There's a party on Saturday," she said. "I need to go to that."

When she saw his face, she added,

"You can come."

His frown deepened.

"Why don't you meet me there," she said, "and then, after that, you can give me the surprise?"

They didn't speak about it for the rest of the week. Johannes didn't bother to ask if she wanted to go together with him; he merely asked the address and the time, and cleaned his shoes and pressed his shirt again. When he arrived, the crowd was larger than he expected, and though he saw a few familiar faces, he could tell that this was not simply the FDJ group. The room, he realized, was murmuring with several foreign languages.

Miriam wore a tight black dress that Johannes had never seen before and she was standing with her back to him, talking to a tall, handsome man in a black turtleneck and a stylish Western jacket. She held a drink in one hand and with the other, she toyed with her hair. Johannes approached them slowly but stopped when he saw her face in profile.

He wanted to be strong, to stride manfully over and place his arm around her waist, to claim her as *his* woman. But instead of courage, he found only a cold hollow of dread at the base of his spine. When he saw the look on her face as she gazed upward at the handsome Frenchman, the only thoughts he could find were: *Please no. Not her. Take anyone but her... you're rich, good-looking, young... you can have any of these girls. Please, not her. She's the only thing I have.*

He didn't realize he had approached so closely until she turned, with no surprise at all on her face, and said politely,

"Johannes, this is Alain LeClerc."

On the walk home that night he told himself that he was refusing to think about it. He thought about nothing else. The way she smiled when the Frenchman spoke, the way she shifted girlishly on her feet, as if nervous before him.

I shrunk away and did nothing, Johannes said to himself as he walked alone. I deserve to lose her, he thought, if I'm afraid to fight for her.

But how do you fight to keep someone who doesn't want to be kept? When she excused herself because she wanted to see the Frenchman's car — that was when he fled. And she would use that, he knew, as an excuse if she ever felt she needed one: Where were you? You disappeared. But he suspected she wouldn't be needing any excuses. And he could no longer bear to watch. So he withdrew to the night and even though it was summer, he felt as cold as he could ever remember feeling.

Johannes detoured to walk the route from her apartment to his, and everywhere, sprouting and blooming from beside the sidewalks the whole way, one thousand gladiolas lined the path, exploding in lemon and fuchsia.

42.

He didn't dare call. For three days he slept only in unsteady snatches at his desk at work, waking and glancing around frantically if he thought he heard the sound of a woman's heels. At night he stood by his window above the street and waited for her to come, to find the flower path and follow it back to him.

"I'll tell her," he said to the glass. When she came back to him, he resolved, he would tell her about their child. Even if she never wanted to see him again, still he wanted her to know.

The nights were warm but he couldn't bear the feeling of coldness that penetrated his bones. He wrapped himself in a coat but it didn't matter. From his eastern window, he saw that the old brick apartment building had finally come down. There was a fenced-in pile of shards and rubble now where its stubborn walls had stood for so long. When did this happen? Did he approve it? Johannes couldn't remember.

One night he walked down to the street and stared at the faded word on the wall. To his left, at the frontier of his sight, a shadow stood beside the curb. Johannes turned, squinted, and saw it move slowly away, then inside a doorway. He walked toward it, down the block and onto the next, and he slowed as he approached the old bank building.

There was no one else nearby, no performance tonight. Johannes stood on the street for a long time, staring at the black maw of its entrance. Then he stepped inside.

In the deep drapery of shadows that covered the ruined lobby, he could barely see the outline of the two of them, leaning against the far wall and regarding him in the pale wash of light from the street. Johannes was silent, unwilling to ask the only thing he needed to ask. Finally one of them answered him anyway.

"She's gone."

Johannes shivered.

"Why?" he asked.

"She left with him."

"It's so cold," Johannes said.

Everywhere it disappears. He walks the streets now, looking at the walls, wondering where it has gone. He is sure he wrote it here, once, in huge black letters. Or here, beside this mailbox, he can remember writing it. But nothing. Not even marks of erasure. All through the city tonight, his words are vanishing from the walls.

He is passing back to the other side, he realizes, where nothing is seen.

He has reached the river, a little south of Palace Bridge. Nobody sees him; he is the only figure in the entire plaza. The floodlights fill the broad stretches of pavement with white and yellow, but he doesn't seem to have a shadow. He is looking down at the black water, wondering if perhaps it will take him finally, after all these years.

I'm sorry, Mother. I should never have run.

He remembered his head coming to rest on something hard and dark. Slimy. He felt with his hand. Concrete, the bank of the river. There was soft motion beneath his back, lapping, the current.

Still, the water refuses to kill him.

He climbed out, realized he had only drifted about three blocks. He struggled in the heavy, soaked clothes as he shuffled home. Once inside, he stripped them off and lay shivering in his bed, naked, feeling for the book of poetry beneath the pillow. It wasn't there. In its place was the pistol.

Johannes pulled out the gun and stared at it for a long time. When the light began to gather in the corners and then filled the room, he rose, holding it in his lap. He stood, walked three paces toward the window, and threw it out into the street. It landed with an impotent *clack* against the pavement.

He did the same with his knot of keys.

He dressed, put on his old raincoat, and went out into the street, not bothering to close the door behind him. He walked to the nearest subway station and without a second's hesitation, he went down.

One day she was there and the next she wasn't. That's all he could remember now.

dark velocity

Berlin, Summer 1992

43.

One of the giant blue pipes was broken. It had burst a joint, one half falling to the sidewalk, an artery severed and left disconnected. Its choking mouth had vomited a brown delta of mud and rock across the pavement, the muck searching for the earth whence it came, spreading out on the street. Daniel stared at the fallen pipe for a minute. The dirt was so thick in it that the orifice was almost completely clogged, with only an irregular murmuring of water escaping, as if he were looking at the inside of the city's heart attack.

Daniel walked to the streetcar. Even if all the deities of Berlin traffic took mercy on him, he'd still be a few minutes late to meet Eugene at *d'accord*. Then he realized that the S-Bahn wasn't running from the Alexanderplatz today and the buses took twice as long as usual, maneuvering through countless detours to avoid torn streets where workmen removed old sewer and gas lines. He finally got off near the Tiergarten and walked the rest of the way.

"Well, there he is," Sabine said. *"Les boys sont arrivés."* Eugene turned, squinted in his direction. Daniel walked to the bar and sat down beside his partner.

"What?" he asked when they continued to stare at him.

"Why are you so late?" Eugene asked.

"You may have noticed that it takes an Act of God to get from point A to point B in this city these days?"

"At least there *is* a point B," Sabine said, preparing Daniel's vehicle. "It's a pain in the ass, but I like having a whole city and not just a half."

He nodded his thanks when she placed the vehicle before him.

"All right," Sabine said, "now that you're both here I'm supposed to tell you something. That man in the gray coat, sitting in the next-to-last booth?"

Without moving their heads they scanned the mirror in the bar, quickly fixed him, and then looked away.

"Miguel sent him," she said. "He told me that when you're both ready, to join him at his table to talk business."

She placed singsong over-emphasis on the last word.

"Have you seen him before?" Eugene asked quietly, studying his grapefruit juice.

"No. But he seems legit."

Daniel and Eugene simultaneously raised their eyebrows.

"Ah, what the fuck." Eugene sighed, gulped the last of his juice. "I'm in a fatalistic mood today."

"How unusual for you," Daniel mumbled.

They rose, Daniel winking at Sabine, and walked to the man's table. He said nothing, gesturing at the other side of the booth with two open hands. Before him was a thick leather binder with a gold clasp, à la DeSoto.

"Gentlemen," he said. "Mr. DeSoto regrets any inconvenience, but if you are prepared, he can meet with you at his Eichenallee office."

"Which one?" Eugene asked, eyebrows contracting.

"Perhaps you're not familiar with it. In any event, if you're prepared, we can leave now."

They looked at each other and shrugged.

"Sure," said Daniel.

"Very good." The man pushed the binder across the table. "You can examine these documents during the trip." He rose. "Shall we?"

Daniel, finishing his vehicle in a quick swallow, was the last to follow.

They drove west along the Kaiserdamm, thick tires whispering through the water on the street. Daniel said nothing. Eugene leafed through the papers.

"Seems like we're back in business," he said in French. "Not even a month. I would have thought he'd have us grounded for at least two. Must be something big."

Daniel didn't respond, his eyes focused on the carpeted floorboards.

"Another weapons deal of some kind, looks like." Eugene turned another page. "In Potsdam, hmm. And four different deliveries. I wonder what these things are...."

"I saw her old man again. On the street in my neighborhood."

"Hm, what?"

"Johannes," Daniel said, turning to look at him, noticing that Eugene had pulled out his glasses to read in the darkened back seat of the Mercedes. "The one that Sabine...."

"*Again,*" Eugene said, lowering the glasses on his nose and looking at Daniel over the frames. "So when are you going to tell her?"

"I don't know. It was very strange. I tried to talk to him...."

"I suppose that will put her mind at ease somewhat."

"Something is very wrong, though."

Eugene said nothing, waiting for him to elaborate. The car turned off the Kaiserdamm and onto a side street.

"There's more to it than... I mean — Shit, I don't know. I've been holding off telling her until I can figure it out. It's like, he *knows* who I am."

Eugene squinted one eye.

"I know," Daniel said. "It's stupid. It's probably nothing. I should probably just tell her."

"I take it," Eugene deadpanned, "you neglected to get his business card so Sabine could remain in touch with him?"

"Gentlemen," the driver said from the front. "We're here. If you'd be so kind as to present yourself to the guards, the rest will be self-explanatory."

The Mercedes glided to a stop in front of a large but otherwise unremarkable house. Daniel and Eugene got out, the car pulling away even before they had shut the doors. A large man in a blue suit emerged from a side entrance and approached them. He nodded in recognition but still stroked them with a metal detector.

"Follow me," he said.

They were led around the side of the building to a back door, which, although it was heavy oak, opened with an electronic click and a noiseless sweep. When they had entered, it closed behind them, leaving the guard outside.

They stood in an elegant foyer with a checkered marble floor. On the walls hung half a dozen Romantic-period paintings, three on each side. At the end of the foyer, an ancient door opened electronically on ultra-modern sensors and they were greeted by a puff of warm air.

The room they entered was a vast study with a vaulted four-meter ceiling. Two of the four walls were covered by oaken bookshelves which climbed well beyond a man's reach, and which were full of heavy volumes. The third wall, facing them, was centered upon a huge fireplace. There were padded chairs and several tables. At a small round one, in front of the fire, three chairs had been conspicuously gathered.

"This is his home," Daniel said, turning slowly.

"I'm sure he has several."

"No, this is it. I can tell."

A door opened behind them, one of two which flanked the entrance they had used. A woman in a black dress entered, bearing a tray. She moved as if the two visitors didn't exist, straight to the table before the fireplace, where she set down a steaming cup of tea and two snifters of cognac.

"Gentlemen," she said, inclining her head toward the chairs. When Daniel and Eugene moved toward them, she left in the same silent rush.

They sat, staring at the table and its three drinks.

DeSoto entered through the third door a minute later, a burgundy cardigan sweater hanging perfectly from the slopes of his shoulders. He sat down at the third chair without greeting them. He stared at the glass for a moment. Then he spoke.

"Our relationship is first and foremost professional. However, that does not, in my opinion, preclude the courtesies one would offer to friends. The time has come, gentlemen, for complete frankness between us."

He turned to Daniel.

"What is the condition of your health?"

Daniel blinked once.

"With the greatest respect," he said slowly. "I prefer to keep that private."

DeSoto appeared unmoved.

"It is a matter of professional as well as personal concern," he said.

"I appreciate the personal concern," Daniel replied. "But with regard to the professional issues, it was my understanding that I was no longer employed by you."

"I fail to understand your stubbornness," DeSoto said.

"*As do I*," Eugene said, alarmed. "Daniel, this isn't time for games."

"Enough." DeSoto raised his hand. His voice lost the timbre of its elegant long vowels, becoming tight and brittle. "There is important business to discuss. I am offering to re-instate you. I demand to know whether or not you are capable of the work I have for you."

Daniel and DeSoto stared at each other across the table.

"I've looked at the papers," Eugene said. "From what I can see, this is fairly straightforward. I can't imagine why we couldn't—"

"I didn't ask you." DeSoto's bottomless eyes remained on Daniel.

"The condition of my health," Daniel said quietly, "is deteriorating. I might have some sort of disorder, I might have cancer, I'm not sure."

Eugene sighed, fingers massaging the bridge of his nose.

DeSoto stared, unblinking.

"You haven't seen a doctor?" he finally asked.

"Not the kind you mean."

"So it might be nothing?"

"It's definitely not nothing," Daniel said.

DeSoto leaned back into the chair. His eyes turned to the fireplace.

"Does Julia know?" he asked.

"No."

"You should tell her."

"Did you tell Sabine everything when she was your woman?"

To Daniel and Eugene's surprise, a wistful smile crept across DeSoto's mouth.

"Sabine learns everything. Telling her was always irrelevant. Still, it's the right thing to do."

"I realize that."

"Well," DeSoto said, still staring at the fireplace. "I need you to answer my question. Are you fit to work?"

"Yes."

"Very well." He turned to the table, lifted one of the snifters slightly. "To business, then."

"To business." They drank, Eugene sipping his tea.

When they lowered their drinks to the table, DeSoto sank back into his chair. His eyes remained on the fireplace as he spoke to them.

"In two weeks a truck with Polish license plates will arrive in Potsdam. You have the time and address in the file. Prior to its arrival, you will secure the area, and upon arrival, you'll pay the driver the sum specified in the papers. I'll arrange to have this money delivered to you, Eugene, in a few days. The usual people. We'll use American dollars this time, though, to muddy the tracks a bit. After paying the driver you will place the goods in the safe house, and you will wait with them until evening when a new truck will arrive with substitute containers. You'll have use of that truck for the deliveries.

"Each container has a numerical code which corresponds to the four addresses of the deliveries. All four of the deliveries must be made that evening. One of them is in Oranienburg, so you should get started as soon as the sun goes down. The other three are all in or around Berlin. It is imperative that you complete all deliveries that night. Information on contacts and locations are all in that folder. The sequence isn't particularly important; you can establish your own order, but all the recipients will be expecting them on that night.

"In the case of the Oranienburg delivery, payment will be on the spot, in cash. I've had no dealings with this gentleman in the past, although his references are good. Nonetheless, feel free to count it. You'll probably want to do that one first because it's important that you leave the delivery truck at our usual vehicle safe-house in the East. In the case of the other three deliveries, I have arranged for secure third-parties to transact payments. The money is a little warm on this end, so it needs to travel via Zurich, Paris, New York, and then back here. Don't trouble yourself with that; just make sure that the right people accept the goods at the right places, nothing more.

"And," DeSoto said, reaching for his snifter, "there is one other thing. You are not to examine the goods at all."

Eugene squinted.

"You mean you don't want them inspected?"

"No." DeSoto took a sip of cognac, letting it slide around his tongue for a few seconds before he swallowed. "Please understand, it's not personal. Quite the contrary. There are precious few people I can trust to obey an injunction of that nature."

"Very well," Eugene said. "How do we calculate our percentages?"

"You won't." DeSoto put the glass back down on the table. "Upon completion, I'll pay each of you half a million, flat. Plus any of the usual expenses, if you feel that's necessary. In dollars."

"A million dollars?" Eugene said.

"You have no objections?"

"No, that's, ah... very generous."

"Just don't give me another of those God-awful American turkeys for Christmas this year," DeSoto said, sighing. "Even the guards wouldn't eat it."

44.

It begins while he sleeps, invades the harmless dream, turns it sour like curdling milk running through him, the sensation of rising heat until his head is roiling and the heat has distended his stomach, and Daniel gasps into the stream of shadows in his room, reaching out for nothing, grabbing at oxygen, sliding snakelike until his head is over the edge, erupting a ruddy stream of blood and acid, searing up his throat, choking out of his mouth, spattering the floor.

His inhale is desperate, short, stealing back the air in the moment before the next explosion roils him, hands rushing to the pain, mouth agape and throat shuddering out the bile.

Now he is scraping on his knees, hand shooting out to the telephone: clasped in four fingers while the thumb dials.

At first, he thought it was the interior of a cloud, so soft and white as he lay on his back, his gaze like radar waves unreflected, lost in its nebula. Then the warmth of a hand, dry, against his cheek. And a voice in a gentle descent, as of disappointment or hope deferred:

"Ah, I think you are stable now."

Daniel licked his lips but his tongue was thick with dried acid.

"Can I have some water?"

He heard the heavy footsteps traverse the room, pause, then return. A plastic cup hovered before his face, floating suspended in brown fingers.

"Thank you," he said, struggling to rise and drink it.

"I don't—" Daniel began, shook his head, drank the rest of the water, fell back to the pillow. "How long have I been here?"

"Only a little more than an hour."

"How did I get here?"

"You came."

"Alone?"

"Yes."

"I don't see how."

"Ah, I don't either. You were in bad shape. You still are. I've given you something for the pain."

"Thank you, Rashid."

"Ah, not at all. The least I could do."

"I can't focus my eyes," Daniel said, blinking heavily several times. "Everything's fuzzy."

The Syrian made a soft growling noise.

"What?" Daniel asked.

"Could be the medicine, could be something else."

"Bet on 'something else.'"

"Are you drinking still?"

"Of course."

"Ah, I'm sure that doesn't help."

"It helps quite a bit."

"You need to get some rest."

"Doctors always say that to you when you're well and truly fucked."

"Ah, well I'm not a doctor anymore," Rashid said.

"No, definitely not. You're much better than a doctor. You actually give a damn. I can depend on you."

Daniel blinked slowly several times, trying fruitlessly to focus his vision. He closed his eyes.

"Danny Boy, have you tried to make sense of any of this?"

"What do you mean?"

"Well," Rashid said, sighing again, "I mean when it comes and goes. And why."

"You said it was like a tide."

"Ah, but the tide has its logic. It has rules. It can be understood."

"Are you saying this is all in my head?"

"No, but—"

"—because that's crazy. It's real. It's very real."

"Ah, pain is real, my friend, no matter where it comes from. I had a patient once, a devout man, a missionary. Ah, but he wasn't a very good missionary, he had no subtlety. He became hysterical about his failure to win any converts, which only made it worse. He couldn't sleep, he had migraines. One day he bled. From his wrist, like Christ. I had to call a Christian doctor I knew in Lebanon to ask him what the hell was happening."

"Stigmata," Daniel said.

"Yes. Indeed."

"Look, I'm not —"

"—No Danny Boy, listen: this man, his pain — his physical pain — was real. He did it to himself but it doesn't matter. He was reaching so desperately for something that he created wounds from the past, bleeding into the present."

"You tell a good story, Rashid. But I probably have cancer. You know it and I know it. Christ isn't involved. I just..." Daniel rubbed his face again, grimaced. "I just want to be able to focus my eyes."

"Ah well," Rashid sighed, "I think I'll take a blood sample. You can rest here for a while."

He turned to leave and had withdrawn a few steps.

"Rashid?"

The Syrian stopped, waited, regarded his friend supine on the white surface of the bed.

"Honestly," Daniel said, "Do you think.... It's not in my head."

"I consider all possibilities, Daniel. I don't have an answer."

"Do you think this, I mean, this episode, is the beginning of... I'm not losing my mind, Rashid."

"Danny Boy. Rest. I'll have a better look shortly."

The splash of colliding beads in the doorway: was it Rashid departing now, leaving after the blood sample, was there a blood sample at all? The medicine is coating something in his stomach, holding two warring parties at bay for a time, a cease-fire inside him.

45.

When the orange digits of his clock flashed 3:00 AM he knew he would not be able to sleep. Daniel had felt himself drifting off once or twice, sliding toward a dream when his mind had suddenly clarified and his muscles had contracted, and then he was lying wide awake again, staring at the unfinished sculpture on his living room floor and thinking about the job in Potsdam.

He rose and sat on the edge of the bed for several minutes. The sculpture head stared back at him as if waiting for some instructions or perhaps ready to convey a message to Julia. Daniel considered what that message ought to be. Marry me? Run away with me? Have my baby? Or perhaps something as simple as: Don't leave me. Every time he rolled one of those things around in his head he felt a cold wash of vulnerability and weakness.

"I've got this... thing tomorrow, or I guess today, in Potsdam." He rubbed his face with both hands. "I don't know. Yevgenny thinks it's fine, or maybe he doesn't and he hasn't said anything to me about it. But I've got a bad feeling. I think that if I can get through this, I'm going to retire. But what I want to say is..." he sighed.

"What I want to say is: I'm in love with you. And if something goes wrong today, I want you to know that."

"I want you to know that," he said again, then sat and stared at the sculpture for most of the next hour without adding a word.

Eugene came by that morning and knocked on Daniel's door several hours early. Daniel frowned at his partner's unusual behavior.

"You want to go get breakfast?" Eugene said, leaning into the frame of Daniel's doorway and stroking his beard.

"Yeah, all right," Daniel said. "Let me get my stuff together."

"Eggs," Eugene said as he walked in, carefully closing the door after him. He wandered the living room as Daniel trudged back to his bedroom to search for clothes. Eugene patrolled the edges of the room, looking over his shoulder at the unfinished sculpture head without surprise or comment as if he had seen it many times.

"What?" Daniel shouted from the adjacent room, his head pushing through a shirt, emerging a second later wild-haired and blinking as if he was giving birth to himself.

"I've been craving eggs. I want to go to Donatello."

Daniel walked from his bedroom, two shoes dangling from one hand. "That's fine," he said, sitting at the tearsplash table and tying his shoes. A few seconds later he stood up, felt his pocket for his keys, shrugged, and said, "Ready."

They stared at the burgeoning plate of deviled eggs the waitress placed in front of Eugene. Daniel lifted his coffee and prepared to watch Eugene devour an entire generation of chickens.

"I haven't checked my car," Daniel said absently, inhaling over the edge of his *demi-tasse.* "I haven't driven it in a while."

"It'll be fine." Eugene grinned at a helpless hemisphere of white and yellow in his fingers. He raised his eyebrows lasciviously as he bit into it. After he had swallowed theatrically, he asked,

"How are you feeling?"

Daniel smirked.

"That's the reason we're having breakfast together," He glanced at his watch. "Three hours before we need to leave. Making sure I'm up to it."

Eugene finished an egg and reached for another. He shrugged. "Fact of life. I need to know. Can you blame me?"

When Daniel said nothing, he added:

"Something's been bugging me about this deal, ever since I looked at the documents. There's four deliveries, right? Three on account, one in cash. The one in cash is the only tricky one, and it's out of town. The others are just schoolboy shit. Anybody could do them. And whatever it is we're delivering, it's obviously not something the cops would be looking for, or else we wouldn't be driving around with it, knocking on doors like Christmas singers. Yet it's worth a million dollars to DeSoto."

"Much more than that. A million's just our share."

"Yeah," Eugene said, squinting. "Our share, for what? To be delivery boys? It's too easy. It doesn't make any sense."

"I checked out all the names," Daniel said. "We're going to keep the list of all the addresses, right, just in case?"

"Yeah, I made two copies. And I checked out all these names, too. Nothing. All wise-guy names, but still none of them sound familiar. Or maybe that's it. Maybe *all* of them sound familiar."

Daniel shook his head.

"I'm not worried about it. And neither are you. The main thing you're worried about is me. And I'm fine." Then he chuckled and added in English:

"I feel like a million bucks."

46.

"I don't know why you bought a new car," Eugene said, staring at Daniel's Peugeot. "You barely use it once a month."

"You'll just have to suffer through it," Daniel said.

"I'm naming this car 'Gigi.'"

"What?" Daniel asked. "You can't name my car."

"Too late, I did. Her name is Gigi."

"Are you ready?"

"Yeah."

"Speak only German."

Eugene sighed, nodded, grasped the handle, and pried himself upward and out of the seat. He looked at his watch.

"See you in an hour," Daniel said, and pulled away, leaving Eugene on the sidewalk. Eugene watched Gigi the Peugeot wait at a red light. Before it turned and pulled out of view, he started walking.

He cut through a brick-paved parking lot where a couple of tourist buses were gathered, having disgorged their human freight at *Sans Souci.* The bus drivers sprawled in their seats, smoking, reading newspapers. One was asleep, wide-mouthed, while his radio thumped techno music through the corrugated walls of his vehicle.

Potsdam was a schizophrenic little town, Daniel decided, too small and insignificant for its personality disorders to generate much attention. One section was utterly miserable. Wounded buildings like cancers untreated for sixty years leaned against decaying blockhouses of socialist realism. One block away a completely renewed section burst in rainbow colors along its pedestrian-only streets, where vendors beneath loud umbrellas competed with minstrels and clowns for the attention of the wandering tourists. Almost everything was for sale. Eugene walked to one end of this carnival, where a white-headed woman was selling ice-cream bars. He chose an almond-peach one and licked it slowly as he strolled the length of the frantically cheerful market district, occasionally stopping to look in shop windows at the expensive things nobody needed and which no one showed any inclination to buy.

Daniel parked the Peugeot at the other end of town. He walked slowly down sidewalks with man-sized craters, beneath façades which seemed seconds from peeling off the buildings and tumbling into the potholes in the streets. As he walked an anemic Wartburg spluttered past him in the opposite direction, its narrow tires navigating around the worst of the various jagged traps in the road. Daniel passed a lonely bar where two heavy-set men drank beer and concentrated on a football match on television.

As he approached the market district he saw the drift-off from a block away. Having strolled the four blocks of vendors, some tourists became curious as to what lay beyond. A few seconds of the mean streets convinced them to retrace their steps back to the world of color and safety until the bus drivers came to collect them. Daniel approached the burble of street noise and turned the corner onto the sudden cornucopia of the marketplace. Almost immediately he saw Eugene walking toward him casually with one hand in his jeans pocket and a half-finished ice cream bar in the other. They passed without acknowledgment as if they hadn't even seen each other.

Each one walked the other's back steps for three blocks, as they always did in a new place, searching for unwanted followers.

At length, they returned to the corner that served as the border between the fake, vibrant Potsdam and the real, dead Potsdam. Before approaching too closely each nodded quickly at the other to signal the all-clear.

Eugene sighed, looking around for a trash can for the sticky wooden stalk in his hand, then tossed it to the curb.

"A crazy place," he said, shaking his head mournfully at the civic ruin behind them. "See, this is what communism did. This used to be a lovely little town. Now it's shit."

"You always say that. What capitalism did isn't much better. All right, did you check the address?"

Eugene nodded. "Not one of the prettier places."

"Well," Daniel said, "we've got... what, forty-five minutes? Might as well go there now."

They found the house three blocks away, peacefully rotting in the middle of a short block of decrepit buildings. They knocked, stood on opposite sides of the door. Eugene turned the key in the lock and pushed the door open.

The decay wasn't quite as bad inside. A recent coat of plaster and paint covered the weary walls. The floors were dirty but not rotten. The place smelled of mildew and heating gas but the dust was irregular as if some surfaces had been recently used or even cleaned while others were touched only by the scurrying of hungry rats in the night.

"The basement," Daniel said, nodding to a staircase leading down. They walked down slowly, Daniel first, as Eugene flipped on a light switch to illuminate the passage. The basement was small and unfurnished, with only the water heater and the furnace occupying the dusty concrete floor. They went back upstairs, found two chairs in what appeared to be a living room near the front, and waited.

They took turns watching the street. Eugene had lifted a copy of the local newspaper from one of the market street displays and they passed it back and forth, one watching for fifteen minutes near the window, the other at the back of the room, reading. It was Daniel's watch when the truck pulled up outside, though Eugene also heard the wind of its brakes and looked up immediately.

"That's it," Daniel said. "Polish tags."

Eugene put the paper on the floor. He unlatched the safety on his Makarov, rose silently, and walked to the staircase. He stopped a few steps down, out of sight of the doorway, and leaned against the wall. Daniel waited, watching the truck driver check a scrap of paper, stare at the house, and then put the paper away.

"One man or two?" Eugene asked quietly from the basement stairs.

"One," Daniel said. "Wasn't that the plan?"

"Yeah, but I like to make sure. I haven't been too happy with plans lately."

"I'm going to go out there," Daniel said.

"What? No. Wait for him to come in."

"Nah, he looks okay."

"Shithead, I can't cover you out there. Wait for him."

But Daniel had already opened the door. When the truck driver saw him standing in the doorway, he nodded once and jabbed his thumb over his shoulder, pointing to the freight concealed in the back of his truck. He climbed down from the cab, a big man in his thirties, a sweaty round face and bulging belly.

"Not so bad traffic," he said to Daniel in heavily accented German. "I am only some minutes early."

Then, when Daniel had approached within arms' reach, the driver lowered his voice and with it, his entire head, to whisper:

"I am to count the money."

Daniel nodded.

"That's fine. It's in the house. Let's open up here..." he gestured with his head at the back of the truck and saw Eugene now standing in the doorway, one hand resting on his belt, a disgusted look on his shaggy face.

The truck driver pulled his keys from the ignition and huffed to the back, where he inserted them into the padlock on the truck's rolling back door. He unlocked it and heaved it up, and the door rose to expose four cardboard boxes, each as long as a small desk, each resting in large, open wooden crates stuffed with Styrofoam padding.

"They are not so heavy how they look," the driver said. "Twenty kilos. One man carries one easy." He clambered in, hauling his stomach up onto the back ramp of the truck. By this time Eugene had arrived, arms folded across his chest, observing.

The truck driver pulled one box out of its crate without difficulty and held it out to Daniel.

"You go, take inside, then we count money."

Daniel took the box, surprised that it indeed weighed only about twenty kilos. The truck driver handed a second one to Eugene, who hesitated a moment, contemplating the wisdom of having all four of their arms full. He put it down on the deck of the truck and waited for the driver himself to lift one before he scooped up his and followed Daniel and the driver inside. Daniel returned for the fourth box, and they carried them all down to the basement.

"To keep on the sides, yes, until the other, ah... ah..."

"Containers."

"Yes, until other containers comes. Easy to break."

Daniel reached under his sweater and produced a thick page-sized envelope he had wedged under his belt.

"The money," he said, handing it to the truck driver.

They went upstairs to count it. When all was in order the driver smiled, shook both their hands, and left into the slowly gathering evening outside.

Eugene sat back down with a sigh, picking up his newspaper.

"When's the second truck?" Daniel asked.

"Any time now."

It was eight and the light was still bright in the streets when the second truck pulled up: a small, noisy old IFA from the East. Daniel and Eugene watched two young blonde men in sunglasses and black turtlenecks scan the block for a few minutes, and then apparently commune in their seats.

"What the fuck is this," Eugene giggled, *"Mad Magazine?* Hey look at me, everybody, I'm a spy..."

"Or a nightclub deejay," Daniel mused as the two finally got out of the truck and walked toward the house. Their heads scanned the block incessantly as if expecting an ambush at any second.

"They look like twins." Eugene snorted and returned to his post on the stairs. Daniel waited for them to knock.

"Is this the house for the Christmas delivery?" one of them asked Daniel through the door.

"Yes, we ordered four presents," Daniel replied.

"We have your wrapping papers in the truck."

Daniel opened the door. The two were twitchy, the muscles in their narrow faces pulsing rapidly beneath the skin.

"The goods are in the basement," Daniel said. "Bring whatever you need down there."

They nodded and lurched back toward the truck. While they were opening it Eugene walked from the stairs to watch.

"Those are some weird fuckers," he said as they returned through the door, each carrying some sort of cylinder wrapped in brown paper. They tramped down the stairs, then back up, returning for a second pair of cylinders.

"You can't come down while we're down there," one said over his shoulder as he passed through the doorway.

Eugene yawned.

"Well, fine. Then you can't come up here, either."

One of them looked at Eugene, alarmed. Daniel chuckled and shook his head.

From the basement came sounds of cardboard being torn apart, then a power drill removing screws from boards. One of the twins returned to remove a large toolbox from the truck and to shut the door. Daniel and Eugene looked at each other in disbelief then settled back into their chairs while muffled scrapes and bumps wound their way up from the cellar.

When he couldn't concentrate on the newspaper Daniel slapped it down to his lap.

"What the hell are they doing down there? What did DeSoto smuggle in, model ships?"

"Top secret pinball machines," Eugene said, listening to the scrape of metal against metal.

Daniel shook his head.

"They better finish soon," he said. "It's almost eight already."

"I'll take the Oranienburg one and that one in West Berlin," Eugene said. "You can do the two East Berlin addresses and turn in the truck when you're done."

"Why do you want to go to Oranienburg?"

"Remember what DeSoto said about this guy in Oranienburg?" Eugene asked. "How he's a cash-only deal, and somebody he's never worked with before?"

"Right."

"Let's do that one an hour before all the others. That'll give me an hour to get back in case something is wrong. And if I don't get back then you know not to do the others. Considering our luck recently in dealing with strangers...."

"Oh, that's bullshit," Daniel said. "They're all strangers. If anything, I should be the one taking the risks."

"I don't agree."

"Look, if I'm healthy enough to do the deal, then I'm healthy enough to take the risks and on top of that, I *owe* him and you for botching it last time. And if I'm not healthy enough to do the deal then I'm certainly not going to be getting any healthier, so my loss is less of a blow than yours."

Eugene frowned.

"Nice try," he finally said. "But I'm still going to take the Oranienburg delivery. There's just something. I don't know. Something's been bugging me about that one."

Daniel shook his head.

"Whatever. I don't see what—"

"We're finished," one of the twins announced, standing in front of the basement door with his toolkit.

"Excellent," Eugene said, a little too loudly.

The other twin appeared from the basement, re-buttoning his cuffs.

"Ignore the cardboard and rubbish down there," he said. "The four metal containers — that's your cargo."

"Now boys," Eugene said, squinting and wagging his chin, "I don't like to leave a messy kitchen."

The twins stared at him, perplexed, apparently waiting for him to say something more. At length they nodded and put on their sunglasses.

"Good evening," the first one said as they moved through the front door, bumping the frame on the way and scurried down the street. They vanished around a corner into the darkening town.

Daniel sighed. "Well, let's go have a look, shall we?"

They walked down the stairs and stood side by side in the basement, staring at the four shining cylinders. Each was about a meter in length and a quarter of a meter in diameter. The twins had arranged them standing on end, four abreast in the center of the floor. Torn paper wrappings, discarded Styrofoam, and various other packing materials were strewn about the floor behind them.

"Should we wait for them to hatch?" Eugene whispered.

"Lasers," Daniel said. "I'll bet you anything. I've heard that ever since that Star Wars stuff got canceled, everybody in the East is trying to buy some. They've got this new kind of metal canister thing — titanium or tungsten or something, I forget — but they're X-ray proof. You can run it through an X-ray and it'll look harmless, but inside you've got drugs or lasers, or whatever."

"I don't know. I think it's the *Alien.*"

"The *Alien* was green," Daniel said, walking around one of the cylinders, stroking its surface. "Here's that numerical plate," he said when he had reached the other side. Eugene was still rooted in place, arms locked across his chest.

"Well," Daniel said, shrugging, looking up at his partner on the other side of the cylinders. "Our cargo."

Eugene came around the other side to check the numbers. He removed a piece of paper from his coat pocket and, frustrated by the poor light, bent down to get a better look.

Daniel shook his head. "Which ones are which?

"This one," Eugene said, patting one with his hand. "Um... and this other one on the other end. Those two are yours. Do you have the addresses?"

"Yeah."

"Okay then." Eugene puffed, bent down to put his hands around one of them. He lifted it without undue strain, his face rising in surprise.

Daniel parked in front of the house. They loaded his car first, then brought the other two cylinders to the truck. The latch on the back was rusted but finally gave way. There was nothing at all in the back except the toolbox the twins had used.

"Where the hell are we supposed to put these things so they don't crash around?" Daniel said.

Eugene stood guard while Daniel went back down to the basement, a total of four trips, carrying up most of the spent cardboard and Styrofoam packing, fashioning a rough nest for the two cylinders. The truck door closed with considerable effort.

"You'd think DeSoto could afford something better," Eugene said.

"He didn't get to be rich by splurging on trucks."

They stood between the two vehicles, hands in pockets. Night had fallen on the street, and Potsdam looked bleak and depressed.

"Well, good luck," Daniel said, switching back to German.

"No problem," Eugene said, in English.

They nodded at each other and got in the vehicles. Daniel watched Eugene drive Gigi the Peugeot down the street. Then, after three attempts, he coaxed the truck into life. It wheezed and trudged away from the curb.

47.

Daniel pushed through the Berlin-bound traffic, the truck sputtering at each shift of gears. The sky was fully dark by the time he got off the autobahn at the Potsdamer Chaussee. The truck's performance seemed to improve as it neared the old East Berlin streets as if going home relieved its inferiority complex. Daniel crossed the river and fumbled with his map on the passenger seat and with the slip of paper on the dashboard which held the addresses. When he located the neighborhood he drove around until he found a late-night store and parked on the street in front of it. The middle-aged Vietnamese owners eyed him suspiciously as he bought a coffee and a roll and then sat at their one table, squeezed between the magazine rack and the window, for an hour and a quarter.

The truck almost refused to start again when he was finished. It succumbed to Daniel's curses and stubbornness and eventually sighed into gear. He drove the remaining few blocks to the first address, among a row of recently-renovated homes which were holding up far better than the majority of structures in the East. He reluctantly shut off the truck's motor after muttering a little threat that it damn well better start up again. There was no indication that anybody was in the house, nor that they had noticed his arrival. The building was unlit and silent.

Daniel got out and walked to the door. Beside a black button, a plaque read:

Prof. Dr. Gerd Kamman

He rang the bell and immediately heard scattering footsteps. Then hands at the door. A segment of the curtain in one of the glass panels was tugged aside for a peek. Then the lock clicked and Daniel found himself looking down at a very round, very bald head, emerging atop a gray sweater.

"Delivery tonight," Daniel said.

"Yes, yes," the man nodded hurriedly, looking around Daniel, either for someone or something that was not there.

"You're supposed to tell me something," Daniel said, slightly amused by this improbable client: short, chubby, thickly bespectacled, his worried face sprouting little rice-shaped beads of perspiration.

"Ah," the man whispered. "Yes, wait." He grasped in one pocket, then another, found a piece of paper which had obviously been folded and unfolded and folded again a hundred times, possibly all tonight. He opened it, his hands unsteady, adjusting his glasses, then he simply handed it to Daniel.

On a badly worn piece of letterhead stationery from the College of Sciences at Humboldt University, Professor Kamman's handwriting jittered out the coded response. Daniel shook his head sadly.

"Fine." He handed it back to the professor. "Do you have a back entrance?"

Kamman looked alarmed, like a man who had made extensive plans but had forgotten one crucial thing.

"No," he said, the pellets of sweat multiplying at his temples.

"It doesn't matter to me," Daniel said, "I can give it to you here."

When Kamman seemed frozen with fear and indecision Daniel turned and went to the truck. He jerked the back door upward, amazed that the ad hoc packing job hadn't disintegrated during the drive. Both cylinders were exactly as they had left them. He examined the number on the plate.

"My God..." he heard Kamman whisper from behind him.

"I don't know what dirty little secret you've got here," Daniel said, lifting the cylinder with both arms, "but I'll carry it as far as—"

"—I'll get it, I'll get it," Kamman pleaded, holding his arms out as if demanding the return of his infant. Daniel handed the cylinder to him, and the professor's eyes bulged at the weight. He shuffled nervously back to his door. Daniel stood at the back of the truck, unsure if he wanted to follow. At length, he simply shook his head and closed up the truck. He was about to leave when Kamman appeared in the doorway again, his face red and moist. He nodded at Daniel, beckoned him over as if he could no longer leave his home.

"Everything, then, is settled?"

"As far as I'm concerned," Daniel said. "I'm not handling the money."

"Yes, yes, no — I mean, the money, well, we took care of the money."

"It's your baby now."

"Excellent. Good, very good."

Kamman wiped his brow with his hand, breathing more deeply, looking around him again.

"You need a drink," Daniel observed.

"What? Oh, yes, ha. Yes."

"Very well, good evening."

"Yes, good. Fine."

Daniel was surprised to see Kamman still standing in his doorway, almost as much as he was surprised to hear the truck start up without complaint.

48.

When he had copied the addresses Daniel assumed that the person making the delivery arrangements was an English-speaker. On the second address, the word "traffic" was written in English, after the street number. Daniel thought it meant that he would meet the person accepting the delivery but then arrange to transfer the goods at a different place because of an excessive number of people or vehicles. But he found himself creeping deeper into the suburbs where traffic was virtually non-existent. People huddled in knots of three or four, sharing a blanket or a lamp, gulping beer from aluminum cans and pissing it back onto the watery streets. Teenage junkies haunted the empty lots, their gazes furtive from behind gnarled walls.

He drove by without slowing, to get a look at the place first, and he smiled when he figured it out. It was a dance club or disco of some kind, and the sizzling orange neon lettering over the faceless bunker-style door read: TRAFFIC.

There was no discrete place to park, so he drove around a while longer to get a sense of the job. Dead cars and trucks, some of them stripped of anything salvageable, were washed up on the curbs, an uneven metal riptide. Now he understood why DeSoto had selected this truck. Daniel cruised the block, then the surrounding area, and finally settled on an alleyway barely wider than the truck itself. He nosed it into the darkness and when he killed the headlights the alley swallowed everything in a deep gray hollow.

Daniel walked around the block. The mechanical thumping of the dance music pulsed bass from beneath the sidewalk. There was no line at the door, but down five stairs a buzz-cut young man waited, silent and glowering, his crossed arms swelling menacingly to fill the passage.

"I'm looking for Michael," Daniel said.

"Do you have the delivery?"

"I have something for Michael."

"Where is it?"

"It's nearby."

The man contemplated Daniel for a moment, then reached behind himself for a tiny phone that was hanging from the wall. He dialed but said nothing, waiting for a voice. When it came, he said,

"Delivery for Michael. All right. I'll tell him."

He replaced the phone. "The alleyway, behind this street."

"I saw it," Daniel said.

"Take it to the back door. And hey — if you're carrying," He paused, arched his single thick eyebrow. "They won't be happy."

Daniel walked out and around the corner again. When he got to the back door two short but immensely broad men waited in front of the door, staring at nothing, smoking in agitated puffs. Above them, a bare halogen bulb illuminated the doorstep and its immediate radius in the alley. As he approached, their eyes fixed upon him.

"You the delivery man?" One of them asked, his accent from somewhere in the Balkans.

"You expecting someone?" Daniel replied, hands in his pockets.

"We need to check you out, and we need the goods," the other one said, nodding at Daniel's invisible hands.

"I'm looking for Michael," Daniel said.

"I'm looking for my Christmas present," the first one said.

"That's better," Daniel said, inclining his head. "I needed you to say the magic words. I'll be back."

He returned a couple of minutes later. When they saw the cylinder against his chest, the two men smiled, simultaneously throwing down their cigarettes.

"Bring it in," said the one with the heavy accent.

"Don't do anything stupid," said the other, holding up a hand, then patting Daniel's stomach, his chest, bending down to squeeze his ankles.

Daniel paused for the search, then shouldered past them, walking sideways through the door to accommodate the cylinder.

"Downstairs," the second one said. "Michael wants to check it out."

They followed him patiently down the stairs, one sideways step at a time, the cylinder hugged against his chest. When he reached the bottom, the accented one said:

"Go right, then right again."

The ceiling shuddered rhythmically from the techno music above them. Daniel walked slowly past empty beer crates. The two followed, unconcerned with his pace. He paused when he found himself at the edge of a surprisingly large and open room, furnished only with large wooden boxes along two of the walls. Here and there crates and broken pieces of crates had been shoved up against the wall, giving the impression that the room was centrifugal: all objects having spun outward to cling to the perimeter. A half dozen swarthy men lounged nervously, they too against the walls, their eyes beaming at the cylinder as soon as Daniel entered. They were dressed in the misshapen polyester coats and cheap dress shirts favored by the mafia of virtually every East European country.

"Excellent," said a small thin man wearing large-rimmed glasses. Daniel couldn't place his accent as he said: "Put it down here, gently."

The small man watched intently as Daniel put the cylinder down on its end. He immediately squatted in front of it, even before Daniel had risen, and searched for the numerical plate. At length he nodded, rose and turned, and said over Daniel's shoulder,

"Perfect."

He could hear the blow approaching in the half-second of swirling air as the bar flew toward his legs. Daniel grunted, legs buckling, falling knees-first as the metal smashed him down.

The little man slid out of the way, moving sideways. Daniel turned over, frantic, saw three of them above him, broad stomachs and thick mustaches, metal bars rising in the air above their heads, about to come down to finish him.

—Wait!

The bars paused in mid-air. The faces turned, all three in unison like obedient birds.

—Not yet.

The other voice, from an invisible throat, was cold and familiar.

They looked back down at him, mouths working, throats thirsting for the kill. They stepped aside once, twice, widening the gap. Daniel raised himself on one arm. He thought he might be able to bolt if his legs would let him. The pain was alive, rampant up and down his spine, filling his head. He was about to try anyway, his only chance. He gathered his strength and flexed his arm when another face appeared over him, eyes blue as ice crystals, hair bristling bullet gray. That face looked down, a tight little smile tugging at one corner of his mouth, watching Daniel gasp, watching him freeze over in fear.

"You little shit."

Alain LeClerc folded his arms behind his back, surveying Daniel's crumpled form beneath him. He was savoring this, almost obscene in his pleasure. Taking his time. Then, in English flat as an American highway:

"Working for Miguel DeSoto these days, are we?"

Daniel lay speechless on the floor.

"He's not as clever as he thinks he is. Not a pleasant thought, is it? Your old man, after all these years, still a bit smarter than Señor Art Collector. And a good stretch smarter than *you*. Well, I might not be able to pick out the finest bottle of Saint Émillion, but I can tell you a few things about your boss. I was doing deals more complicated than this back when he was moistening sorority panties at Columbia or wherever the fuck it was he went. I don't care how many diamonds are on his Rolex, kid, he's still a fool, and *you're* a fool for taking his side against me."

LeClerc spread his arms, sweeping to encompass the room.

"Gentlemen," he said grandly in French, "I present: My son."

Nobody in the room knew how to react. They stepped back a bit from Daniel, uncertain what LeClerc intended.

"He thinks he's my son, anyway," LeClerc said, turning back to look down at Daniel. "The joke was on me for long enough, now it's on you. I married that crazy dancing bitch, your mother, God help me. Thinking with my dick. I paid a fucking fortune to get her out of here. I had no idea she already had *you* in the oven. So I raised you."

"Can you believe that?" LeClerc said to the men. "Not even my own kid, and the bitch went and died on me, but no! I raised him. Paid for everything." Then, turning back toward Daniel: "And how did you repay me? Took my money and went to America, well good riddance. But now, what, a decade later? You're trying to set me up?"

LeClerc's tone became more climactic as he rested his palms on his hips.

"That's how you repay me? Working for some fucking Spaniard, trying to set me up? You think you're smart enough to kill me? Think that DeSoto is even smart enough to protect you? He doesn't know who he's dealing with, who he's really dealing with. It's bigger than you think, kid. You're just my little part of it."

LeClerc paused, tilted his head. For the first time, a full smile broke across the hard lines of his mouth.

"Look at him!" He turned, speaking to the room, the smile spreading. "He doesn't believe me. He can't believe it. What?" He turned back, to glare down at Daniel with bottomless disdain. "No smart-ass comments now? Huh? *My son....* Good God, I'd forgotten how sick I was of those words."

Daniel saw some of their faces shift around, as if trying to find something, brows furrowed, heads raised upward listening to something Daniel couldn't hear. Some kind of movement from above them, on the ceiling? LeClerc seemed annoyed, glancing around at his men.

"What?" he demanded.

They were silent, listening, faces drawn upward like guilty children. Daniel's eyes settled upon a piece of pine board, some strip from a heavy packing crate. It sat against the wall a meter to his right, two bent nails clawing outward from one end. But then he heard it, too: something scraping, scattering across the floor above them.

LeClerc pivoted, frowning. With his chin he commanded them into motion. The two who greeted Daniel at the door stepped forward, but he ordered them away before they advanced to him:

"Go up there."

They nodded in unison, vanishing around the corner leading to the stairs.

LeClerc exhaled heavily, turned to look at Daniel.

"Nothing to say? No last words? I'd be disappointed and disgusted with you if you were actually my son, but since you're nothing more than a bad judgment call thirty-odd years ago...."

Their heads rotated upward again, the flesh of LeClerc's face simmering with anger.

"What the hell is that?"

But it stopped before the words finished passing his lips. And now, silence. The thudding bass of the disco evaporated, although they could still hear its rhythms, residual in their ears. Nothing at all now. Iron bars fell to the floor, hands reached inside coats, waistbands. LeClerc looked at two of his men, guns tight against their stomachs. He gestured to the exit, this time with his nose. They departed quickly, turning through the corridor, out of sight. LeClerc stood above Daniel, as if keeping him on the floor solely by the weight of his presence. There were two armed men remaining, and the small foreigner, now hunching in the far corner. Daniel listened to the heavy fall of four feet ascending the stairs.

A pinched whistle, a muffled pop. LeClerc's eyes widened, then constricted. His head turned.

The sound of something, some things, thick, coming down the stairs, rapid, awkward, thudding to the floor. Bodies. The men turned. Daniel dove for the board, reached it in one motion. They weren't watching, good, his legs didn't work the first time. But then he was up, rising, seeing the terror on the small man's face, the only one who has yet to notice him. He drew the wood back in both hands.

LeClerc felt the motion in the air too late. His face turned as the wood arced toward him, breaking against his cheek, an impossibly loud *crack!*

It made the others spin around to look. They didn't see the small figure flying in, slipping sideways, red ponytail flying, Makarov out in both hands. A bullet cracked through one's ear. The last one spun back toward the explosion. He saw the red swish of hair, not the gun, not the bullet in his mouth, then he fell backward on rubbery legs, arms flaying the air, crumpling to the floor.

The small man gasped, threw both arms around his head, teetered back against the wall. Daniel hobbled, his legs unsteady, grabbed him by his scalp, threw him down.

"Move and you die," he said, heaving for breath, fighting the pain of standing up.

Alain LeClerc groaned from the floor. One of the others began to convulse. Eugene turned toward him, his mouth screwed up in anger and disgust. He put another silenced bullet in the man's head. It popped when it cracked through the bone and struck the concrete. Deep red spread from the shattered skull. Only LeClerc and the small man remained, lying down in the center of the floor.

Eugene looked at LeClerc.

"Live or die?" he asked, training the Makarov on the slowly rousing form. LeClerc was breathing heavily, his legs moving.

"Wait—" Daniel said.

"We don't have much time."

"Wait."

Daniel kicked at LeClerc's arm, turning him over. The cerulean eyes blinked several times, finally focused on the pistol. For the first time he looked old, his eyes squinting, wrinkled.

"Get up," Daniel said.

LeClerc almost smiled. He rose, sitting up, a swelling line of red the length of his face. Then he snorted and rose between them. Even now, bleeding and half-dazed, he was terrifying.

"Well well," LeClerc finally said, slurring a little. "Do you have the balls to kill me?"

"There's a Makarov pointed directly at your brain," Daniel said. "It's being held by my friend, who has already killed all of your men. Whether or not I have the balls to kill you.... it's no longer an issue."

"Then," LeClerc said slowly, "do you intend to stand here all night?"

"Daniel," Eugene whispered angrily. "We don't have time. Fifty people saw me come in here and start shooting, and they're all out on the street."

"There are no cops out here," Daniel said, walking over to one of the corpses and picking up the .38 that had fallen beside it. "We have enough time for one thing."

He turned back to face LeClerc.

"What you said. About me. Now would be a good time to tell the truth."

"I've already told you the truth."

"You're not my father."

"No, you goddamned *bâtard.*"

"Who is?"

"I have no idea." LeClerc's head jittered involuntarily as a trickle of blood fell to his neck. "Some kraut. You're all German. You never were French, that's your problem."

Daniel was silent for so long that Eugene finally shook his head and demanded:

"Live or die?"

"When did you come to Paris?" Daniel asked.

LeClerc laughed. "I was born in Paris, you idiot."

"With *her*! When did you come to Paris with her?"

"What? Good God, you must be kidding — sixty-two, sixty-three? I don't remember. I was young and stupid back then."

And then, lips tightening, eyes filling with frost, he added:

"She was just a piece of ass, and I should've known it."

Eugene's stare remained on LeClerc's head until he heard Daniel breathing so heavily he thought he might be getting sick. When he looked, he was shocked to see that Daniel had raised the gun directly to LeClerc's face. The older man was unflinching, staring straight at Daniel with glacial dispassion.

"Die," Daniel whispered and pulled the trigger.

The silence, invisible, traveling immediately behind the bullet is what does it — the vacuum in the wake of that terrible speed — dark, annihilating with its emptiness, ripping out all life that it touches, sucking it away instantly before you can see, the speed of nothing.

Daniel watches the darkness as it pulls from the barrel, a black dart behind the steel. It opens the ice of the face, devours and destroys as it moves away from him, nearing the dark velocity where the possible and impossible trade places, a scream in the hollow before the dream.

Go to it now, *he says to the destroyed face, broken and falling away before him in a spray of red too bright, too alive to have ever passed through that heart.* Go to nowhere.

The small man shivered, moaned from the floor. They had forgotten he was there.

"What about him?" Eugene asked.

"I don't know."

"We can't leave him as a witness."

"Hey," Daniel kicked at him, making him gasp. "If you want to live, get up."

"I'm a scientist," he wheedled as he rose. "I'm not a gangster."

Eugene squinted.

"You're Russian."

The man looked at him, swallowed heavily.

"You're a fucking Russian. I can tell from your accent," Eugene said, and then berated the man in his native tongue. Daniel stood, his leg throbbing, understanding only a handful of words as Eugene's voice rose in anger and the small man's rose in his increasingly hopeless defense.

"This motherfucker," Eugene said in English, "was going to sell his services to terrorists who wanted to blow up a whole city."

The man shook his head vehemently, splashing the air with his hands.

"What are you talking about?" Daniel asked.

"That's what you were going to do, isn't it?" Eugene demanded, shouting at the cowering figure. "You were going to help them do what? Which one? New York? Moscow? Tokyo?"

"Yevgenny! What the fuck are you talking about?"

"It's a nuclear bomb, Daniel."

Eugene nodded at the cylinder.

"We've been carrying four nuclear weapons, hauling them around like goddamned milkmen. They're artillery shells. Nuclear-tipped artillery shells." He turned his rage back to the man. "Made in the Soviet Union."

"We've delivered nuclear weapons," Daniel said, incredulous.

"Isn't that a lovely thought?" Eugene said. "I can't believe we didn't think of that. I can't fucking believe we were so ignorant." He shouted in Russian again, apparently asking questions whose answers he interrupted with more shouted questions. Finally he spat furiously on the floor.

"We've got to get out of here. What do you want to do with this guy?"

Daniel stared at their captive for a moment, was about to say something, then Eugene said:

"Fuck him"

and pulled the trigger.

"No—" Daniel said, then grimaced. "We might have needed him."

"He gets away and ten million people fry," Eugene said. "No way. And it's too complicated for us. He's a witness to too many things. And what the hell would we have done with any other information he might have had?"

Daniel shook his head.

"All right."

"Let's get that fucking bomb and get the hell out of here," Eugene said, shoving the Makarov into his belt.

"What are we going to do with *this?*" Daniel asked, grunting in pain as he lifted it.

49.

They left the truck a block from the arranged drop site, just in case. Eugene drove Daniel's Peugeot and Daniel slid into the passenger seat. The face of Alain LeClerc, silvery as ice in the air before him, shattered, shattered again, shattered a thousand times. Daniel could see nothing else. It was only now dawning upon him, how close he had come to dying, that Eugene had saved his life yet again. And again, Eugene seemed indifferent to it, babbling in English as if talking was a form of therapy.

"So I made good time out to Oranienburg and I got there, and it was a private home. And this guy — he's forty, fiftyish. Looks like a scientist. Thick glasses, the works. And that was a little strange, you know. What's this fucker doing with suitcases full of cash? American dollars. You know how much?"

"Two and a half mil, right? Four deals are ten million, DeSoto gives us ten percent." Daniel swallowed, trying to clear his head..

"*Genau*. Two and a half million dollars. In hundreds. I counted out five hundred bundles of them. And this guy's so nervous, all sweaty and pacing, checking the numbers on that canister over and over again.

"See, originally I wasn't thinking weapons at all. Then you said something about lasers, but when I saw the money... for two and a half mil you can walk into a hospital and buy one right off the wall. It had to be something else. Then I got to the second place in Berlin.

"It's two guys, Germans. I was there for a couple of minutes and they're doing the same thing, checking the numbers, looking at me real nervous the whole time. But they're definitely not college professors. I can see that they're carrying; they've got big bulges under their coats. Then I caught a glimpse of a third guy pacing around in the next room. The door's ajar and he's walking around. I don't want to stare, but I'm peeking in there, trying to get a better look, and he turns around. And I nearly shit my pants. It was Scherbatov."

"Who?"

"Nikolai Scherbatov!"

Daniel squinted then his eyes widened.

"Yeah..." Eugene said, his head bobbing. "Nikolai Fucking Scherbatov in the next room. He didn't see me. But I'm starting to think: what does Scherbatov do? He does clubs, discos, that kind of shit. And what did he use to do? Weapons. And if he wanted to get back in business, who would he have to beat? Who's Numero Uno in weapons deals around here?"

"Miguel DeSoto Ramos," Daniel said.

"That's when I got worried. So I moved a little bit closer to the door. And I had my hand on my piece and I said, 'You guys heard from Sergio lately?'

"And they fucking froze, man. One of them reached, and I drilled him—"

Eugene made a finger-and-thumb gun in the air above the dashboard.

"I plugged both of them and I ran. Didn't look back. I had no clue this car could move so fast. That's when it all came together for me. Everything we've been doing these last couple of deals — we're not working weapons deals for Miguel DeSoto, even though he thinks we are. We're the dummies. Part of a *hit* on DeSoto."

Daniel squinted.

"How could DeSoto not know any of this?"

"Third-party, fourth-party shit, all of it," Eugene said, shrugging. "DeSoto thinks he's got four separate deals working, but it's only one. Nikolai Scherbatov and his pet Russian and German scientists — about to land the biggest coup in the history of weapons smuggling."

"With the help," Daniel whispered, "of his loyal lieutenant Alain LeClerc."

"That's how I knew," Eugene said. "That disco, *Traffic*? It's a Russian disco. I remember when it opened last year. Man, I should've known. I should've *known.* Ever since that Polish deal — you were right and I didn't listen. It was too easy, the stuff was too new. It was Scherbatov the whole time, pulling us in."

"Arrange the cash in circles," Daniel said, "so DeSoto thinks he's got it in the money chain coming around to him through names he trusts. Throw in just enough immediate cash to make it look legit, and to make it look like different customers. Scrub both of DeSoto's delivery boys, get the nukes, and grab the cash. All in one night."

"The man thinks big," Eugene said.

"They must have thought we'd do all the deliveries together; they didn't expect us to split up. They were waiting for us in *Traffic* and were going to kill us both. I just got 'lucky' and got Alain LeClerc to myself." Daniel exhaled slowly through his nose. "We have a problem."

"Yeah, you noticed."

"I mean, even if DeSoto believes us, we have a problem. Scherbatov...."

"Who knows what he'll do now," Eugene said. "He's got three nukes. He might decide to call it a day."

"And we've got one," Daniel said.

They considered this for a full minute.

"I can smell you thinking," Eugene said.

"He's going to protect the nukes first and foremost."

"Mm-hm."

"He'll only move against us after he knows for sure we're not moving against him. After he's secured his babies. We've got two days at the most."

"That's *if* he moves. He might declare victory and head back to Paris."

"Do you want to gamble on that?"

"No," Eugene said. "But what I'm saying is, we've got something else. We've got information."

"You're thinking of giving somebody those addresses and numbers."

"It crossed my mind."

"Then we'd have a war with Miguel for sure."

"We're businessmen," Eugene said, "not mass-murderers. Do you want to turn on the news some morning next week and see a fucking crater where New York used to be?"

"If they're nuclear-tipped artillery shells they can't be that big. I mean, we carried them in our arms."

"Okay, fine, so they'll only kill a million people instead of ten million. You're right, that's better."

"Yevgenny, what the hell business do you think we're in? We sell machine-guns to people or trade them for grenade launchers. Do you think that stuff's being used for party favors?"

"It's being used," Eugene was almost shouting now, "by wise guys to shoot other wise guys. Nuclear bombs are a little bit different, Daniel!"

Daniel stared out the window at the jagged blur of the city.

"We can't go off half-cocked on this," he said. "We need to think carefully about what we're going to do."

"All right." Eugene shook his head sadly. "All right. First of all, we need to put our little pal here somewhere safe."

"Nina," Daniel replied, so quickly and surely that Eugene stared straight ahead and said only,

"Okay, good."

When they got to the Prenzlauer Allee, Eugene asked:

"You're going to sleep at Julia's?"

"No, my place."

"That may not be the best idea, very shortly."

"We've got a little time."

"All right. What do we tell DeSoto?"

Daniel sighed. "I don't know. Think of something."

"Tomorrow," Eugene said, "we can ask for a private meeting. That'll buy some more time, so he won't come looking for us. Whether we tell him the truth or not."

"All right. Fine. Tomorrow, then."

"But first," Daniel said, "Turn here, go south for a bit."

Eugene parked on the street half a block from the subway station. Daniel saw another immense communist-era apartment building fenced off at the sidewalk, with plastic yellow-and-black signs warning of yet discovered another bomb beneath the foundation. The authorities had apparently decided to demolish this one and let the bomb complete its work after all these years.

More buildings earned these death sentences now every day. Their asbestos-filled walls and ceilings were too heavy, too moldy, too expensive to save. It was cheaper to annihilate them. Their pocked grey shells stared aghast at the fencing around the edge of the block, the way a zoo animal might consider its cage. The signs warned pedestrians to keep their distance. Water had already risen from the pierced foundations and was running through the street.

Daniel's shoes crunched broken glass on the platform as Eugene opened the hidden door behind the vending machine and then stood guard as Daniel descended the steps of the service entrance, carrying the bomb in its silver cocoon in both arms against his chest like a corpse. Now that he knew what it was, it felt very much alive and he was the one who felt himself to be dead.

At the alcove he set the cylinder down on its end, leaned against the wall and breathed heavily for a minute, resting his arms. Then he fumbled for his key. He found it and was about to open the lock when he sensed someone in the darkness to his left. He turned to look but could see nothing.

He waited and listened. Is he imagining this too? In this darkness, he might be moving or standing still, alone or haunted by any of a million of Berlin's innumerable ghosts.

He opened the alcove and muscled the bomb inside, then locked the door. He stood and strained to see into the blackness but there was only a feeling.

"Johannes?" he asked.

Daniel heard water dripping quickly somewhere as if falling from the ceiling onto the tunnel floor. He surmised that the excavation for the doomed apartment building across the street had penetrated the tunnel or opened some sort of fissure.

"It will all be destroyed," an old voice whispered.

Daniel shuddered.

"Johannes?" He squinted, increasingly frustrated. "I can help you. Sabine — you remember Sabine? She'd like to help you, you know, get back on your feet. She'd give you some good hot meals, medicine, maybe even some money. I swear, if you'd—"

"The water is coming," the old man said.

"Why are you here?" Daniel asked.

"The water is coming back," he answered. "This time there's no escape."

Daniel closed and locked the alcove then turned to stand in front of it. He waited and listened in the silence for so long that he knew Eugene would start to get worried. He took a pair of steps forward then listened again.

"You're not here," he said finally, almost convincing himself, and then he went back out and up.

50.

When Daniel came home he called Eugene and made sure everything was secure at his place. They agreed to meet the next night.

He was leaning against the frame of his window when he realized the difference. On his floor, the plaster sculpture head was complete, its holes filled, its surface smoothed. He walked across the room to study the face. A trace of the antiseptic aroma of paint rose from the sadly clamped mouth, the downturned eyes. Daniel squatted down beside it, inhaling the drying chemicals, closing his eyes and imagining her perfect hands against it, massaging life into the cold muck, a gentle birth in the compilation of elements.

He sighed and rose, walked to the bedroom. He had kicked off his shoes and was unbuttoning his pants when he felt a lump in the left pocket. He extracted a vial.

It was narrow and black, the length of all the others Rashid gave him, but he hadn't given him this one. Had he? No, he decided, unconvinced the moment he thought it. No, this must have been in the pocket for some time, I must've forgotten about it.

He opened the lid and the pills quivered, looking up at him, awaiting his decision. He shook two into his hand, then slapped his palm to his mouth and choked them down without a drink, closing with a gasp.

He slept deeply, dreamless, for the first time in weeks.

51.

Sabine saw him the moment he entered. Her mouth had been open as if she was about to say something to somebody but then closed, lips vanishing in a single troubled line.

Daniel hesitated two steps in, eyes boxing the room. No Eugene, none of DeSoto's men. At least none he recognized, and if DeSoto was going to pull your plug then he probably wouldn't send somebody you knew.

"Miguel is looking for you," she whispered as he sat at the bar.

Daniel smiled.

"But you're making my vehicle."

"Yeah?" she said, stopping.

"No, that's good. That means... well, you don't pour drinks for a dead man. Or maybe you do."

"Fuck," she said, shaking the mixer beneath her chin. "You're giving me gray hair. I don't know what's going on with you boys anymore. Miguel had a man in here for hours, waiting for you. He just left half an hour ago. Eugene came by earlier, got one foot in the door, took a look at him and left. The guy didn't notice him."

"Maybe he's not looking for Eugene. When did he come by?"

"Who, Eugene? About, uh... I guess about two hours ago."

She thumped the glass down on the wood.

"Daniel," she said, her face lined with worry. "Don't start something with Miguel."

"I didn't. Don't worry."

She nodded, hands on her hips.

"I'm going to go sit down," Daniel said, rising, tipping his forehead toward a back booth.

Sabine came over a while later, sat down beside him.

"You're still alive," she observed.

"Thus far," he said.

"I'm so worried about you."

"No... you shouldn't be. I'm not—"

But she had taken the far side of his head in one hand and pulled his temple to her lips, kissing him softly behind the eye. His words collapsed into an embarrassed chuckle.

"You'd tell me if you were in real trouble, right?" she asked.

"Yes," he said.

"You'd apologize for lying to me about saying you weren't in real trouble, right?"

"Sabine."

"Daniel. I'm too old to have my heart broken. Don't you dare. I love both of you stupid boys, and I need to know if I'm about to lose you."

He shook his head, smiling.

"Where do you get all your courage?"

"Women are braver, men are more romantic," she said. "Everybody thinks it's the other way around. Nobody's figured it out yet but me. Men are crazy romantics who get themselves killed for beautiful ideas and fall in love with vague concepts. Women are the stalwart ones, always sticking it out stubbornly when they'd be smarter to run away."

"So," she said. "Are you getting ready to run away?"

"Believe me, it's better for you if you don't know."

She stared at him a moment longer, biting her lip. Then she stroked the back of his head once and rose to go.

"Sabine," he said. "I found him."

She stared at him quizzically.

"Johannes," he said. "I found him."

Her back stiffened, her voice dropped to a whisper.

"He's all right?"

"Yes," Daniel said. "I don't think he wants to be 'found,' though. He lives out near me. I think he sleeps in Friedrichshain or at a shelter on the Leninallee."

"Did you speak with him?"

"Yeah, a little. He told me to get lost."

"He's okay, then?"

Daniel smiled.

"Yes," he said. "I'm pretty sure he's okay."

She was staring at him, didn't hear the phone ringing. Daniel watched over her shoulder as the Russian cook exited cautiously from the kitchen, saw the rattling receiver on the wall, and carefully lifted it. A moment later, he called across the room, shouting Sabine's name, holding out the telephone. Sabine turned to look, then back to Daniel. She nodded slightly.

"All right," she said and walked away.

A moment later, she was gesturing to him.

"It's for you," she said as he walked over. "Yevgenny," she whispered.

"*Ça va?*" he said, taking it, curling toward the wall.

"Push these numbers," Eugene said in English and rattled off six digits. Daniel pushed them. The phone squawked and sizzled for a second, finally making a wet-sounding *cluck*.

"Okay, we're clear, no bugs," Eugene said. "I assume Sabine told you?"

"About some guy waiting here for us."

"Yeah. I might have been too optimistic earlier. Maybe we don't have very much time."

"What do you think?" Daniel said, hearing Eugene sigh.

"Well, I have an idea."

"But it's not a good one?"

"It's the least bad of the ones I've had so far," Eugene said. "I can call tonight and tip off the cops about the names and addresses, give them those numbers on the canisters."

"The cops?"

"The *real* cops. You know, Federal guys. I could use some of the different mobile lines, scramble it up, but spread out the calls so that three or four guys get the message."

"Then what?" Daniel asked. "That only increases the number of people trying to nail us."

"It might hurt Miguel, it might not. We can give some info to him, too, so he'll at least be prepared. But I'm not willing to take the fall for him. It was his fault, not checking his back on these deals, that almost got us killed."

"Agreed. But this means we leave town."

"Yeah, most likely," Eugene said.

"I mean, even if Miguel agrees that it's fair, and decides not to kill us, we'd still never get work here again. Not in Berlin, maybe not even in Germany."

"Or France," Eugene said. "Don't forget Scherbatov."

"Yeah."

They were quiet for a moment, Daniel listening to the low sparkle of electrons dancing through the line: Eugene's scrambler frying any eavesdroppers.

"Back to Mother Russia?" Daniel finally asked.

"It's crossed my mind," Eugene said. "Not my first choice, but probably the best place for me right now. It's big, it's disorganized, I can lay low for as long as I like. And you?"

"I don't know."

"Listen," Eugene said, "if you've got a better plan, I'm open to suggestion."

Daniel exhaled slowly.

"No," he said. "No, you're right. That's the only way."

"It's the only way I can think of to stop Scherbatov without taking him on — make it the cops' problem. Anybody could've given them that information. All he knows so far is that LeClerc fucked up last night and something went wrong."

"Yeah," Daniel said, "All right. I'll take care of Miguel. I'll call him tomorrow, maybe even tonight."

"*I'll* call him tonight," Eugene said, "and arrange a meeting for tomorrow. That'll give us some time. Then you can call him tomorrow, instead of us going down there. I'm going out right now to get some of our things from the stashes. Do you want me to get yours, too?"

"No, that's all right. I'll take care of it."

"There's one more thing we have to take care of."

"I know," Daniel said.

"What are you going to do with it?"

"I don't know. Maybe I'll call the cops and tell them where to find it."

"All right. I'll leave it up to you."

"Are you leaving tomorrow?" Daniel asked.

"Yeah. First to Prague for a couple of days, then to St. Petersburg. I don't know. Come winter, I'll probably lose my mind. Maybe I'll start learning Spanish, so I can go somewhere warm for a change."

Daniel smiled.

"So this is it for us."

"I think so. Unless you want to learn Russian."

"Not a chance."

"Pushkin, Chekhov... you don't know what you're missing."

"I read some Tolstoy in high school. That'll have to do. Listen — we've still got our secret numbers, right?"

"Yeah," Eugene said. "You remember yours?"

"Yeah, yeah," Daniel said, trying to recall the digits he had memorized a year ago. "I got it."

"We can still send signals," Eugene said, "like spies in movies and shit."

"When we each get... wherever. We can make contact then."

"I haven't told Sabine," Eugene said. He sighed. "I guess I'll call her soon, after this is settled. I feel bad about that."

"It's been a wild ride, hasn't it?"

"Yes, it has."

"Yevgenny," Daniel said, but found that his lip had fled into his mouth, blocking the rest.

Finally Eugene said:

"I would do it again. Even if you only had fifteen more seconds to live."

Daniel swallowed heavily.

"Merci."

"Au revoir, mon vieux. Bon chance."

When he put the phone down, Sabine was staring at him, standing near the door which led up to her apartment. She looked at his face for several seconds, assessing the weight which tugged downward at the corners of his eyes and mouth. Then she turned, opened the door, and disappeared up the stairs.

By the time he had finished his fourth drink, the noises from the kitchen formed a mechanical tempo to the murmur of voices in the room. Daniel floated somewhere beneath it, his head awash in dull rhythms, his thoughts bubbling up slowly through a chilly vodka swamp.

He was stagnant in his own frosty murk, vaguely aware of the opening front door, of the turning of male heads, the nods, the ascending key of their mumblings. But he didn't see her until she had crossed the room, until she was standing above him at the table. Narrow praying mantis arms hung at her sides, her mouth in a troubled still-life kiss. His eyes rose slowly, disbelieving, along the gentle slope of her stomach, her chest, up to her face.

"Are you okay?" she said.

He nodded sloppily.

"You're such a liar."

She smiled, lowered herself into the seat beside him, arms enclosing his head as it tumbled to her breast, his ear against the warm stroke of her heart.

"I think I'm losing everything," he whispered.

"Ssshh." She kissed his head, clutched it against her. "No, you're not."

"Oh, God, Julia."

"Come on," she said. "Enough of this. I'm taking you home."

They went by taxi, Julia generally uninclined to use the S-Bahn. The entire journey — swerving, swishing through water around construction sites — she held him, both of them silent, breathing steadily. She paid the driver when they stopped, then guided Daniel from the street into the courtyard, where he finally realized that they had come to his apartment.

"We should go to your place," he said. "It might not be safe here."

"No one's going to hurt you," she said, palming the key.

"Why did you come?" he asked as they walked up his staircase.

"Sabine called."

"You finished the sculpture," he said dreamily as they entered.

"I know. I think you should have it, that's why I left it here. I know you don't like decorations, but there's something about this that's just... you. I've had it in my hands enough to know. It feels like you."

Daniel stood in his living room, staring at the side of the head. Julia shrugged off her coat, laid it on the tearsplash table, and walked to the bedroom. She emerged a moment later tugging his bedsheets across the floor like an immense and unruly bridal train. She left them in a heap in the center of the living room and vanished again to return with his pillows. By the third trip, she had created a nest of bedding on the floor.

She unbuttoned his shirt until with a push it fell away behind him. She crouched to his feet, untied his shoes, slipped them off, tugged away the socks as he wobbled over her. Then she rose to his stomach, kissed it quickly as she drew the trousers down, pulling them over his feet. She rose and pointed to the nest.

"Lie down."

Daniel complied, transfixed as she knelt over him, the thin curtain of her dress rippling by degrees above her form.

She began at his temples, little finger points of warm pressure, sliding downward. She circled his cheekbones with her thumbs, kissing his nose when she departed south across his throat.

"I don't know why I've always liked your face so much," she said. "It's almost like I can see the angry little boy walking the streets of Paris. He grew a bigger body and learned some different languages, but he's still... pure."

"No one's ever used that word to describe me," Daniel said.

"Shhh. Lie still. I understand the word to mean un-corrupted," she said. "A part of the world, but not dissolved into it." She massaged his neck and shoulders.

"I'm a career criminal, Julia. I can't be un-corrupted."

"Don't be so simple. And lie still! Obeying laws and systems doesn't make you pure. Disregarding them doesn't make you corrupt." Her fingers spread across his stomach.

"I know," she said as she kissed him beneath the navel, "what I have felt inside me." She took him in her mouth, her fingers ascending his torso, her hair fanned out across his waist. When she finished the long motion, teeth dragging up his length, lips joining at the end in a kiss, she rose and hovered over him again. Then she lowered herself upon him, the tumult of him rising inside her slowly, disappearing into darkness.

She rose some time later when he was deeply buried in sleep. A rare reversal of their roles. She turned off the light and curled beside him, pulling the nest up at the sides, so that it sealed them in.

52.

He dreamt of a staircase twisting into the earth. He woke and she was gone.

Daniel's hand fell to cold crests of bedsheets. His head dense and strumming, he was not yet fully awake when the first wave of pain came, spurting up through his stomach into his chest. It unwound inside him quickly and he could feel it returning, receding, regrouping, preparing another ascent. He was naked and cold, swimming the exploded pond of sheets on the floor. It was still dark as he rose, his hand on his gut, dreading the next assault.

It caught him as he stood, took him back down to his knees. It surged up through him like a wave at high tide, hot and angry. He stood again and staggered to the bedroom, to his phone. He held it and dialed with his thumb.

Rashid didn't answer. The machine intervened after five rings: breathy Arabic syllables apologizing. Daniel put the phone down. He didn't know what time it was, couldn't see the clock. He was staring around the darkened space of his bedroom when it seized him again.

"Oh! God!" His head bowed low enough to bump the stripped frame of his bed. Gulping air, he found himself laughing, then laughing at the oddity of laughing. Then understanding, as if reminding himself of a superb joke:

"Are you early or late?" He shouted. "Trying to kill me before anybody else can? Or does it not matter now? Well? Come on, hurry up before someone else beats you to it."

He hobbled into his trousers, stomped into his shoes. He pulled a shirt around him and slammed the door as he left.

As if he could outrun it for a while, as if it were chasing him along the stairs, following him down the spiral through the darkness.

Out on the street, he pushed ahead through the pre-dawn chill. At the base of his stomach it waited, coiled and ready, perhaps amused by his sudden resolve.

Streetlights were irregular phenomena now except on those blocks where the water hadn't risen to infest their wiring. Daniel plunged ahead past heaps of garbage alternating with fences and cranes in front of the buildings on either side. Rats squealed at the rude interruption, fled for a moment until he passed, then resumed their work. He walked a dozen blocks, turning now and again, leading himself by feel.

As he approached the subway station he saw a cluster of lights around the condemned building. The old frame was covered in some sort of mesh. Were they working on the demolition at night? Daniel didn't see any workmen, but it appeared ready to go. Its foundation bled now in several gushing streams of brown, oily water.

The subway entrance was fenced-off but Daniel simply climbed over. There did not appear to be anyone around to notice or object. He descended into the darkness of the station. The platform was lit only by the red emergency lanterns above the exits. Water from the broken foundation above streamed in now, slapping against the tracks. More dripped through cracks that had formed in the ceiling, plunking into thin puddles everywhere. Silent trickles emerged from the walls, running down like glass tendrils across the stone face to the floor. The air was heavy, cold, and red like blood.

He found the service tunnel mostly by feel. Even after his eyes adjusted he could barely see forward to the alcove.

He patted the slimy wall with his palms, feeling his way toward the lock. He thumbed through his keys, felt the shape and threaded it in. He pulled the door open but there was no cylinder.

He was confused for a few seconds, unable to remember what he had done and when he had done it, then a stripe of panic ran down his neck into his boiling chest. He felt water flowing around his shoes, cold, seeping gradually through the leather and touching him. The alcove was locked, he had the only key, could someone have taken the bomb, or did he never put it here in the first place?

Daniel exhaled slowly, forced himself to calm down. He closed the alcove door, turned, and retraced his steps to the platform. And there, in the middle of the murky river that now covered the tracks and filled nearly up to the platform level, he saw not the cylinder, but the weapon itself, unpacked, upright in the midst of the subway line, its nose still above the rising water.

"I am not losing my mind," Daniel insisted. Had he unpacked it and placed it here? Had somebody else, somehow, for some reason? He realized that the only way to get it now would be to climb down into the flooded track and hope that no electricity still coursed through the rails. As he stared and thought about that, he watched the water rising steadily, to lap now at the edge of the platform. Only about a hand's length of the shell's cone remained visible.

Then the red light died. The platform was almost perfectly black as he felt the water filling his shoes. He reached into his pocket and felt for the flashlight but it wasn't there.

I was facing the tracks, he said to steady himself. *If I turn around I face the wall.* He tried as carefully as he could to turn exactly 180 degrees, and then he started sliding his feet forward one step at a time, hoping that if he were headed the wrong way, he could feel the cliff-edge in time not to fall into the river. The water rose to his ankles.

At last, his foot bumped something just as his outstretched hands felt the wall. Now he turned to his left and walked more quickly, knowing he would collide with the staircase. After another terrifying stretch of time, with the water now at his shins, he felt the banister collide with his armpit. He searched with his foot and found the first step.

The platform sounded like a waterfall, invisible liquid pouring in curtains from the cracked ceiling, running along the walls, rushing into the tunnel. He climbed now, up the stairs and onto the street. He was bent over panting, resting his hands on his knees, when he saw the old man standing perhaps ten meters away, in front of the fencing that surrounded the condemned building.

Their eyes met. Johannes said something that Daniel couldn't hear. Then the grey figure stepped carefully through the water running through the street, one shaky foot at a time, until he stood before him.

"I know you," Daniel said.

Across the old face, a dozen lines stretched in as many directions, a long current of pain running out from beneath the gray scalp, creasing down across weary bones to the neck. Johannes said nothing.

Daniel found his arms shaking. He tried to stuff his hands in his pockets, but that felt worse than the shaking. Finally he clenched his fists and said,

"Her name was Miriam."

"Yes," Johannes said, "You must have been very young."

"I was... five, I think. When she died."

"There was a time," Johannes said, "when I thought I would die. I wanted to die. Somehow I just went on living."

Daniel was shaking now, unable to find any refuge for his hands. He thought of his own age and wondered how old Johannes must be.

"Do you know who I am?" Daniel asked.

"Yes."

"My mother's name was Miriam."

"I know."

"Oh, Jesus." Daniel gasped. "I'm sorry. I'm so sorry." His hands rose frantically and he stuffed them into his armpits to stop them instead. "I want to live now — this is the first time. I want to live, but I can't."

He didn't see Johannes close the remaining space between them. When he looked up, he saw the old man before him, frail arms taking him around the back, closing him.

"My son, my son. We must be strong."

Daniel yelped like a wounded dog, then wept, loud shuddering sobs.

"I'm so sorry," he choked into the old man's shoulders. "I've wasted my life. I wasn't ready to do anything good until now, and now it's too late."

"It's almost time for me to go," Johannes said.

"What? No — why? Not yet."

"My son. I always knew it would be a son."

"Why do you have to go?"

Daniel shivered as he felt the water sloshing inside his shoes. For the first time, Johannes smiled.

"It's the only thing left to do."

"But, no— I need you."

"It's too late for me," Johannes said. "But you no longer have to choose. You don't have to choose between staying and escaping." He pulled his arms away and took a step backward.

"Would you like to say anything?" he asked.

Daniel shook his head slowly.

Johannes smiled.

"My son," the old man said, still smiling as he turned and made his way to the fence. It opened for him without struggle, as if he knew exactly where and how to touch it. Johannes walked across the demolition site, into the black cavern of the doorless frame. For a moment he was there, a grey shadow against the black outline, then he vanished inside.

Daniel stared for a moment then felt a shudder. The pavement moved, and it seemed as if the entire city was buckling. He felt the shock waves through his bones as the huge building groaned and screamed, then its bricks collapsed, beams and boards shattered and letting go, and howling, for an instant, into the descent.

All that remained was an immense pile of rubble, from which water burbled insistently, seeking its escape from the destruction above the ground.

53.

Daniel walked through silting puddles in the first hour of daylight. At an intersection, a yellow-coated road crew bulldozed rubble from the street. Three dump trucks waited at the sidewalk to haul it away. A knot of green-shirted street repairmen was up ahead at the next turn, shoveling sand into potholes. At the end of the block, Daniel stopped beneath one of the huge blue water pumps. It was rumbling with the weight of millions of liters coursing through it. He stood for a minute, listening to the sound of its effort.

Daniel's shoes squirted with each step as he walked south and east toward his neighborhood. He turned and looked when he heard the wheels of a streetcar. It had stopped a few blocks up from him, and people were getting on. Half a block from Daniel was the next stop on the line, with a glass-roofed shelter at the street corner. A woman waited, holding the hand of a little boy, who in turn was holding a bundle of schoolbooks. The tram rolled down the center of the street toward them, blocking Daniel's vision of them when it stopped. He saw the boy getting on alone, sitting by himself and staring at the rubble. When the blue streetcar pulled away, Daniel saw the woman, her back to the shelter, walking home.

He wanted to visit Rashid. The burning in his stomach was gone, crushed out like a cigarette, cold and dull. He wasn't sure what he felt in its place, but it was different, of that he was certain. But it's too early; the Syrian wouldn't be there for another two or three hours. He decided not to put off the only thing he absolutely had to do today.

At the first pay phone, he found he lifted the receiver and discovered to his surprise that it was working. He inserted his card and dialed.

"Who's calling?" someone answered tersely.

"Daniel LeClerc, calling for Mr. DeSoto."

There was a pause, a series of clicks.

"I'm going through a scrambler," Daniel said. "You can't trace it."

The man on the other end said nothing.

"Trust me, it's important," Daniel said. "He wants to talk to me."

"Wait," the man said, and immediately put him on hold.

He stood and watched the morning swelling through the street. Then at last the voice, cool and impenetrable.

"Daniel."

"Miguel."

"Eugene called me last night and set a lunch appointment, but I believe you're calling to give me your regrets."

"I'm calling to tell you several things."

"Well then. Business."

"First of all," Daniel said, "I have to ask you a question, and even though you don't owe me anything, I'm hoping you'll give me an honest answer."

"I have never lied to you, Daniel, although I suspect I can no longer say 'vice-versa.'"

"I know that's how it looks, but it's not so."

"Perhaps you should ask your question."

Daniel swallowed.

"Did you... not put a hit on me last night because Julia was there?"

"You're being vulgar, Daniel."

"Eugene is gone."

"Indeed," DeSoto said. "And you?"

"I'm still in Berlin."

"Why don't you get on with what you wanted to tell me."

"All right. I'm going to tell you these things," Daniel said, "but I have no idea whether or not you're going to believe them. I've been trying to put myself in your position. I don't know if I'd believe it or not.

"It's been a set-up. Everything, from that weapons deal in Poland last month, maybe even before that. That thing with my... ah, father, all of it. It's Scherbatov, making a move on you. I came within a millimeter of my life the other night. Eugene saved me. If he hadn't caught a glimpse of Scherbatov at one of the deliveries and been quick on his feet, we'd both be dead.

"You can figure most of it out if you haven't already. But there are some things you should know. Scherbatov has three of the bombs. Eugene has called the feds and given them names, addresses, number-plates, all of it. He didn't say anything about you, but if it comes back to you, we wanted you to be ready."

"How very considerate. Who has the fourth one?"

"I don't know."

"Rather than losing my temper, I am going to ask you again. Where is the fourth device?"

"It was in a service tunnel on the U-1, but the tunnel flooded last night. It's gone."

"Is there a particular reason that you have decided I am an imbecile?"

"Believe me, Miguel, if I had it, I would be incredibly happy to give it you. I'd never have touched it in the first place if I'd known what it was. That was your fault for not being frank with us. You left us in the dark and we were almost killed."

"You're not going to have me believe that a nuclear... device is floating somewhere through the Berlin subway."

"Scherbatov doesn't have it, and neither do I."

"What makes you think that Scherbatov doesn't have it?"

"If he did, I'd be dead right now."

"Well then, Daniel. You wanted frankness? I shall be frank with you. At the moment, your being non-existent does not seem like a particularly bad idea."

"That's the other thing I wanted to tell you. I'm staying. If you want to clean me, you know where to find me. I'll be in Berlin, all the usual places. If you want to do it discretely, so Sabine and Julia won't be upset, you can arrange it somewhere. I'll come. It can be tidy. I'm not going to run away."

DeSoto was silent.

"I'm finished, Miguel."

"The fact of your unfortunate illness does not particularly incline me toward forgiveness."

"That's not what I mean."

"Oh, I see. You were planning to take up a new career, then?"

"That's it exactly. I'm done with it."

Daniel could hear the crunch of leather as DeSoto leaned back into his chair.

"Do you know," DeSoto said, "that during the entire course of my relationship with Sabine we had only a single argument? That is, admittedly, one more than I normally tolerate from a woman. One fight in two years, and none thereafter. Until last night."

"She has nothing to do with any of this," Daniel said.

"Rest assured that I agree with you, for once. She, regrettably, feels otherwise. She called me last night to plead for your life."

"Are you telling me this to make me feel ashamed?"

"To be perfectly honest, I don't care how you feel about it. And as far as your retirement plan is concerned, you still owe me a missing... device."

Daniel shook his head, stared down at the pavement.

"No. I've told you everything," he said. "I'll give you everything Eugene gave the cops, so you can have an edge on Scherbatov. You can deal with me as you see fit. I'm not going anywhere. But I'm never going to do this work again. For you or anybody, or even for myself."

Aside from the occasional cluck of the scrambler, the line was so silent that Daniel thought it might be dead. At last DeSoto said,

"I have been very poorly served by you."

"I'm sorry you feel that way. I did my best."

"Well. Everything grows rotten with time, doesn't it. Imagine that a year ago I considered the two of you to be esteemed colleagues. Now you're just former employees.

One has jumped ship, probably skating back to Russia at best possible speed, and the other one — not satisfied with simply failing me — is openly defying me to kill him."

"You know that's unfair," Daniel said. "You never let us in on—"

"Irrelevant. I've made up my mind. If I so much as overhear a single syllable of anything you and I have shared over the last four years...."

"There's no need to make threats. I told you already, if you don't want me alive, go ahead and do it now. I've given you my word that I'm out, completely. If you think I can't be trusted, if I'm too much of a risk or a pain in the ass to have around, you know what to do, and you know how to find me."

"Well, go on then. Go away and leave me alone. You and Julia both. We shall never speak again, Daniel."

Daniel hung up and walked down the street.

54.

He stopped on the curb, watching a bald Turkish man sweep muck from the floor of his shop. He looked up at Daniel, nodded his recognition.

"I'm not open yet. Come back in another hour. I've got to clean all this up. The water crested last night, there's mud everywhere."

"That's okay, I don't need anything," Daniel said. "I'm waiting."

The man continued sweeping, glancing up suspiciously from time to time. Finally, Daniel sighed and crossed the street.

Julia answered the bell on the second ring, croaking into the intercom.

"What?"

"It's me. Can I come up?"

The door buzzed and clacked open. By the time he got to her door, she had retreated to bed. He walked into her room, sat down on the edge of the bed beside her.

"You smell funny," she said.

"I got wet. I'll take a shower."

"Like medicine," she said, sniffing. "Are you okay?"

"Yeah."

"Promise?"

He nodded, stroked her face.

"Yeah, I think so."

"Where've you been?"

"I had to talk to Miguel. We worked some things out. I'm going to retire."

"I'm sleepy," she said. "We can talk about it later." She placed her hand lightly on his forearm. "Come to bed."

He kissed her ear.

"I'm going to go to the bathroom. I'll be right back."

Naked, hunched over her sink washing his hands, he realized that his face confronted him in the mirror. He stared at it, puzzled, as if he had never come to terms with his own face before. It appeared whole, undamaged, alive. He placed his hand on his stomach and held it there, feeling for something, wondering why it felt empty. He was sure something was in there but he sensed only stillness, calm, at the center of his body.

She groaned slightly when he lowered himself beside her, draping his arm across her chest.

"Julia?"

She turned over on her back, eyes barely open, her face sweet with the benign innocence of sleep.

"Mm?"

"I want to stay with you."

"Good," she said and kissed him. Her eyes fell closed again, her mouth smiling. Her breathing became deep and steady. Daniel laid his head carefully against her stomach.

55.

Daniel awoke thinking about the conversation with DeSoto. He looked at Julia's clock and realized that they had slept until nearly 10:00. It appeared that he was going to live. He was not entirely sure what being happy felt like, was not sure if he had ever been, but an unfamiliar lightness and optimism propelled him up and forward, out of the bed and into her living room. His trousers had not yet dried, and as he tugged his clothes on he found himself smiling involuntarily.

Julia snored determinedly from the bedroom. Daniel decided to walk down the block to the bakery and get some breakfast for them. Berlin's heavy white sky parted to reveal a few tentative slices of blue. A tall woman pushed a baby in a stroller and Daniel smiled at them as he passed, then shook his head and laughed at himself.

Across the street from the bakery, the sidewalk ended abruptly in a cage of wire fencing. Another old building was coming down. Daniel looked up at its sad and broken façade, like some vertical desert landscape full of jagged rocks. He squeezed around the fence and was about to cross the street when something caught his eye.

On one of the tall foundation stones around the building's base, he saw a fragment of old graffiti. It looked as if it had been painted with a brush rather than a spray can. It was not a gang tag or a logo, but the remains of a single word in red paint. Daniel squinted to read it and made out: *Escape.*

He shrugged and crossed the street.

ABOUT THE AUTHOR

Sam A. Mustafa is a professor and historian who divides his time between the United States and Germany. He has published several books on German history. *Vanish Like Water* is his first novel. He lives in the New York City area.

Made in United States
North Haven, CT
10 May 2022

19087927R00183